To Nick

Happy reading

Magnum Opus

An extraordinary tale of friendship and love that
transcends the horrors of war

NIGEL MESSENGER

Best Wishes

Nigel 23/1/25

Published by Nigel Messenger in 2024

ISBN 978-1-8383569-6-5

Book Cover Design and Typeset by The Daydream Academy, Stroud, Gloucestershire.

Contents

Prologue

The forest, with its trees, heaths, wastelands and open spaces, had been unchanged for more than 1,000 years. It had been designed to create a hunting ground for the king, protected by law, so its purpose was to accommodate the boar and deer. The penalties for poaching, taking wood or produce from the forest ranged from fines to, in the most severe cases, execution.

For young boys, the forest was a giant playground, and the youth from nearby Milton took every advantage. Today, they played soldiers beneath the tall oaks and hid amongst the bracken in the dappled autumn sunshine. Sticks became swords and rudimentary bows and arrows. They built fortresses and hideouts, and time ceased to exist as it had done for generations of boys before them.

But on this particular day, loud screams and shouts interrupted their play. Alarmed, the boys lay prone, crawling carefully through the bracken in the direction of the skirmish. They came to a roadside, where four men were attacking an elderly couple with knives. Their two horses whinnied and bucked, throwing the unfortunate man and woman to the ground. They were dead in moments, and the villains calmly wiped their knives on the clothes of the victims before stealing their few possessions.

The country had begun its descent into lawlessness and violence, and there seemed to be little anyone could do about it.

***

She was the most beautiful woman I had ever seen, the loveliest being on earth, and I would never meet her like again this side of heaven. She ruled over our neighbour France and was worshipped by all her subjects. I too worshipped her with all my heart and soul and with every ounce of my physical being. She was like a beacon of light, a child of our Saviour, a wraith, a spirit, and yet a commanding lady, a queen of nations.

Her bright golden hair flowed freely, making exquisite shapes in the breeze. Her eyes were of the deepest blue and when she set her gaze on me, they almost blinded me with their brilliance and caused my insides to become soft and fluid. When she spoke to me, she made me feel I was the only person in the world. Rather than walk, she floated with immense grace and style, and all eyes turned towards her. I had never known a woman who could use her sway to such devastating effect. Many feel it, but few men understand the power and attraction of a woman's demeanour. But power is the ultimate attraction.

Her smile illuminated a room, making it sparkle with exquisite happiness, and all smiled with her. Her laughter tinkled, cracking the air like a starburst. She was irresistible, her charm and charisma inspiring total devotion, and thus, whatever she asked of anyone, they readily, loyally and enthusiastically complied like an obedient puppy.

I loved to watch her dance: she and the music became one as she glided around the floor as if supported by currents of air. I loved her fragrance, which came from the pressed flowers of Grasse, so soft and gentle. A slender wisp of that incense would transport me to a divine place. A small bottle would cost me more than a year's wages, but I would gladly pay that price and more to gain one single glance from her.

And yet, she had recognised my miserable existence. The few words she spoke to me would stay with me for a lifetime. She asked me to look after her safety and I blustered a stuttering reply. Oh, how I wished I could have that time over again, not only to hear her voice, but to reply in a more confident, positive manner. If only I had been able to rehearse my response before I was required to spill it forth.

Oh Eleanor, your essence will be with me always. I will never forget you, be disloyal or cease loving you. I will follow you to the ends of the earth and will catch you before you fall off the edge, so we may be together in paradise for eternity. Or will that delight elude me as well? You will never know the depth of my pain, wanting you and never being able to sate my passion. All I can do now is to serve you to the extent of my abilities – nay, double that.

Why would you choose me above the strong and tall royal knights and noblemen, muscular and tanned from 1,000 suns and sculptured by 100 battles and tournaments? Such a decision could bring your nation and mine, and indeed Europe, to its knees with laughter and derision. The lands would flood with tears of scorn.

But while they were laughing, you did indeed choose me. Why did you do that? Even though I am weak and useless, was there something you saw in me that others could not?

Even though I am but a cripple?

***

She could hear the shouts from her bedroom window high up in the castle, the screams of terror as the attackers forced their way into the stronghold. She heard the cries of the people as they were slaughtered and the cruel laughter of men who would show no mercy.

Heavy boot treads sounded on the stairs and in the corridor, coming closer, coming for her. She shuddered with an awful sense of foreboding. There was no hope of escape, no chance to protect herself.

With a terrible crash, a huge man burst into her room. One glance at his cruel eyes, devoid of any kindness or compassion, and she knew she was staring at her doom.

Even by the low standards of the day, it was an unusually brutal and violent attack. Crossing the room in long strides, the man slapped the woman viciously across the face, his large fists beating her head until her ears rang and blood poured from her nose and lips. Weak from the pain, still she fought, her nails uselessly scratching at him as he tore off every stitch of her clothing, pulling the final strands of cloth from her body with desperate urgency. He pushed her down on to the bed, loosened his belt. As she started to sit up, he punched her in the face repeatedly, causing her injured nose to explode in agony. As he hit her again and again, she no longer tried to sit up. Instead, she remained perfectly still, awaiting her fate with dread.

Her screams of despair went unheeded, there was no one left who cared. He pushed apart her legs and entered her roughly. Her pain was so severe that she longed for oblivion.

Then it was all over. The man got up, pulled up his trousers, notched his belt. Without a backward glance at the stricken woman whimpering softly on the bed, he walked to the door. Pulling it open towards him, he walked out of the room.

But her torment wasn't at an end. Two henchmen entered the room, picked up the stricken woman and threw her out of the open window.

Part I – Shiva

Chapter 1

Outremer

A name applied to the medieval French Crusader States: Edessa, Antioch, Tripoli and Jerusalem

I stopped and looked around at the endless land and sky. The day was burning hot as the sun shone directly above our tired army, the sky cloudless and the air still. The earth was dry and dusty and bare of trees and grass. We were desperate to find verdant land and water, but the heat was relentless, as was the empty landscape. The hills and contours of earlier days had flattened and the green had disappeared.

We found it hard to believe that we had travelled so far and for so long, simply to end up in this empty, arid desert. We had already passed Jerusalem, but unfortunately had not been invited inside its walls, instead joining forces with its army and travelling north to our new objective.

Our army consisted of hundreds of knights and their entourages, in addition to a ragtag mass of hangers-on numbering many thousands. We were a mix of several European nationalities, but there was no overall leadership. The two kings, Louis of France and Conrad of Germany, along with various European nobles couldn't agree on a combined way forward. Our so-called leaders had arrived here from different places, taking different routes, some with varying degrees of success, most with failure and disaster.

As a result, we had suffered hunger and drought, betrayal and enemy attacks. We had lost far more than half our numbers and were all exhausted. And that was before we had even arrived at our promised land. We dreamed of home and our families and the normality of everyday life. Our aspirations of salvation and redemption were long forgotten, our morale could not have been any lower.

This fiasco was the Second Crusade, and my companions and I were dreading the outcome. The first, some 50 years before, had been a success in that the European armies had captured Jerusalem and formed four Crusader states, known as Outremer. We were told that the fall of one of them, Edessa, to the Muslims had necessitated this second wave, although our objectives weren't clear. The various leaders had differing opinions, and one of them thought that it would now be a brilliant idea to change tack to attack and take Damascus.

We were on our way there.

* * *

It might have been a small explosion or merely the crack of a whip, but it caused the huge white stallion to rear up on his hind legs in fright, expelling a sharp neigh that sounded more like a deep-throated scream. We all jumped in alarm as the rider tried to control and calm the magnificent beast.

The stallion appeared to recover as his front legs landed back on the dusty ground, but then he stamped his hooves and rose once more in fright before crashing down again. The rider – sitting side-saddle, which was not unusual for a lady – was nearly unseated as the stallion raced off ahead, crossing the rough ground at speed with the rider desperately clinging on, working the reins and using all the skills she had practised since she was little more than a baby. But this horse was testing even her expertise and she wasn't able to slow him down as he kicked up clouds of dust, which blew into our faces.

I knew immediately that she was in serious trouble, and I ran forward intent on catching the horse and rider. It took me a few moments to get into my stride; after months travelling by ship, and then walking for miles over foreign lands, my limbs were not used to the strains of running. Others followed behind me, but I was a better runner than all of them and I soon pulled away. No one had beaten me in a race for several years, so I had the best chance of saving the rider. The horse was, of course, much faster than I was on the flat ground, but I was relieved to see he was approaching a low hill and rockier terrain. Both elements would slow the stallion down.

I had recognised the rider immediately the horse had first reared. She was known and admired across the world and was integral to our journey and quest: one of the leaders of our army and a driving force behind our objectives. Why had she been given such a huge brute to ride? No one could have controlled the stallion in his current state of agitation.

After what seemed to be an age, I gradually got closer to the horse and rider. He had slowed down to about half speed, but I had not, and I was more confident of catching them. I was relieved to see that she was now sitting more comfortably, but still seemed to have little control over the startled horse.

I could feel the sweat on my head and face, and small rivulets were running down my back and legs. My muscles were straining to keep up the pace, but I could catch them if I increased my speed a little. The gap was twenty paces, and then ten. Moments later, I was level with horse and rider.

At the first opportunity, I grabbed the reins with my one good hand and the horse reared up, pulling me off the ground for a moment or two. And then, I landed back on my feet and pulled. The horse pushed forward again, and I lost my balance and was dragged on my toes.

The great beast turned his head towards me and for a moment, I thought he was going to attack and trample me. Fortunately, he turned forwards once again, but was still pushing ahead. Gradually, the horse slowed, and I was able to run and then walk until he came to a standstill, panting and snorting in frustration and anger.

The rider turned to me, smiling with relief, and spoke to me in her native French. I had knowledge of her language, but I replied in English. Her gratitude and captivating smile made me wilt with pleasure and immense shyness. I thought my heart would melt in her gracious presence. The pale blue covering on her head left her beautiful face exposed in a style favoured by titled ladies. The soft cloth flowed down into a long dress covering her body and legs.

She dismounted slowly and carefully with great elegance until she was standing next to me. I was trying to calm my breathing after my exertions. When I was fully recovered, we walked together; I led the beast while she rested a gentle hand on my shoulder, still a little in shock after her frightening encounter. I wanted the short journey to last forever as I had never before been in the presence of such a beautiful and graceful lady, nor one so regal and powerful.

She pointed to where she wanted to go. The exhausted stallion did not resist, but meekly did as I commanded. As we approached the camp, I could hear the cheers and applause from her countrymen and women, relieved to see their special lady back safely. People rushed over with arms outstretched to guide her back to her tent. Two men took the reins away from me.

I walked the short distance to my people and sat on the ground with a small group of friends, boys of my own age. Exhausted and drained, I was nonetheless grateful that I had succeeded in stopping the horse and saving the gracious lady. A boy brought me a flagon and I gratefully drained the precious stream water. Water was in short supply, so I was very thankful for his kindness.

More of my friends joined me as we sat in the still warm sunshine of the late afternoon. They were impressed with my good deed and turn of speed, while I tried to play it down.

We were enjoying easy conversion when one of my friends jerked his head in the direction of my lord's tent.

"Look out," he warned, "there's trouble approaching!"

My lord, wearing only his chainmail shirt and woollen hosen as I had removed his armour earlier, was walking towards us from his tent. A tall man, certainly the tallest I had ever known, who carried no spare weight, he was in his middle thirties. With the arrogant look of the gentry – his thin, long and slightly bearded face wearing a permanent sneer, and his large nose betraying his Norman origins – he was a man I would have preferred not to have had to serve. When he spoke, it was in a rather annoying lisp. I had known him all my life and hated him with every sinew of my being.

"Well done, Crispin! Do you realise you've probably made history today? D'you know who that lady is? She is none other than Queen Eleanor of France, the wife of King Louis. Did you have any idea who she was when you gave chase?"

"Yes, sir, I know who she is, but I would have done the same for anyone."

"You did well. I didn't know you could run so fast."

"I've been practising all my life and I'm now the fastest runner in Milton. I've won the annual race from Marston to Milton for the past three years."

I spoke this as a statement of fact as I didn't want him or my friends to think I was showing off. This was the most my lord had ever said to me and I was surprised he even knew my name. Although I had lived in his castle all my life and now worked for him, he usually gave me orders through other people. This had never bothered me as it tended to be safer *not* to be noticed by him and to keep our heads down when he was around. My friends and I all knew he could be unnecessarily ruthless and cruel.

"Well, your speed is remarkable. I'm sure she'll want to speak to you later to thank you."

He turned around quickly as if he didn't want to be in the presence of lower order people any longer than he needed to, and strode away back towards his tent. Everyone in my home village worked for him or paid him tithes and rent. As Lord of the Manor, he owned Milton Castle and all the buildings and the land for miles around. If he didn't get his dues, or even if they were late, he would come down heavily on the offenders.

My hatred of him was mirrored by hundreds of others.

***

Later that evening, a messenger came to find me. He was very young and approached my people with some hesitation, asking for the boy who had rescued the Queen. He was dressed like a French courtier in a light silvery chemise, his funny hat, made of the same material, fitting his head like an oversized cap. He spoke English in a rather stilted manner, his voice soft and high, his accent strongly French. His seriousness and cultured demeanour made me smile.

"You must come with me to see our Queen. She wants to speak to you. If you follow me, I will take you to her."

He didn't look at me, keeping his pert nose in the air, appearing to dislike carrying out this task he had been given. Here was another bursting with his own self-importance!

But that was of no consequence to me. I couldn't believe that Queen Eleanor of France wanted to see me. I knew I had probably saved her life, but I was a lowly English boy who had nothing to do with royalty. Nonetheless, I couldn't wait to be in her wondrous presence again.

The boy led me the short distance to her tent.

"Your Majesty, I have the English boy here with me as you asked." The French language was still spoken in my country as well as English, and had been since the arrival of the Normans around 80 years earlier, so I understood his words.

Two huge men, armed with heavy spears and wearing helmets with massive nose guards, held open the tent flaps. They must have been her bodyguards. Both looked at me with some surprise, and then stood aside to let me in.

Inside, the tent was as big as the largest room in Milton Castle. I blinked to get my eyes used to the duskiness; there were only a few dimly lit lanterns dotted around the huge space. A carpet covered most of the floor, and the wooden furniture – delicate armoires, dressing tables and chairs – did not look like the heavy oak cupboards and benches I was used to in my English home. The pieces were light and pretty with intricate carvings and curved sides – the legs of the chairs and tables had been sculpted into delicate shapes, some resembling human limbs. Beautiful materials covered some of the pieces, silks of red and green and purple, and vast cushions had been plumped up to accommodate any shape or size of arse lucky enough to be supported by them.

I fleetingly wondered who'd had the awful job of carrying all this furniture across so many hills and seas, visualising several fed-up oxen moaning about the heavy wagons they had to pull. Did they wonder what on earth their load would be used for? Did they ever dream of tipping the wagon down a hill into a lake and losing the burden? How many carpenters and polishers were travelling with the French to keep Their Majesties' furnishings in prime condition? We had heard that Queen Eleanor had brought with her 200 chambermaids and a long trail of carts and carriages containing trunks of clothes, as if she was going on a glorious excursion instead of one of the most fearsome journeys ever undertaken.

I was so distracted by my surroundings that for a short moment, I forgot I was in the presence of my lovely lady. I peered through the gloom to find the vision I'd helped earlier.

A gentle and soft voice interrupted my daydreaming. "Thank you for coming to see me. I wanted to offer my gratitude with my heart full for your quick and selfless action. I still can't believe how fast you ran. You've certainly saved my life. What is your name, brave man?"

I hesitated, reeling with shock and joy at the beauty and timbre of her voice. The sound reminded me of the haunting music I had so often heard in church, choirboys singing, their treble voices effortlessly soaring to the heights. But this voice was lower, more sensual and somehow shocking. To this day, I don't know how I managed to reply.

"Er, Crispin, Your Majesty," I stuttered.

Queen Eleanor was sitting on a low lounger, leaning back against the rest with one leg on the seat and the other on the floor. She was almost indescribably lovely and charismatic. She had changed since her narrow escape, now wearing a long dress of the most magnificent golden material I had ever seen. The hem had risen a little, exposing a very elegant ankle. Her blonde hair had been brushed, flowing across her shoulders. I guessed she was in her early twenties, so young for such an important person.

I had heard the men talk about her before, saying she was the most beautiful woman in the whole world. I did not doubt that. I was smitten and thought my legs would give way. My body swayed and I struggled to regain my composure.

Her most arresting feature was her captivating eyes. They were a brilliant shade of light blue that I had never seen before in a human face, lighter than the sea or sky. They were a powerful weapon which could reduce the most important man, even a king, to a quivering wreck, confessing to the most heinous crimes whether he had committed them or not. There was no point at all in trying to resist her commands.

When I finally managed to tear my eyes away from her, I saw a man resting on a second lounger. Wearing rather scruffy pale undergarments, he looked like he had been asleep and only stirred when I entered. He seemed somewhat older than she and strangely out of place, like he should have been on his knees in a church or monastery.

I almost leapt with fright when I realised this was the French King Louis. But surely a king never looked like this. He was short, skinny, balding, and very pale, which made me wonder how he had kept the sun and wind away from his face on this long trip. He sat up and looked at me with practised disinterest, and then lay down again, closing his eyes, ignoring me.

Queen Eleanor gave me the benefit of her brilliant warm smile. "Come and sit down," she said. I was stunned once again by the sound of her voice. She spoke with clarity and authority, and yet there was a kindness and sincerity about her. "You are probably tired after your extraordinary performance." She pointed to a small chair close to her and I obeyed and stepped forward, sitting with gratitude. The King didn't open an eye. She raised her right arm and immediately a servant came to her side. Queen Eleanor ordered a glass of wine for me, her guest. The drink was placed on an intricately carved table next to me in no more than a few moments.

"Where are you from, Crispin?"

"I... I live in a castle in England with my mother. My lord is here, and we are part of the Crusader Army."

"What's your lord's name?"

"Lord De Beaumont of the Manor of Milton."

"And what do you do for him?" Her beautiful eyes rested on my short withered arm with concern.

"I look after my lord's armoury." Then I decided to answer her unasked question. "I was born like this, and they told my mother to dispose of me, saying I wouldn't be able to bring any money into the family. But she wouldn't let me go."

"Well, you can certainly move very fast. I've never seen anyone so quick. That is a great talent. How do you manage to work with Lord Milton's weapons with only one arm?"

"I've spent years learning how to do all the jobs I need to do with my one good hand and sometimes with my feet as well. I worked so long and hard on my skills that my lord was not able to find anyone better. There is no job I cannot do, and I am proud to work more quickly and better than anyone else. I've also practised hard to become the fastest runner in our area."

I think she was impressed. "Perhaps one day you will work for me," she said. "I need someone to protect me, someone who is clever and resourceful."

I couldn't believe I was hearing this!

"I would be very honoured to serve you, Your Majesty, but I doubt my lord will ever let me go."

She went on to ask me about my long and dangerous journey from England and across Europe.

"This is the first time I've ever been away from home and it has been an amazing adventure. I had never seen the sea before, and to travel across it was very exciting. But I didn't expect so much warfare and danger, and that was before we arrived here."

"And how was your journey across the land?"

"Exhausting and dangerous. Many times, I thought we would all be killed or die of hunger and thirst. We lost many to disease as well."

She nodded sympathetically and smiled, and then she stood. It was time for me to go.

"Thank you so much, Crispin. I am forever in your debt. I do hope we will meet again and that I can do something to repay you for your courage and kindness."

I stood, bowed and thanked her, and then moved backwards towards the entrance to the tent. Once outside, I made my way back to my camp. I must have walked, but the sensation was more like floating on a cloud. I felt exhilarated – nay, thrilled – and my blood was fizzing through my body. Her final words echoed in my mind.

"Thank you for saving my life. I will never forget you."

I hoped and prayed that I would meet this lovely being again. So absorbed had I been by her presence, I realised that I had forgotten to taste the wine I had been served.

***

We had departed from England nearly two years earlier. Even though the excitement of my new adventure had since worn a bit thin, I never forgot the thrill of leaving home for the first time. My mother and I had cried and hugged; I loved my mother so much and often recalled all she had done for me and the sacrifices she'd made. I hoped we wouldn't be apart for too long. I missed her terribly.

I didn't have a choice about going on the trip. My lord had decided we would all do our duty for Christ and, of course, the Pope had demanded our service. We would be needed to fight the infidels and drive them out of Jerusalem, restoring the Holy Land to Christendom. When we departed my home village, I had no idea where the Holy Land was or how we would get there. Apparently, we would have to cross the sea, but I didn't even know what that was. I was told that it was like the pond near the castle at home, but much bigger, perhaps 100 times bigger. We would float across it on a boat. This all sounded terrifying to me.

We had been visited by churchmen who had been touring the local towns and villages, ordering all men to do their duty. Once the Holy Land had been freed, we would be absolved of all our sins. That sounded good to me, and from then onwards, I longed to visit the land of the Bible.

My lord ordered us to travel with him as we made the journey to Dartmouth. I had never been out of Wiltshire before and if I hadn't been so sad about leaving my home and my mother, I would have appreciated the beautiful countryside more. We travelled the roads with my lord's knights and servants in dozens of carts for the few days it took us to get to the sea.

Dartmouth was set on the sparkling river Dart, which would take us out to the wide sea just beyond. Our jaws dropped at the beauty of the vast stretch of blue water, much bigger than the village pond we had left behind. We couldn't even see the other side.

There were dozens of ships in the harbour and we wondered how they could possibly transport us up the river and across the sea. What would happen if our ship sank? All of a sudden, I wasn't looking forward to the future quite so much. I just wanted to go back home to the castle and my mother.

We watched as one of the ships set off. Lines of oarsmen rowed her towards the sea. Once she was on the open water, the sailors on deck rigged up huge sheets to catch the wind. I was told the sheets were called sails.

We spent the whole of the next day piling our stores and horses into three of the ships. I didn't enjoy the way the vessels rocked, creaked and moved as we loaded them. The horses shared my trepidation. They didn't like being led across the wooden planks on to the ships, and one of them screamed and stamped his front legs in terror. He was in danger of skidding into the water, and I was called forward to calm the beast and lead him across the walkway. I was quite used to working with all kinds of animals and some said I had a natural affinity with them. Luckily, I succeeded, and no harm came to the poor horse.

We then had to carry three heavy metal trunks on to the ships. These contained my lord's armour and weapons. I had spent days carefully wrapping each piece in cloth to prevent damage, having been told I would have to allow for excessive movement caused by rough seas and storms. One of the knights said that my head would be on the block if any piece was damaged. I hoped he didn't mean this literally!

It took several of us many hours to carry the trunks on to the ships. We then had to ensure that each one was tied in position so that it wouldn't move. After that, we loaded the ships with food, weapons, tents, medical equipment – indeed, any gear we'd need for the coming months and maybe years. We also loaded many barrels of stream water because apparently, we couldn't drink the sea water. It would first make us mad, and then kill us. I fervently hoped the fresh water wouldn't run out!

Finally, we were ready to depart. Several rowers took their positions and slowly, the huge, heavy vessel moved towards the mouth of the river and the endless ocean beyond. Already, the choppy waters were making the ship move up, down and round in every direction, and as the waves grew bigger, she seemed to lurch forward every few seconds. I thought she was going to dive into the deep, but she righted herself just in time. Strong winds forced the ship on to her side, and then pulled her over to the other side. I thought we were going to topple over. No sooner had she righted herself than she was forced over once again. At that moment, I gave up on any ambition I might have had to become a sailor!

Once the men had rigged the sails, the rowers were no longer needed, and they were grateful to take a rest. I wasn't prepared for the noises from the wooden planks of the ships as they rubbed together. How on earth would we be able to sleep with this constant creaking and groaning? Many of us, including me, suffered from sickness caused by the rolling and rocking of the boat. We spent hours leaning over the sides and I will never forget how wretched I felt. I just wanted to die.

I had assumed that we would reach land in an hour or so, but when the darkness came, the ships were still moving forward and the horizon just carried on for ever. We made our way below decks.

I had been warned that rats always found their way on to every ship and we could hear their squealing and scratching all through the night. I had a lifelong fear of rats and I was terrified that they would run over my head and body. Sleep was impossible for me.

We had been sailing for only a few days when the weather turned awful. We had to help to take down the sails as the winds were too strong, dragging the ship over until the mast almost touched the sea. The rain was constant, and the ship was heaving so much that the dreaded sickness had spread to all the men on board. Hating the insecurity of the wood and water beneath my feet, I longed to be on land again where I felt safe. I think I passed out several times over the days the dreadful ordeal lasted.

Before travelling to the Holy Land, we would be visiting the Iberian Peninsula, but I had no idea what or where that was. At last, we reached a safe harbour at a place called Porto. We had been at sea for a month.

We were told to stay on the ship while my lord and several of his knights went ashore. After a few days, they returned and my lord told me and all his men to gather on deck to listen to him.

"We're going to help my friend King Alfonso to take Lisbon back from the Moors. When our armies seize the city, we can take the treasures for ourselves and that means we can all share in the spoils. We set sail tomorrow at first light."

This attack took four months of our precious time. Despite my dislike of sea travel, I was so relieved when at last we set sail to the Holy Land to rescue the country of Jesus from the infidel. I had by then killed a man with a sword for the first time, and then killed dozens more. It was their life or mine, which was at risk many times. I hated the violence and hoped I would never be exposed to it again.

My hopes were in vain. And we never did get our share of the spoils.

Chapter 2

Prison

Days after my meeting with Eleanor, I helped my lord get dressed and prepared him for our journey to Damascus, considered to be one of the most important Muslim cities in the world. I'd worked hard to burnish and polish the metalled parts of his extensive armour and to ensure all his clothing was clean and fresh smelling, but my lord stood in his quilted undergarment, tall and strong, looking into the middle distance, ignoring the presence of a lowly servant. I was well used to his ways by now and just concentrated on doing my duties as I had done several hundred times before.

He held his arms forward as I threaded them through the mail shirt openings one at a time, before securing it to his upper body. Then came the hood and collar of mail which covered his head and shoulders, thereby protecting the exposed areas of his upper body. He was so tall, I had to stand on a box to complete this task.

I helped him into the flexible mail which covered his legs and thighs, then enshrouded his armour with white material to protect the metal from the fierce sun. Without it, the armour would become as hot as an oven and my lord would roast like an ox. The image made me smile inwardly, but I kept my expression impassive as I completed my tasks.

When he was fully dressed, three of us had to help my lord on to his huge destrier. I had to admit he was an impressive figure as he set off towards the city, and we followed dutifully.

***

When I woke up, I was in unimaginable pain. I hardly dared move. With trepidation, I touched my left side and winced at the tenderness of the wound I found there. I wondered how serious it was and whether I would survive it. Would my wound get infected? I had witnessed many a poor soul withering away and dying days after a cut or thrust.

I had no idea how long I had been here, or indeed where 'here' was. Opening one eye, I dimly saw a gloomy room with little streams of sunlight filtering through a barred window. I opened the other eye.

The meagre light coming in was enough to allow me to see around the room. Men were lying alongside me on the floor in piles of dirty straw, moaning softly. The smell of their bodies nearly caused me to gag and choke, and I struggled to get myself under control.

Right now, I didn't want any of the men to know I was conscious. First, I needed to learn more about my current circumstances and how I had got here. A miasma of flies and various unpleasant bugs were enjoying the environment rather more than the human occupants were. The men had used a corner of the room as a latrine. The smell was indescribably bad and getting worse by the hour.

I counted the bodies. There were thirteen men lying in rows on the floor. They were dressed in long shirts, as I was. I guessed we were all wounded Crusaders who had been captured during the battle for Damascus. From this, I assumed that we had lost.

I was immediately afraid. Would I ever get out of here and back home to my dear mother? There had been many terrifying moments during my months of adventure, but none had been as bad as this. And I was sure it was going to get worse.

I was right.

My throat was parched. I must have been hungry as well, but my stomach's needs were not a priority. I wondered if our captors had provided any water, but I still didn't find the courage to speak.

I didn't need to.

"What happened to your arm? Did you lose it in battle?"

The man nearest to me turned towards me, guessing I was awake. He was small and bearded, tough looking like a foot soldier. He spoke with a deep guttural accent, and I had some difficulty understanding him. I guessed he was with Conrad and his German army. I knew they'd had a worse time than the rest of us, having been savaged by the Turks on their way here.

"No," I replied, "I was born without it. But I have been wounded, I think by an arrow. Look here." I pointed to my side, just below my ribs.

"Let's have a look. Turn towards me and show me the wound." With some difficulty and a lot of pain, I did as he asked. His sharp intake of breath did nothing to ease my fears. "My – looks nasty. You'll have to keep that clean." The man laughed, but it was a bitter sound. "Goodness only knows how you'll manage that in this hell hole. I'm Hans, by the way, a simple farmer from the Rhinelands. Now I'm an archer with the Holy Roman Emperor. Or rather, I was!" Another humourless laugh "Who are you with?"

"My Lord Milton of England," I replied. "I look after his armour. He ordered me to be part of his attacking force, although that's not what I have been trained for. What on earth happened back there?"

He looked at me sadly. "It's a big mistake to go into battle under two leaders with two different ideas. First, we were told to go here, and then told to go there. The worst thing was when we were ordered out of the orchards and irrigated areas on to the southern parts. We had no food or water and we dried up in the hot sun."

My memory of the disastrous past few days was now slowly coming back to me with horrible clarity.

"Yes, we had no chance there at all and the Muslim army attacked us with ease from all sides, while our armies dithered," I replied. "I think that Louis and Conrad should have had a firm plan agreed before all this went ahead. What's going to happen to us now?"

He stared at me for a few moments, his face mournful.

"Haven't you heard? The bastards came in here and demanded to know our functions in the army. I stupidly told them that I was an archer. Four of us were dragged over to that corner and had our middle fingers chopped off." He held up both hands to prove his point. "You've no idea how painful that was. A finger doesn't look like it's going to hurt much, but bloody hell, it was agony!"

Men who had wielded swords in battle, Hans told me, had had their right hands cut off, their blood spurting everywhere. Our captors had staunched the blood flow with hot plates and the men's screams had been terrible.

"We are now useless to our armies. I suppose we were lucky to have survived, but losing a hand may be even worse than dying."

A sharp tremor ran from my lower back up to my shoulders when I heard this. I didn't want any of this to be done to me, I didn't think I could survive the pain. I remembered a story I'd heard in school about the first King Henry locking up one of his nobles for disloyalty. The usual punishment was blinding and castration, and the nobleman could not bear to face this suffering. In desperation, he beat his head against the brick wall of his prison until he had killed himself. Like that nobleman, I would rather die than face any more pain and mutilation.

I shuddered in awful terror. "What will happen to me?"

"Dunno, it depends on what you say your job was, and whether they believe you or not."

"I will tell them I merely looked after my lord's armour," I replied rather shakily.

"Perhaps they will spare you, thinking you already had your arm taken off."

"Is there anything to drink in here?"

Hans just laughed bitterly once again, shaking his head.

***

Hours or perhaps even days later, I awoke from a deep sleep. I now knew what it felt like to be old. My body ached and creaked when I moved, and my head hurt terribly. There was no point in getting up as nothing had changed.

Time passed. Each time I awoke, I felt increasingly hopeless and depressed. I looked around for food and water, but there was barely enough to go round. The kindly Hans would save a low level of water in a bottle for me. It was usually brown and disgusting, but I was so desperate, I drained it eagerly.

As I descended into a deep mental and physical depression, visions of my mother and home flashed in my head. I saw green lands and a river of cool water. But they were all out of reach and only added to my suffering.

However, even in my depths of despair, I managed to keep hope alive. Somehow, I believed, I would survive whatever the world and its worst people could throw at me. I had experienced low periods before, when bullies had made my young life worse than hell. Many times during my travels here, on the ship and during the battles in Iberia, I had confronted pain and terror. And now in this horrible prison, where I should have had no expectations of survival, I believed that instinct, faith, optimism, perhaps a guardian angel would save me. Although I came very close, I never lost hope completely.

As a child, I'd had an imaginary friend who, for some obscure reason, I'd named Era. Particularly, but not exclusively, in times of trouble, Era would sit on my shoulder, above my one good arm, and talk to me. He was a loyal friend and a faithful advisor. Looking back, I know this sounds odd and somewhat deranged, but he always gave me good advice. Now he was telling me that I must have faith.

***

It was the early hours of the morning when I next woke. Something had disturbed me. Something had changed, finally.

A flickering of dim light. I looked at the barred window and wondered for a moment if I had imagined it. No, a definite shadow, blocking the light briefly. I stood up and moved closer to the window, looking outside. I peered from every angle and saw nothing.

I went back to my place on the floor and looked up at the window again. A small body appeared. I went closer, and this time it did not move. A local boy was watching us poor prisoners from outside the gaol. He was a few years younger than me, probably around ten or eleven, and stared at me with his bright brown eyes. But he wasn't a typical street urchin, that much was clear. He was well dressed in a white cloth covering most of his head and body, with only a few patches of brown skin exposed. In daylight hours, we could see thousands of Arab boys in the street, playing games, fighting, searching for food or for something to sell to make a coin. At first glance, he looked like one of them. But something was different about him.

This boy was on his own. He kept looking at me with enquiring eyes. I glanced around to see none of the other men were taking any notice of him, or me, so I walked up to the window. I smiled at him and held my hand up.

"I'm Yusuf. Franj?" he asked, pointing at me.

"Crispin," I replied, patting my chest with my good hand.

"Grippen?"

"No, Crispin," I said.

"Crippen?"

"OK, that's near enough." I had picked up enough Arabic from listening to the guards to be able to carry on a basic conversation, and hand gestures did the rest.

"Yusuf is Joseph," he explained. The name Joseph was popular in England and, of course, we all knew about Joseph in the Bible, but I didn't know the Muslims used the same first names as we did, albeit in different forms.

"How old are you?" I asked, holding up five fingers. He held up ten fingers, closed his hands, then opened one hand again, showing one finger. "Oh, you are eleven years old, are you? I'm fifteen," I said as I flashed five fingers three times using my one good hand. He held up his left arm with a questioning look, wanting to know why I only had one. Using gestures and words, I told him that I had only ever had one. He shook his head in pity.

"Who is that brat you are talking to?" a guttural voice called out behind me. I recognised the tones of my neighbour, Hans, his harsh words contrasting with his generous spirit.

"Just a local boy. He might be able to help us."

"Well, be careful. Wouldn't trust any of those bastards."

"Yusuf, we are very thirsty," I said, turning back to the boy and pointing to my mouth and throat. "Can you get us some water or milk?" I used my fingers to indicate milking a cow.

Without a word, he rushed off. I hoped I hadn't scared him or put him into a difficult situation. We had been given minimal stale rations by our guards, just enough to keep us alive.

Yusuf didn't return and I went back to my small space on the floor with great disappointment. Without help, it seemed unlikely that we would survive more than a few days.

"Why are they keeping us in these dreadful conditions and how long will we be here?" I asked my German neighbour.

"Well, it depends on what you are worth. I'm only a lowly archer with a missing firing finger and no money, so I guess I will be thrown out with the garbage. I gave up all hope days ago. Some of these swordsmen might be worth a coin or two, even those who have had a hand chopped off, if they are related to a knight. But I don't hold out much hope for you," he added bluntly. "You're not much use with one arm, are you?"

"Do you think my lord will put up a few coins for me?"

He didn't answer me. By the expression on his face, I could guess his opinion.

I lay my head down. I didn't think I had felt this low before, having been given a glimpse of hope only to have it snatched away. The future seemed bleak. I missed my mother dreadfully. What was the point of my miserable life? I had no control over events. Even at home, I was treated little better than a slave by my lord, and it had been worse on our long campaign.

Then I heard a voice from the window. "Crippen, Crippen, wake up." I raised my head to see Yusuf through the bars, holding a metal jug. "Crippen, come here, I have brought you some milk."

Going eagerly to the window, I put my hand through the bars to take the jug from him, but couldn't pull it into the cell. It wouldn't fit. I turned and called to my German friend to come and have a drink. He did so quickly and pulled the lip of the jug to his parched mouth through the bars. Others pushed forward to have their turn. They ignored me and the jug was empty in moments.

"Crippen, you must drink," said Yusuf in dismay. "You are more important than the others. I will bring some more, but this will be just for you."

He was back in moments and passed me a tall metal cup which fitted through the bars. The others pushed behind me for their share, but now it was my turn.

"Thank you, Yusuf," I said when I handed him the empty cup. "You have saved our lives. Can you get us food as well?"

***

Drifting off again on my filthy floor space, I was transported back to the tiny room in the castle in which I had grown up with my mother. I gazed up into her honey-coloured eyes and bathed in her smile. I wanted to tell her that she was the best mother in the world, and I couldn't have wished for a happier early life.

She kept me warm and healthy, always feeding me well, although food could be very hard to get, and we were never thirsty. We had porridge and bread most mornings and I looked forward to our weekly cheese treat. She took me for walks in our beautiful countryside and showed me how to look for food growing wild, which belonged to everyone. There were so many varieties of greens, berries and fruit, and I could never get enough of the mushrooms. She taught me all the names of the different types and, importantly, the ones to avoid. I remembered having bad stomach pains when I hadn't been careful enough.

Mother was good friends with the cook, and we often enjoyed extra food as a result. The cook had a daughter around the same age as me, called Mary. We were allowed to fish in the river, and Mother made me a basic line. I was so happy when I landed my first trout.

I enjoyed my early life in the countryside. I loved most of the seasons: the spring with its colourful floral displays, the long hot days of summer, and the mild autumn with its abundant fruits and nuts. Winters were harsh and the ice and snow could last for many months. During the cold, dark days, we were all hungry most of the time.

We were supposed to be a united people, ruled by King Stephen, but everyone seemed to be fighting each other. It was unsafe to travel any of our roads without a full escort of armed men. I remembered witnessing an old couple being murdered on the edge of the forest while they were riding to the town. I was with a gang of boys playing in the forest when we heard their screams and, hidden by the undergrowth, watched the terrible attack unfold. It was a horrible experience for us, but it must have been far worse for the victims.

Mostly, though, we were fortunate to be protected by our community and the sturdy walls of our castle. We were often told England was the best country to live in, but at times, this was hard to believe.

I attended school in our local Benedictine monastery. Instantly, I was transported back to the airy schoolroom with its high ceiling. The monks were strange looking men with their black habits and their oddly cut hair, leaving rather silly fringes. They taught us Latin and made us repeat the verbs until we were word perfect: "Amo, Amas, Amat, Amamus, Amatis, Amant." Whenever we made a mistake, a quick rap over the knuckles with a monk's stick usually encouraged us to improve. Today, I can still recite those verbs to perfection. In fact, more than that, I can speak whole passages in Latin, translating from English and French books. I remained grateful for the monks' guidance and wished I had studied even harder than I did.

I would never forget Brother Wilfrid who taught us about the incredible history of our islands. He was a very small man – we boys were all taller than him – with a badly bent back, which further reduced his height. He seemed to be an old man, although young people are not always good judges of age, but he was a wonderful teacher and we all looked forward to his lessons.

"We were first overcome by the Romans around 1,000 years ago, but they left after 400 years. And then in 1066, The Conqueror, William the Bastard, brought his soldiers over from Normandy across the narrow sea in hundreds of boats. He defeated the Saxon King Harold at the Battle of Senlac. The Normans are now our rulers."

"What's a bastard, sir?" one boy asked.

I heard another at the back of the class whisper, "Just like Crispin." I knew exactly what a bastard was, and I could feel myself reddening deeply in embarrassment.

Wilfred pretended that he hadn't heard the whispered comment, explaining that it meant William was not a legitimate son. In other words, he had been born to a woman to whom his father was not married.

"The conquest happened fewer than eighty years ago. I remember my father telling me that he saw William during a service he attended in Winchester Abbey. William was already a man in middle age and he had put on a huge amount of weight. He was vast! When he died, his body was too big for his tomb."

I knew that the Normans, descended from the Norse Vikings, could be brutal. After all, my lord was one of them, and so was true to type. But I also knew that Wilfrid wouldn't dare to say so openly.

Wilfrid told us that the current trouble in England started with the sinking of the White Ship, which had just left Barfleur in Normandy. All but one of the 300 passengers drowned when the ship hit rocks. The sole survivor was a butcher, who had gone on board to collect some debts. This happened only twenty years ago.

Another hand shot up. "Someone told me that the passengers were drunk. Can that be true?"

"Yes, they were all very drunk, including the ship's crew. That's the reason the ship sailed off course and struck a rock just a mile away from Barfleur. The waters were very cold, and few could swim. They would have died quickly. The cream of English and Norman society were wiped out.

"Henry, the fourth son of William, was King. His beloved son William Adelin was one of several nobles who drowned, and he was the heir to the English and Norman throne. Legend has it that he was actually rescued by his bodyguard, who had taken a small boat from the ship, but as they were rowing back to the safety of the shore, William heard his half-sister screaming in terror. He ordered his bodyguard to return to rescue her from the sinking ship, but their boat ended up going down with her.

"It is said that King Henry never smiled again after his devastating loss. It's this one catastrophic event that has led to our terrible unrest, albeit indirectly."

"But why did it cause so much trouble?" asked a small boy with his hand in the air.

"Henry was a great King who brought peace to England and Normandy. He ruled his kingdoms ruthlessly, but fairly, although he was brutal to those who were disloyal to him. It is said that during his reign, a young girl laden with gold could travel unharmed through the Kingdom of England.

"But this changed the moment the King died, and many say his decline came about as a result of losing his son to the sea. England has become lawless and violent. It is unsafe now to be out and about in the land."

We knew this to be true.

"In the vacuum left by Henry's death, many men, and women, wanted the power and wealth that kingship would bring. As you know, Henry's daughter, Matilda, claims the throne is hers, but many people do not want a Queen. A woman has never ruled in England on her own. Our King Stephen was Henry's nephew, and he and Matilda have been fighting for the throne for years. I can't see this being resolved soon. Stephen had been on the White Ship before she sailed, but he was sick and had to be carried back to the harbour. History would have been very different if he had not been ill on that fateful day."

We were all fascinated with his story, told in Brother Wilfrid's engaging style.

"Who do we support, Matilda or Stephen?" Another boy, another hand pushed high.

"That's enough for one day. We will continue the lesson next week."

We all groaned with disappointment. I couldn't wait for the next lesson as I was keen to know more about why we lived in such terrible times.

***

"Our Lord Milton has been supporting King Stephen." It was a week later and Brother Wilfrid was continuing his history lesson. "But now this is uncertain as the King has just captured Roger, Bishop of Salisbury, confiscating his wealth and property. Roger was perhaps the most important man in England after the King and was greatly valued by Henry. He ran the country's finances and devised the Exchequer table – and before you ask, this vast table, covered in cloth, is laid out like a giant chessboard with various counters that indicate monetary values, income and expenditure, as well as amounts owed and owing. At a glance, the King could see the extent of his considerable wealth and treasury, and money owed by his nobles and tenants. Those who didn't pay him on time would be ruthlessly dealt with."

I remembered Bishop Roger visiting my lord at the castle once. His power had been evidenced by his magnificent clothes and subservient entourage. My lord provided a huge banquet for them, with whole roasted bulls and pigs presented at the tables, accompanied by vast amounts of expensive wine. At the time, I had wondered why Roger was treated with such reverence.

And now, Stephen had taken all his wealth and privilege away from him. Why?

"Roger had become too powerful," Brother Wilfrid answered my unasked question. "And Stephen felt threatened by him.

"Do you think there will ever be a Queen of England?" one of the boys asked.

"Yes, it will inevitably happen sometime. Matilda is determined to seize the throne, but as you know, she is not popular with the people. They say she is arrogant and aggressive, and she has upset too many. Others say that there will never be a Queen of England because a woman is incapable of fighting in battles, and how else can someone gain power and riches? But I believe women have their own powers and gifts, and these are not the same as a man's."

I also loved the lessons about Our Lord Jesus Christ and his family in the Holy Land, and how He had given up His life for us so that we could be redeemed from our sins. I was never quite sure how He did that, but I believed what I was told.

Forty years ago, the monks told us, armies from Europe had captured Jerusalem from the infidels (whoever they were). Our armies still held that city and this was a source of great pride to us. Wouldn't it be wonderful to visit Jerusalem one day?

When the lessons were over for the day, we couldn't wait to get outside into the fresh air, especially in summer when the weather was hot and humid. We would run to the small river while peeling off our clothes and squealing with excitement, then we jumped into the cool water, splashing and pushing each other. When I looked back, these should have been the best days of my life. But my excitement and enthusiasm were often crushed by one boy. He was big and tough, and his name was Fulke.

He took every opportunity to put me down and encouraged his friends to bully me too. I was beaten up on a regular basis and insulted every day, my one arm often the focus of their torments. They also called my mother a slut and our lord's harlot. I wasn't sure what they meant at first, but it didn't take them long to make their meaning absolutely clear. I didn't believe them, but their words hurt me much more than the physical beatings, and they knew it. This encouraged them to hurl more abuse. I dared not tell my mother, or anyone else.

The physical bullying also increased. I hated it when they caught hold of my one good arm and swung me round faster and faster, and then let go to see how far they could throw me into the lake. It was demeaning and incredibly painful. I was terrified that my arm would be pulled out of its socket, and then I would be completely useless.

Their horrid actions spoiled what could have been an idyllic childhood. As a consequence, I stopped playing games with the other boys and started running on my own. I pushed myself hard and ran faster each day. Running with one arm was difficult, but I practised more than anyone else until I was the fastest runner in the village.

But I still wasn't satisfied, and so I started running longer distances. I was determined that no one in the county would be able to match my pace or stamina.

***

"Crippen, Crippen, wake up."

I raised my head to see Yusuf peering through the bars once again. He had been as good as his word, showing me a large basket full of many kinds of fruits and vegetables. The men were all alert at once and crowded around the small window. We reached through the bars, taking as much as we could, then ate like wolves. There were apples, melons, oranges, juicy peaches – the biggest I had ever seen – and plenty of olives. I spat out the first one I tried, and then swallowed the next one whole.

"Crippen – you should take the stone out first," Yusuf called, but too late!

I had never eaten a lemon before, and I eagerly bit into the yellow fruit and chewed half of it. I didn't think I had ever tasted anything so bitter, but too embarrassed to spit it into my hand after having done so with the olive, I had to swallow it. But despite the unfamiliar flavours, I can't tell you the relief this food gave us. The sweet moisture of the fruit revived our spirits and brought new life to us. Conversations started between the men after days of silence, and the smiles and laughter we shared cheered us up enormously.

Yusuf seemed very pleased with the happiness he had created, and we all made sure to show our gratitude to him. I went back to the window and told him that he had saved our lives with his generous gifts. I was concerned for him, though.

"Yusuf – will you get into trouble?"

He smiled and said, "I don't get into trouble. My father loves me, and we are a close family. I will receive praise and blessings for my actions from my family and from God."

"But we are your enemies. Surely your people would rather we were dead."

"No, you don't understand. We are taught to respect all peoples and to share our worldly goods and the goodness from the earth, even with our enemies. You Franj invade our lands and attack us, and of course we fight back and kill you when we have no other choice. Franj are very aggressive and cruel, unlike us Muslims. Some of your soldiers are extremely violent and dishonourable, much more so than any of our other enemies."

I thought about his statement before answering him. "But we are told very different things about your people. We are civilised while you are savages. Franj are Christians and therefore better people. Our Lord and Saviour came from these Holy Lands, and we are here to claim them back. That's why our people had to take Jerusalem and protect the city from the heathen."

"Is that why you massacred thousands of people from different nations when you took the city? You even killed your own people. Were these Christian acts? No, they were the actions and behaviours of brutes and animals. We only fight in retaliation."

What he was telling me completely contradicted the stories I had repeatedly been told by our leaders and monks. I just couldn't accept that he was right, but I was prepared to listen to him and question him more closely. Perhaps my education had been too one-sided. Maybe it was now time to see the world from a different point of view.

"You asked me if I would get into trouble for bringing you gifts," Yusuf continued, "and I told you no. My father Ayyub is a very important man, a great general in our country and the bravest of them all. He is the fiercest fighter in the land and he will bring all the Arab nations together. He will force you Franj people into the sea and you will never come back here to trouble us. This is our country – not yours. I will follow him to achieve this dream; we will become the strongest people in the world."

"Where is your father now?"

"He is away fighting with the great Nur-al-Din, our leader, but he will return and take charge of Damascus. I look forward to introducing you to him.

"Have you seen Damascus yet? No, of course you haven't. We have the finest buildings, paintings and materials, the best bookshops in the world, and our Mosque is the most magnificent anywhere. If you like, I could tell my family about you, and then I will be allowed to show you around."

I wasn't too sure about this. If his father was indeed as important as Yusuf said, I was certain he wouldn't let me wander freely around his city. It might be better to keep my head low and go unnoticed, just as I had done with my lord back in England. I didn't expect to live more than a few days anyway, but I didn't want to suffer unnecessarily before my death. Thanks to my upbringing, I still believed Yusuf's people were vicious and cruel, despite what my new friend had just told me, so if I became the focus of their attention, I stood a chance of dying a painful death. I didn't want to take any undue risks with my life.

"No, Yusuf, I don't think that would be a good idea. I am safer in here."

Without another word, Yusuf rushed off and I went back to my space on the floor. The atmosphere in the prison was greatly improved after our wonderful feast and I seemed to have gained a level of respect from my fellow prisoners.

Early the next morning, Yusuf reappeared with a glass of milk for me. He also carried a jug for the others.

"I spoke to my family and told them I have a new friend – a Franj, but a boy like me, who only has one arm. As I don't have many friends of my own age, I said that I would like to show you around my city. They said that as my father is not around, they would have to speak to the authorities. Whoever these authorities are, they said yes! But they also said I must have a chaperone. He is standing just over there."

I saw Yusuf point to someone behind him who I couldn't see from the cell window.

"My family has already sent a message to the prison governor to put you into my care. I just have to ask for the one-armed boy as none of the guards will know your name. In fact, I don't like it – Crippen." Yusuf wrinkled his nose. "So I'm going to change it. From now on, you are Shiva – like the many-armed God from India."

"But I only have one arm! That is really silly."

"Well, I think it is funny and that's what I'm going to call you."

A jailer came to take me out of the prison. As I left, a dozen pairs of goggling eyes witnessed the event and jaws dropped all around me.

"Enjoy your freedom and bring some food back for us," my neighbour called out.

"I will do my best, Hans."

Then the others chimed in with their requests.

"Don't forget to bring us all presents."

"We want to know everything you do and see."

"Tell us all about the girls in the city, and make sure you tell them about all these wonderful men in here."

For once, the jailer treated me with kindness and respect, probably due to his orders having come from the senior authorities of the city, and I began to realise just how much power Yusuf's family must have. The jailer led me along a passageway and out into the very bright sunshine. I gasped at the intensity of the heat and the blazing sun, and was briefly dazzled and disorientated. I hadn't been outside for weeks and the jail had been relatively cool, sometimes even freezing cold, so the contrast was a shock. But it was wonderful to breathe in the delicious fresh air, without the taint of bodily smells.

Yusuf came running towards me, followed by his chaperone. I guessed this man had been appointed to keep an eye on me rather than him. No one wanted a Franj on the loose, trying to escape or causing trouble.

Yusuf looked excited to see me and gave me a big hug. His face was beaming with smiles.

"Shiva, it's great you are out of that horrible place. Now look, what would you like to do first? No, first you are going to drink. This bottle holds water from the top of a mountain. Look, the snow is still in it. Go on, drink, it will do you good."

I didn't need any further persuading. I took the bottle from him gratefully and, with several swigs, drained the delicious nectar, leaving a large piece of ice at the bottom that wouldn't fit through the neck. As the ice melted, I greedily drank the rest of it. I was so relieved, I couldn't speak for a few moments.

"Come on, Shiva, we need to get you some clean clothes next."

Yusuf led me to a shop across the road. It was a wooden structure painted a pleasing shade of light blue, but it was so dark inside that I had to blink several time to adjust my eyes. As they grew accustomed to the gloom once more, I saw that the place was vast. I was amazed to see hundreds – nay, perhaps thousands – of clothes of all types and colours. Many were bright, made from different materials and animal skins. Some were heavy and dark, and some were so light, they would keep you cool on the hottest days.

On the opposite side of the shop, I saw carpets piled up on the floor, others hanging from the walls. The variety and vibrancy of the colours was breathtaking. I briefly thought how glorious they would look in my lord's vast dining room. In fact, the shop was probably larger than that room.

I would have liked to stay and wonder at all the other delights in there, but Yusuf had plans. He ordered an elderly man to find me a kaftan, and the shopkeeper passed me a very expensive looking wrap, made of the most lovely, light material. The brilliant white would deflect the sun and keep me cool. Next, Yusuf ordered the man to find me some matching headgear.

All the while, the chaperone watched, never once speaking or smiling. He was tall and rather sinister looking, dressed in a black shift which was so long, it swished on the ground as he walked. His brown leather belt carried a huge and evil-looking curved scimitar. I didn't want to get on the wrong side of him; I could just imagine him raising it high in the air and swishing it down at lightning speed.

I shuddered briefly.

The chaperone stepped forward and gave a few coins to the shopkeeper, who bowed in thanks as we left the shop.

"Look, Shiva, you are a sack of bones," said Yusuf, prodding me in the ribs. "You need feeding up and I know just the place to take you. This café is my father's favourite place. Just you wait until you taste the delicious dishes they make."

Juices rushed into my mouth and my stomach rumbled in eager anticipation. Yusuf was not exaggerating. We went into another dark place and as our eyes slowly adapted to the gloom, I could see rows of brown wooden tables and chairs in a space much bigger than I'd expected. Most of the tables were occupied by families and small groups. The buzz of conversation and clatter of cooking utensils filled the room, giving the place a very inviting atmosphere. I couldn't believe how fast the waiters moved around the room and in and out of the kitchen.

A small but very fat host with a huge smile rushed up to us, bowing several times. I guessed he knew Yusuf and his family, and respected their importance locally. The three of us were shown to a table on the far side of the room, near the kitchen. The cooking smells and waves of aromas from the spices almost made me faint. It was all a lot to get used to, but at this moment, I was too hungry to care.

Yusuf whispered a few words to our host. In moments, he'd brought us huge plates of small delicacies. I couldn't wait and started gobbling down mouthfuls of the sweet and spicy goodies.

"Shiva, you are supposed to wait to be invited to eat," said Yusuf, laughing. "But of course, you must be starving, so I forgive you."

The chaperone was not so amused. Under the intensity of his glare, I apologised in Arabic to both Yusuf and the grim-faced man.

As more plates arrived, some with larger portions than our appetiser, I waited for Yusuf to invite me to get started. Our dour chaperone didn't eat a morsel. Yusuf helped himself to small mouthfuls, but didn't eat anything like as much as I did.

"Go on, Shiva, eat, eat, eat!" he encouraged, waving a hand at the food. "I want you to make up for all those weeks when you had to survive on hardly any food in that awful prison. And what you had looked disgusting and smelt even worse."

I did what I was told. After many minutes, my stomach began to fill to its maximum capacity. The feeling was almost indescribably pleasurable.

Finally, I couldn't eat any more and leant back with great relief.

"Shiva, your stomach has swollen. I hope I haven't given you too much to eat."

Before I could reply, a wave of tiredness overcame me and my eyelids drooped. I put my head on the table and slept.

***

I woke up with a start. Yusuf was shaking my shoulder and speaking to me, words I did not want to hear.

"Shiva, it's time for you to go back now."

Someone – probably the chaperone – had taken me to a side room and laid me on a couch. I felt so much better for my sleep, but I was horrified to hear that I was going to be taken back to that awful place.

Yusuf and the chaperone walked me back to the prison, a few minutes away. I had experienced precious moments of freedom and, perhaps more importantly, I'd felt cared for, for the first time since I had left my home. The sustenance made me feel better than I had in weeks, but I dreaded returning to the grim reality of my existence.

Yusuf must have picked up on my low mood. "Shiva, I'm sorry, but I don't have any choice. I will come back to see you soon, I promise."

The problem was that he didn't come back. At least, not for a very long time.

How can your hopes be raised up so high, only to tumble down again like the ships riding the huge waves? I recalled my voyage from England, our vessel hammering down into the sea, seemingly never to rise again. To say I was disappointed would be a huge understatement. I had never felt so down and depressed, and the feeling of helplessness and hopelessness crushed me.

I had believed that this Muslim boy would rescue me, but now I knew how stupid I had been to think that. Why would Yusuf and his family want to help an enemy of their people? They had thousands of their own people to care for, so why should they bother about what happened to me?

I resigned myself to a slow death. I just hoped my end would come with as little pain as possible. Close to panic, I called upon Era, my imaginary friend, for support. And as ever, he gave me positive words of advice. He told me to be strong and have faith.

My energy was low, but I knew it was important to keep communicating with my fellow prisoners.

After all, I had become a minor hero among them due to my association with a small dark-skinned boy who had sustained us all.

I spoke to my neighbour. "Hans, do we have any hope?"

"I am only a simple man. But at home, I was a successful farmer, owning a large piece of land. How do you think I feel now in this stinking place? My religion comforts me, though, and when I close my eyes, I see my grandmother. She is speaking to me now, telling me to keep strong and have faith.

"Don't forget, Crispin, that we have that Arab boy to feed us, if he comes back. And we must believe he will. His food and drink will keep our bodies and souls strong. I pray for our future and eventual release. You too must be strong."

I was shocked and surprised at his humanity, even in this awful situation. After his kind and warm words, I rested my head on a smelly rag and started to relax. Yes, I would stay positive and have faith for the future. After all, faith is the basis of my religion, of Hans's religion, and as devoted believers, we know that Our Lord will keep us safe.

I was worried, though, about all those who had been killed and wounded on our way here. Why had they not been protected? It's so hard to keep your faith when you see friends falling by the wayside. Did that mean that we would be safe in the life hereafter, but not in this one? The Pope had promised that we would be absolved of all our sins if we joined the campaign.

I felt so confused. Surely my Saviour would not let me down.

Conditions in the prison got even worse. Without Yusuf, food and water were in short supply again, and two of the men grew seriously ill. Hans kept asking me if I could contact Yusuf to come to help us.

"Crispin, we all urgently need food and drink to keep our bodies going. I am afraid that some of us are near death. Have a word with the prison guards and the governor to help us."

But of course, I could do nothing without Yusuf's help, and he was nowhere to be seen.

***

Days and then weeks went by without any change. We begged the guards for help, but it was no good. They ignored us and couldn't care less.

As we'd expected, the two men who had sickened soon died and I was sure more would follow. The room smelt worse than ever. I now knew what was meant by hell. We had arrived there while still on earth. All I wanted to do was to sleep forever, never to wake up.

Three more men died, then another three, and each time, the guards came in to drag their bodies away. There were only six of us left. Perhaps they were waiting and hoping the rest of us would hurry up and die.

But once again, Era had not let me down. I was awoken by a voice that filled me with hope.

"Shiva, Shiva, over here! Come quickly, I'm at the window. Shiva, wake up!"

I opened one eye, tried to move my stiff body, but failed. Eventually, I pushed myself up with my elbow. The pain was horrible. I managed to stagger to the window and saw Yusuf's concerned features.

"Yusuf, where have you been? We are all nearly dead in here," I croaked.

"Here, Shiva, here's some water. Go on, take it. Take it!"

I drained the bottle in seconds without a thought for my fellow prisoners. I didn't need to worry as none of them stirred.

"Here's another bottle, Shiva, take it. I am going to get you out again tomorrow. I'll call in the morning."

I was so shocked that at first, I couldn't answer. I wanted to say that I needed to leave this hellish place for good and I couldn't bear it if I had to go back inside. But the words would not come. Instead, tears fell from my eyes, and I couldn't stop blubbering.

"Shiva, don't worry, it will all be good. I will look after you."

And with that, he was gone like an arrow shot from a bow.

Chapter 3

Free At Last

Yusuf was as good as his word. He was at the prison at first light. Before I was led out of the cell door, I took one last look at the room and at my few remaining companions. But they were too tired and ill to move.

Hans was lying on the floor, unconscious, and I doubted he had long to live. I touched his head for a few moments, my way of saying goodbye, then left him the bottle Yusuf had brought the previous night, still half full of water. But I doubted he would have need of it. I hoped with all my heart that this time, I would never have to come back to this hellhole ever again. I would rather be dead.

The jailer rattled the big door and pushed it open. Once again, he led me outside into the very bright sunshine. Once again, I was disorientated, but extremely relieved to be free after so long.

Yusuf was waiting for me. "Oh, Shiva, I am so pleased to see you. Come on – it's time for food and drink!"

I was crying with relief at being out of that ghastly place. My tears fell freely. My body was so weak, my limbs were screaming in pain, so any movement was agony.

I didn't like to ask Yusuf why it had taken him so long to come back, and I never would. It was just a tremendous relief to see him again. Even the ever-grim chaperone was a welcome sight.

Yusuf held out an ice-cold bottle. I drank greedily.

"Look, Shiva, you are a sack of bones again. We need to feed you up, but that will happen later. I'm not sure how to tell you this in a nice way, so I'll say it bluntly. You stink! I know just the place for you."

The road was busy with traders' stalls of all kinds and the smoky air filled my nostrils with the scent of spices, all of which were new to me. Yusuf told me that the strongest aroma was caused by cannabis, which almost everyone smoked. I had no idea what he was talking about, but Yusuf promised to explain all to me later.

I was fascinated with the sights and sounds of the market. Traders were holding up their goods and shouting over each other about the benefits of their wares. One man was singing about his array of bottles and lamps. Another was talking about the finest shoes this side of Africa. I laughed when I saw they all had long pointy toes.

There were thousands of stalls with merchandise from all parts of the world. Yusuf excitedly told me about all the strange foods, and I recognised the brightly coloured lemons, shiny apples from the local orchards, huge round melons, sweet peaches, rich olives. There were sticky dates, green figs, and nuts of all sizes. I had never seen anything like them before. Hard green coconuts, Yusuf told me, had been brought from the east. He asked a trader to drain the milk from one so that I could taste its delicious sweetness.

Another stall holder peeled a long yellow fruit and broke off the top, exposing its soft white meat, inviting me to eat it. I thanked him and told him it was delicious, and it was. And then he offered me green and red grapes. It was all too much.

Further along the market, spices were beautifully laid out in trays with their bright colours and aromas charming all the senses. Yusuf insisted that I taste each one of them, letting them fizz and sparkle on my tongue. I was dizzy with all these new experiences.

I had never seen so many different types of people before, filling every street. Some were tall, some short; some were healthy, but too many were ill or lame, and some had limbs missing like me. Most were dark skinned, but some were as black as the night.

Yusuf pointed to a group of these black men who were tied together by rope. "These are our slaves. We buy them at the slave markets. They work in the fields and build our houses. The auction prices are very high at the moment and it's a good business for the traders who bring them from the south."

I was horrified, but had the good sense to keep my mouth shut. My attention was soon distracted anyway by men and women who looked as if they could not open their eyes properly. They were much smaller than the other people around.

"These people travel many miles from the east," Yusuf explained, seeing my bewilderment. "It takes them months to get to us. They are also traders, dealing in precious herbs, spices and perfumes, but they are most well known for their beautiful silks and porcelain." Then he pointed in another direction. "What do you think that black powder is for? Yes, the stuff in that box."

I looked at him blankly.

"It's called gunpowder. You can destroy buildings with it. These people from the Far East invented it, and they bring it here to sell to us."

"I hope it doesn't catch fire in this heat." I scuttled away as fast as my aching legs would carry me. The warmth of the sun had eased my suffering somewhat, but I was still stiff from my months of confinement. Glancing back at the gunpowder, I decided I would find out more later, and at a safe distance.

A group of boys ran past us, screaming and yelling with excitement. They had armfuls of fruit and were racing away, just out of reach of one of the traders. He shouted and chased them, waving a big stick, threatening them with a beating. But it was no contest between the aging man and the nimble young boys.

A man was sitting cross-legged on the ground, playing a pipe. To my horrified fascination, a snake rose slowly out of a sack. I was mesmerised by the sound of the pipe, which filled my head and senses and made me feel dizzy and disorientated.

Without warning, I fell to the ground.

***

I woke up in a darkened room, lying on a huge cushion. Several faces, including Yusuf's, were looking down at me with grave concern.

"What happened? I suddenly felt so tired, did I fall asleep?"

"Yes, Shiva," replied Yusuf. "I expected too much of you after your long and terrible ordeal. I should have arranged time for you to rest. But we still need to clean you up. I was suffering quietly while walking next to you! I am going to treat you to a relaxing massage in our local steam rooms. It's a great treat and you will love the experience. I am sure you will smell much better when it is over."

Yusuf pulled me to my feet and walked me outside. Just a short distance along the same street, he led me through an unassuming door on our right. Attendants came and took me into a very hot and steamy room. The steam was so dense that I could hardly see. I had never experienced such a place before and was scared. Was I about to be boiled alive?

Three men approached me and grabbed my good arm and my shoulder. They were big men – not tall, but very wide, wearing towels around their expansive waists. Sweat and steam poured off their bodies. I thought at first they were overweight, but it soon became apparent that they had enormous muscles. They reminded me of wrestlers who'd come to our town many years ago. Their faces were wreathed in smiles as if they were looking forward to my imminent treatment.

My terror grew!

"These men will scrub your body down and make you feel lots better," Yusuf told me. I should have been more grateful to him, but all I wanted to do was sleep. Unfortunately, there was no chance of any rest at all in this place. The massage Yusuf had described as relaxing was anything but. Within moments, I was screaming as severe pain shot through my body. The three men pummelled, prodded, bashed and punched every part of me. They even pulled my fingers so hard, I thought they would be ripped from my hand. For once, I was grateful to have only one arm and smiled at my thought through the pain.

They attacked my legs with a fierce chopping motion using the sides of their hands. Then they turned me on to my back and continued their onslaught on my front, pounding and belting my arm and legs, and massaging my chest and stomach. I cried out and begged them to stop, but they just grinned back at me.

Thankfully, they left my wound alone. Perhaps Yusuf had told them what had happened to me or maybe they already knew. Nonetheless, I thought this torture would never end.

After a very long time, they stood back and finally, my dreadful punishment did end. Every bone in my body was bruised and battered. For a silly moment, I wondered if I would have suffered so much pain from my jailers, but I knew at once that would have been many times worse.

Lying on my front again, I looked sideways and saw Yusuf smiling at me. Perhaps my friend had been enjoying my suffering. Perhaps I had been wrong to trust him. But I just closed my eyes in grateful relief that my ordeal was over.

"Come on, Shiva, I am going to take you home to rest and eat, and then I'm going to show you my beautiful city."

I stood, swaying slightly next to the bed, my legs wobbling like one of my mother's jellies. Again, I collapsed to the ground, unconscious.

***

Many hours later, I woke up in a huge room with radiant sunbeams shining in through the windows. I was lying in a bed fit for a king with a depth of comfort I had only ever dreamt of. Or probably, I had never even imagined such a heaven could exist. This was all so far above my life's experiences. At home, I had slept on a hard wooden cot with a thin cover. After all, I was only a poor English boy, plunged into luxury not even my lord would have known. I didn't deserve this, having been born into servitude. This was not part of my world.

I tried to drift into a beautiful sleep filled with dreams of mystical creatures and exotic lands. But an excited voice brought me back to reality.

"Shiva, how are you? Do you need to sleep some more? You can if you want, because you are in my palace now. You can do whatever you like. But you have been asleep for hours and hours, all evening and all night."

I did indeed want to sleep for a very long time. In fact, I didn't want to get up at all, although I was feeling horribly hungry. I was so tired and drained of life.

"If you are able to get up, we can eat before I take you to visit my beautiful city. You just cannot imagine how lovely it is. I am so excited you are here with me and my family. We have so much to show you."

After a healthy and hearty breakfast of creamy milk, peaches, melons and other delicious fruits I couldn't name, I was looking forward to my tour. Yusuf and I were sitting on the fattest cushions I had ever seen, fatter even than those in Queen Eleanor's tent. The sun was shining on the huge dining table in a room far bigger than any in Lord Milton's castle. I could hardly see from one side to the other. I pinched my leg and chin just to prove I was still alive!

I never did go back to the prison.

***

Yusuf had not exaggerated about his home city of Damascus; it was indeed the most beautiful place I had ever seen. I was sure there was nowhere better in the whole world. And I was lucky to have such an enthusiastic and educated guide.

"Many of the houses are made of wood," Yusuf told me, "while buildings of bricks secured with mud are the choice of wealthier residents."

We walked down a long street and moved towards an area of shops and markets.

"Have you ever seen so many bookshops, Shiva?" asked Yusuf, waving his arms excitedly. "How many are there in your city? How many do you think there are along this street alone?"

I started to count them, but gave up when I reached forty-five.

"Sixty?" I guessed.

"No, you are wrong, there are over 100. I will show you some of the magnificent books on display here. You won't see anything like this anywhere else. Now, let's go to our magnificent Mosque. It is the largest and most beautiful in the world."

My life had taken a dramatic turn for the better, but I wondered how long this would last. Suppose Yusuf became bored with my company and decided to abandon me.

"What's going to happen to me when your father returns?" I asked him. "I am frightened for my future. Here I am in a foreign land full of strangers

– apart from you, of course – a long way from my home."

"Don't worry, Shiva, I have a plan for you and me. I am going to become a mighty warrior. My dream is to be like my father and fight for the unity of our nation. You are going to be my helper."

"But I am a poor English boy with one arm, and these are not my people. What will they do to me when I don't have you to protect me?"

"You worry too much. Have faith in me and my strength. I have ambition and purpose and I need you to help me. We will support each other. You will look after me and my horses."

"But why me?"

"The power you have in your one arm and the rest of your body is greater than most. You have developed skills which only a few have. Yes, you will be my faithful friend and we will support each other all our lives. We have a saying here: 'When one eye is lost, the other becomes sharper.' When one arm is missing, the other becomes more powerful."

"Yes, that's exactly what has happened to me, but I have had to work hard to become better than all the others. I never used my deformity as an excuse."

"I know that, Shiva. Another saying goes: 'When our faith in people is diminished, we look upwards, and our view becomes clearer and more perfect.'"

Yusuf really did surprise me with his maturity and clear vision for the future, so much so it was hard to believe that he was still so young. I had no doubt that he would realise his purpose in life to become a great leader. I felt comforted by his words, but would still rather be thousands of miles away from here. I wanted to be back in the castle in familiar surroundings.

Then I remembered the punishment I'd suffered at the hands of Fulke and his gang of bullies, how they had restricted my life and happiness. In that moment, I resolved to make the most of the opportunities Yusuf had offered me.

Chapter 4

The Journey to Egypt

Ten thousand riders kicked up clouds of dust which completely blacked out views of the path we had taken. Fortunately, the wind was in our faces, otherwise we would not have been able to see the hazards ahead.

We were travelling south from Damascus alongside the right-hand bank of the River Jordan, and going at an incredible speed; we had been commanded to get to our destination in record time in order to outsmart the enemy. The constant drumming of the horses' hooves drowned out any possibility of communicating with anyone, apart from arm waving and pointing, which wasn't that helpful. I observed the land gradually changing from luscious green to the browns and yellows of the desert. The pace was terrifying and exhausting.

I was, of course, aware of the biblical history of these parts. This river had witnessed Jesus's baptism by his cousin John, later known as The Baptist. I could imagine him preaching to his devoted followers on the bank, and then taking them into the river and pushing their heads below the surface for their baptism.

We had been riding close to Jericho where the walls had been flattened by the sound of the

Israelites' trumpets. I pictured Moses leading thousands of people towards the land of milk and honey, which had been promised to them by God after they'd escaped slavery in Egypt. Could they really have taken forty years to get here? We were told we had to reach Egypt in a couple of weeks!

The sheer exhaustion I was suffering ended my daydreaming. It took all my strength and concentration to keep up with the others. I could see Yusuf riding nearby, but there were several horsemen separating us. Still, I endeavoured to keep close to him as he had requested. Yusuf was an excellent and experienced rider, but I was concerned for the health and fitness of his wiry brown horse. After all, the beast was my responsibility and I resolved to do my duties to my best ability.

Of course, I had had as much riding experience as Yusuf, but for once, I was fully aware of my disability and my limitations. I had great difficulty keeping up the pace over the rough ground with only one arm to support me, so I needed twice the strength of other men in that arm and my legs to prevent me from losing my balance and falling off.

The ground to my right rose up high and transformed into huge overhanging cliffs and imposing mountains. To my left, the Jordan drained into the vast Dead Sea. I had read about this in the Bible, but was seeing it for the first time. Looking at the mountains, I instinctively knew that we were in the place where Our Lord had spent forty days and nights alone. He was tempted by the devil, who told Him that He could jump off the highest mountain and be saved by the tempter. Jesus resisted and reinforced his faith.

Further along, I spotted a huge mountain which I guessed was Masada, where a few wretched Israelites held out against the formidable Roman army for more than two years. They committed mass suicide rather than surrender. I would love to have had more time to explore this extraordinary location of a momentous event, which took place not long after the execution and resurrection of our Lord Jesus Christ. However, I didn't think my new friends would have been very sympathetic. And anyway, we had urgent business in Egypt, and didn't have a moment to spare.

We climbed higher. I hoped that a rest would be ordered soon. Horses and men were now exhausted. I was near to breaking point.

Moments later, a rider broke away in front, waving his arms, riding from side to side. We were becoming used to this routine. Gradually, the grateful cohort slowed down and came to a halt. We dismounted awkwardly with stiff legs, sore arses, creaking backs and painful shoulders and arms. We urgently needed water and rest to prepare us for another long day tomorrow.

A huge area of hard, flat ground had been prepared for us and tents were already in place. Teams of boys came for our horses and took them out of our sight to a place of shelter. Another team brought us jugs of very cold water, which I guessed had been brought down from local mountains where the tops were covered in snow. We drank gratefully. Huge sheets were raised on poles and I wondered what these were for. We were ushered underneath, and the purpose was made clear.

After we had stripped off every piece of clothing, gallons of water were sprayed on to the top of these sail-like structures by a method which was not clear to me. As the cooling liquid cascaded down on to our burnt bodies through small holes, giving us all a deliciously cooling shower, I no longer cared how it had been achieved. I wanted to stay under the water for hours, but unfortunately, the blissful process was over in minutes.

We came out into the cool evening air with the sun setting in the west, over the lands the Israelites had travelled from. I dearly wanted to eat, but I was so tired that I didn't think I would have the strength. All I craved was sleep.

"Shiva, you must eat," Yusuf insisted. "You won't have the strength for the long ride tomorrow if you don't. Go on, make an effort."

I forced myself to have a few morsels of the delicious grilled lamb, but it was hard work. My eyelids were drooping.

***

The call to rise seemed to come within seconds of my head resting on a cushion. After a glass of cool milk and a piece of hot bread, it was time to remount for another long day in the relentless southern sun.

The pattern repeated itself day after day. Although I was well-used to riding and the exposure to all weathers, I had experienced nothing like this before. I wondered if I had the stamina to continue.

There was little time to talk to Yusuf or anyone else, but during a rare moment, I mentioned my worries to my friend.

"Shiva, this is very hard for all of us," he replied. "I cannot remember when I have suffered so much. But my uncle Shirkuh says it is imperative that we reach Egypt before the Franj. We must ride fast to avoid them attacking us on the way. This venture could go either way, he says, but he is determined to win."

I knew Shirkuh and was rather afraid of him. He was a terrifying figure; I saw him lose his temper with a soldier once, for no apparent reason. He punched the man again and again until he couldn't get up on his feet. I'd felt sorry for the poor soldier, and after that, I kept my distance, not wanting to get on the wrong side of Shirkuh. If I failed in his opinion, I would be in big trouble.

Short and fat with only one eye, Shirkuh was very tough; he would endure this long journey better than any of us. He had a reputation as big as his belly. I'd heard that he had killed Eleanor's uncle, Raymond of Antioch, some years before by chopping off his head. Shirkuh was riding close to Yusuf, perhaps to keep an eye on him. Yusuf had told me that he was keen to make a good impression on his uncle.

The Franj were from the European countries that had raided Yusuf's lands and taken Jerusalem, a city which was sacred to both Muslims and Christians, and they now ruled the vast area around the city. Brother Wilfred's mesmerising voice echoed in my mind.

"The tomb of Jesus Christ and the Holy Sepulchre had to be protected and the city was taken by our armies forty years ago. Good Christian people still hold this precious possession and must do so for evermore. People from all over Europe, including

England, took the Cross and swore an oath to become pilgrims. They all joined an army which swelled in size as it travelled towards the Holy Land, driven and emboldened by its clear mission."

The paradox of my situation was apparent to me: I would be fighting against my own people, against all I had been taught at school. I had known I would be put into this position sometime, but as I became part of my new society, it seemed to matter less and less.

***

Over the past few years in Damascus, I had been to Muslim schools and places of knowledge, learning how to appreciate Islamic beauty in all its forms. Most days, I visited one of the hundreds of bookshops in the city, as Yusuf had recommended. I read prose and poetry and became proficient in the language. I loved the bright pictures that illustrated the books and began to draw and paint some of my own.

The owner of my favourite bookshop was impressed with my work. "Why don't you create your own book with writing and pictures?" he suggested. "I can help you." He gave me a huge book with hundreds of blank pages, and I eagerly took advantage of his generosity, visiting the shop once a week to work on my exciting new project.

The people of Damascus had a magnificent new hospital and medical school, the care of which I experienced for myself shortly after I was freed from prison. Yusuf became concerned for me after I'd passed out several times with no warning, becoming violently sick. This went beyond exhaustion; my ordeal – the terrible journey and all the deprivations – had clearly caused long-term damage to the health of my body and mind. In addition, the wound in my side had become infected and the pain was horrible.

"Shiva, you need to see a doctor. I will arrange it," Yusuf told me eventually.

The doctor was a rather morose elderly man who came to the house and gave me a thorough examination. When he left, Yusuf hurried into my bedroom to find out exactly what had happened.

"Your doctor spent around an hour examining every part of me," I replied. "He checked my head and body for heat and peered into each orifice." Both Yusuf and I winced at these words. It hadn't been pleasant. "He made me sit up, bend over to touch my toes, breathe in and out, and jump up and down. He prodded my stomach, my neck and chest, and then listened to my heart for what seemed like an age. He was most interested in my withered arm and when I told him I was born this way, he nodded his head in understanding. He took away samples of my bodily waste and promised to come back in a few days."

"Oh, I'm glad I wasn't here to witness that!" Yusuf said with an expression of disgust.

True to his word, the doctor did come back and told me he had arranged for me to go into the city's hospital. I needed expert medical help to become fully well again.

"But I can't afford to go," I replied sadly. "I have no way of paying you."

"Don't worry, Yusuf's family has arranged my payment. In fact, they have been very generous. There are no charges for your hospital stay and treatments. We will keep you there until you are fully recovered."

"But I am not from here. I am a Franj."

"This does not matter. We treat all people wherever they come from without charge, and they only leave hospital when they have fully recovered, not before. The magnificence of our deity provides for this service. We have the most advanced medical practices you will find anywhere in the world. Our doctors have studied in Rome, Babylon, Greece and the Far East. Our expertise and skills have been learned from both ancient and modern times. We are far more advanced in medicine, sciences and the arts than your people. I can assure you that you are in the best place for your restoration to full health."

He was not exaggerating. The hospital was a bright, happy place staffed by caring people and I couldn't fault the way I was treated. The doctors came round every day and checked my medicines and diet; they were so thorough, I doubted anywhere in the world could match their incredible high standards. And, of course, Yusuf visited daily with fruits and sweet cakes.

I was in the hospital for six months. As the doctor had promised, by the time I came out, I was restored to full health.

***

Yusuf was so proud of his city that he took every opportunity to show me around, pointing out the highlights enthusiastically. I loved the bright colours and the way they were reflected in the waters. I had never seen such beautiful buildings, and when Yusuf told me the best architects worked in his city, I did not doubt him.

"I want to show you our most sacred place, a building inspired by God."

As we walked across the city, I was sweating profusely as the sun burnt us through the muggy air.

"This heat is terrible," I said to Yusuf. "How on earth do you survive it? It's like walking through a furnace. I've never known heat like this in England or in the many countries we passed through on our way here."

"Don't worry, I have brought plenty of water with me," was Yusuf's only reply. He lifted his water skin and handed it to me, taking the stopper out.

Our thirst slaked, we walked along streets that were becoming increasingly familiar to me, and came to the huge and magnificent Mosque.

"This is the most sacred building in the world," said Yusuf, spreading his hands in an expansive gesture. "Our famous Umayyad Mosque, and I am going to show you around. Look at all the gold in the stones. See how the sun is reflected off the pictures of plants and trees."

It was indeed magnificent and vast, it's beauty almost impossible to describe. English castles and churches were very drab by comparison, built from stones of plain grey or black. This huge building dazzled the eyes with its bright colours.

"I have arranged special permission to take you for a full tour," said Yusuf.

My excitement must have shown as we walked through the huge entrance. I marvelled at the vast space beyond, the rich creamy marble and gold, green and blue mosaics. Nothing in my experience could compare with this magnificence. Our places of worship in England suddenly seemed tiny.

"This site has been a place of worship for over 1,000 years. Did you know that we used to have a Roman temple here, and then a Christian cathedral? You look surprised. Yes, this place was dedicated to your John the Baptist. His head is in that box over there." Yusuf pointed and my eyes followed the direction of his finger, widening in awe. "We greatly respect John. Did you know your Bible's Abraham is buried not far from the city? He is our Abraham as well."

We walked around the beautiful courtyards with their sparkling fountains and into the mighty dome. I felt quite dizzy looking up. Yusuf smiled at my reaction.

Many of the walls had intricate geometric patterns in bright reds, greens, blues, yellows, interspersed with black. Pure gold and silver shone in abundance from the decor. We walked on over paving stones in a magnificent variety of different colours. I was fascinated with the hues and bent down to touch and feel each one. The texture of these stones evoked powerful emotions in me, feelings of beauty and wonder.

"Yusuf, these designs are beautiful," I murmured. "I love the way that the landscape mosaic spreads over this vast area. The vines and plant pictures are amazing. But why are there no images of people and animals?"

"Our prophet didn't want our people to worship idols, so those images are not allowed. Our Mosque here is one of the most celebrated in the world. You are very privileged to be here."

"What is this Mosque used for?"

"Well, it has many uses. It is, of course, a place for prayer and quiet contemplation. People also come here to talk, listen and learn. Look at the hundreds of people in the courtyard. Mostly, they come here to experience its beauty and mysticism."

I was mesmerised by the designs, which transformed into huge three-dimensional spaces as I stared, and after a while drifted into visions of mystical worlds and spirits. As we walked around the colonnades, every border was blossoming with exotic plants and flowers, their fiery perfumes flavouring the still air. These heady aromas fuelled my imagination and dreams.

"Yusuf, what on earth is that contraption?" I asked, pointing with my one hand. "I've never seen anything like it before." It was a huge box with an enormous wheel and rows of doors. I could hear swirling water and mechanical noises, then two huge brass falcons dropped metal balls into bowls. I was enthralled, but very confused.

"That is a water clock. It has a clever mechanism designed to tell us the time. This is yet another magnificent Muslim invention and the only one in the whole world."

Eventually, we left the building and walked on into the city.

"Damascus is famous for its water," Yusuf told me. "Walk with me along the banks of the river and canals. Look at the beauty of my city. This is surely the most special place in the world."

Although Yusuf loved to show off the great achievements of his countrymen, he wasn't exaggerating. If only the invaders from Europe had knowledge of the achievements of his and nearby countries, we could share learning and skills across all our peoples, rather than attacking and fighting. One day, I hoped, I would have the opportunity to return to England to tell everyone about what I had seen and experienced.

"Thank you, Yusuf," I said. "I do love your city and I am very happy here, and your Mosque is the most magnificent place I have ever visited. I hardly miss my home at all, except for my sweet mother. I worry about her daily, but I don't miss the others. I hope my bullies rot in hell!"

***

Most mornings, Yusuf took me and a group of friends to stables outside the city, close to the walls. The horses were skinny creatures, unlike the huge chargers the Crusader knights rode, but they were fast and nimble and could twist and turn in and out of trouble. I could see that this would be a huge advantage in battle. They also seemed to enjoy racing and exercising and were less prone to moodiness, which was another advantage.

"Shiva, you must understand that we love our horses with all our hearts," Yusuf told me. "They are more important to us than our wives, but don't tell them so. The wives, I mean! You must look after them like your own children. Your people use horses like slaves and don't respect them. Always give them your love and care. Feed and water them before you look after yourself."

If I was struck by the irony of my friend showing such respect for the animals who served him while thinking nothing of using human beings as slaves, I was wise enough not to give voice to it.

We took the horses out and rode them hard. Mostly, we went hunting, seeking out wild deer and other small animals to run down with our spears. Yusuf and his friends used their limbs to control their horses more than my people did. This suited me well and I practised to become like them, quickly learning the skills and gaining competence.

"Shiva, now you must prepare for battle," said Yusuf. "We call the next exercise pegging. I will show you how this is done, and then let you have a go."

The men who were accompanying us rammed around thirty small wooden stakes into the ground in two rows facing each other, a couple of hundred yards apart. When they had finished, Yusuf sat straight on his horse and raised his lance upwards. He waited a few moments to increase the drama, and then slowly lowered his weapon until it pointed at the first stake. Digging his heels into his horse's sides, he flew at the first target with a high-pitched cry. Within seconds, he had split the first stake, and then he whirled his horse around, charging towards the other row. He was also successful with his second target.

Backwards and forwards he charged until he had split all but two of the stakes. Finally, he rode towards me with a satisfied smile.

"That's how it's done! You have to imagine that each stake is a Franj invading our country. One day, we will have killed or chased out all of them."

"But what about the ones you missed completely?"

"Shiva, you have a wicked tongue in your mouth. Let's see if you can do any better. Go!"

I copied his starting position and with a cry, charged down the first stake. I missed it completely. And I missed the second one.

"Very poor start!" I heard him call out. I split number six right down the middle, but only managed to hit three more before I came to the end of the rows.

"You need much more practice," said Yusuf, laughing. "Wait until the next two rows are ready, and then try again."

I was a little more successful the second time, but it would be many weeks before I could approach his achievements.

Another day, we would practise with our scimitars. Setting up dummies dressed in clothes, we would ride towards them at speed, and then cut their tops off. We had to turn about sharply, repeating the stroke on the lower parts. Our men had to move fast to replace them.

"Shiva, you have to imagine these as Franj, and then you will become more skilful."

"But Yusuf, we live side by side with the Franj and even trade with them. They are permanent residents in our country. How can you talk about them with such savagery?"

"You must understand that we are peaceful people, defined by our religion. We are not like the Franj who come here to slaughter us for no reason. We have to fight back. But the Franj who live side by side with us here are generally peaceful and good neighbours. And we trade with all good neighbours. However, they have taken our most holy city by force, and one day we must take it back for our people. I told you before that I will unite my people to claim back these lands which are rightfully ours. I was born to do this. I hope you will always serve me in my holy mission.

"Shiva, you have become one of us. Your skin has browned from 1,000 suns; you dress like us and have deep knowledge of our customs and traditions. You have developed a love for our art and buildings. I believe you love our religion also, but you have not yet bowed before our God. Perhaps this is too early.

"We all trust you and welcome you as one of us. I have not heard any adverse comments about having a foreigner in our midst for quite a while and I hope never to do so again. I want you to be my second in command and together we will achieve brilliance."

I was pleased to hear him say this. I often wondered what would happen to me if his men thought differently. If they turned on me, I would have very limited options.

Yusuf held his scimitar high and declared in an authoritative voice, "This is a far superior weapon to your heavy sword and much more subtle. It is easier to handle and is more effective to kill someone. Imagine you are in the middle of a battle. You must kill or be killed. With this scimitar, I can kill many men and my arm will not tire. Using the sword your people favour, you will tire easily and your arm will ache after a few strokes. And then you will be at risk."

Eventually, I became almost as skilled as he was with the scimitar.

Yusuf was passionate about polo and would play most evenings. Even when he was losing, which wasn't very often, he just loved playing the game. Sometimes, he would play against just one opponent, usually me, and he was never interested in stopping.

"I can't see very well," I would grumble as the sun set. "It's too dark."

"Did you bring those candles?" Yusuf would call out. "Please set them up around the field."

Half a dozen men would spring forward, setting up and lighting the huge candles so we could carry on playing for another hour or two.

"Now, Shiva," Yusuf would say finally, "we must go into the city for some fun and sport with the ladies."

I dreaded this request. Always careful to keep a low profile and not highlight my western features, I definitely didn't want to draw attention to myself. And behaving in a debauched manner was a sure fire way to do exactly that.

***

Yusuf was growing up fast and had just celebrated his sixteenth birthday. I had been honoured to be invited to his family party to celebrate. Even though food was scarce due to strife in the country, the fare was magnificent.

As Yusuf rightly predicted all those years ago, shortly afterwards, Ayyub came back to the city at last with his brother Shirkuh and a small army. Negotiations for the peaceful surrender of Damascus from the current authorities to Ayyub had been going on for years, but now, Yusuf's father was growing impatient.

"My father is a great man, brave and noble," Yusuf assured me. "He will take this city and rule the people with intelligence and generosity, unlike the idiots in charge now. He will easily overcome them. Come with me, we need to help them gain entry."

Ayyub's army had settled just outside the city walls. Yusuf led a dozen men, myself included, up the steps to the top of the battlements, each of us carrying a long rope. We tied one end around a battlement and threw the other over the side to the ground. In moments, soldiers from the army had seized the ropes and were climbing the walls.

We let out a huge cheer when the first man reached the top, soon joined by a dozen others. Engineers rushed down to the gates and broke the locks. The gates were pulled open. The army poured in, along with wagons of food and supplies for the inhabitants. It was a glorious homecoming.

We rushed down to greet the army with huge excitement, Yusuf scanning the crowd for Ayyub. It occurred to me that he might not recognise his father after so many years, but when we saw two men striding towards us, Yusuf gave a cry of joy and ran straight into the arms of one.

When his excitement had calmed down somewhat, Yusuf called me over for introductions. He was now as tall as Ayyub, who welcomed and embraced me. But he and his brother Shirkuh were anxious to ensure that the current leaders of Damascus were removed as soon as possible.

Yusuf and I walked with the two older men to the palace, the army following behind us. We were told to stay outside while Ayyub and Shirkuh walked through the massive doors with their guards. Within an hour, they came back out and Ayyub spoke to the waiting crowds.

"We have arranged the peaceful but immediate departure of the leaders, together with their families. They will not come back here. We can now return this city to its former prosperity and abundance."

The cheers of the crowd were deafening.

Yusuf and I walked with Ayyub and his brother the short distance home. Yusuf's mother and siblings were standing outside the house and she ran into her husband's arms. The excitement was contagious and everyone joined in the huge celebrations, people of the city and soldiers alike. The feasting and dancing went on until the sun rose the following morning and continued well into the next day. I had never attended such a happy and magnificent gathering.

However, what should have been pure enjoyment was marred by one thing. His brother might have welcomed me like a son, but every time I glanced over at him, Shirkuh returned a menacing look. He clearly didn't approve of Yusuf's foreign friend, and he was an enemy I didn't want to make.

I definitely needed to ensure I did nothing to upset this man.

Chapter 5

The Nile

"Reckon it's goin' to rain later."

"Oi don't know about tha'. Were no red sky last night. Anyways, them crops need it, as long as it don't pour next month or it'll rot the 'arvest."

"It will tha', to be sure."

"But wha' a beautiful Spring day. Them lambs will be dancing in delight. Good job they don't know we will be feeding on 'em later. They wouldn't be frolickin' about so much – haha!"

The gentle burr of the Wiltshire accent echoed in my mind as I recalled how people back in the marketplaces and villages of England would always talk about the weather before any other matters. Here, things were very different. There was absolutely no point in talking about the weather because it was exactly the same every day. The sun rose in the east, climbing higher in the sky, then sank again until it rested in the sand to the west. Every day, the clouds were burnt away, and the clear air was scorching. There was no variation to discuss.

As I thought about my homeland, the sun was just setting, but its fierce burn was still as powerful as it had been throughout the day. I tried to pull the cloth over my bare head as it had slipped off once again. Even five minutes of exposure to this sun would cause burning and headaches. What an extraordinary contrast to the conditions I had grown up in.

In fact, nothing was the same as I was used to. I had now experienced several years of warfare and extreme violence, and I hated this above all.

I had been horrified by the severed heads of the Franj we had been sent. We were ordered by Shirkuh to display them on the battlements of the city of Bilbeis to discourage the enemy, which I found a disgusting proposition. Not that I would dare argue with Shirkuh, and I had to admit this horribly violent act worked. The attacking Egyptians and Franj immediately called for a truce and an end to the terrible hostilities. For a little while, anyway.

But peace did not last long. Now, the Franj and Egyptians were on the warpath once again.

My mind was drifting as I rode along the banks of the Nile, heading back towards Cairo from where our horsemen had come. The land was cultivated, and crops grew as far as I could see, watered by the flooding of this mighty river. Vast fields of grain and greenery covered unending flat spaces alongside the beautiful blue waters of the Nile, which twisted and turned for hundreds of miles on its journey south. Many thousands of people laboured on both of its banks, looking after the river's prolific produce.

The cultivated land of my homeland was miniscule by comparison, but many of the crops were similar. I recognised onions and leeks, which were like those we grew at home, and I had become used to fig plants and date palm trees. The spikey grassy leaves, I had been told, were papyrus plants, which had been used to make paper and woven goods and eaten since ancient times.

Yusuf had ordered me to find out exactly where the attacking army was and what they were doing. He had told me very clearly that I must not go near them or let myself get into any danger. The Franj had joined forces with the Egyptians to push us out of the country. The struggle had been going on for months with both sides in fierce combat.

Yusuf would often update me with the ebbs and flows of our campaign. I questioned whether this effort and incredible loss of life was worth it, but he was adamant that it was.

"If we let the Franj take over Egypt," he would argue, "they will have extraordinary wealth and be able to stay here forever, ruling vast areas. They will eventually take over all of our lands. Don't forget that this is not their country. This is our home. If we win against them, they will have a limited time here. As you know, it's one of my long-term ambitions to remove them. If we control the wealth of the Nile, then I can begin my life's work."

"But Yusuf, I still don't understand why Egypt is so valuable to you. Surely it's just the same as anywhere else?"

"No, the Nile is worth its weight in gold – well, almost. Many tons of goods are shipped all the way from Upper Egypt, and then on to Alexandria. From its two ports, goods are shipped on to many places all over the world. The Nile Delta produces enough food to fill all of us and plenty more to sell to others. There is nowhere so valuable. We must take the country and not let it fall into the hands of our enemies."

I was amazed at his vision and determination, especially as he was still climbing the political ladder. His uncle Shirkuh oversaw the army and was responsible for taking Egypt, and he was answerable to the great General Nur-al-Din. I wondered if Yusuf was getting above his station. He had an immense amount of work to do before he could prove himself worthy of promotion.

But Yusuf had no such doubts. "I have told you before, one day I will become the greatest and strongest ruler the Arab world will ever have. I will unite our nation to the glory of God. We must prevail here, and you will help me."

**

Our campaign hadn't been going well lately, and Shirkuh had explained his latest plan to his commanders.

"We must trick the enemy army and draw them out of Cairo by retreating. I know they will follow. When we reach land which is favourable to us, we will trap and attack them."

This was why I was heading back in the direction of Cairo on my horse to look for the enemy, with Yusuf's words filling my head. I had a long time alone to think about my own situation and I tried to form an image in my mind of my dear mother's face, but the vision was so blurred now that I couldn't recognise her. This really upset me. Would I ever see her again?

I had been away from home for so long now. How many years had passed since that precious day when she hugged me for the last time, wishing me God speed? We clung on to each other with tears falling out of control. She was crying and I just couldn't help myself.

I had only been fifteen when I left home, and I reckoned I was now in my mid-thirties, perhaps thirty-five. How old would my mother be now? I never knew her age, but she must be well into her fifties. I wondered if she was still alive. I really hoped so and couldn't bear the idea of any harm coming to her. I could still remember the smell of the lavender perfume she made for herself and wore every day.

Under the guidance of the bookshop owner who had first suggested the project, I had been working on my book for many years now, whenever I had the chance to spend time in Damascus. I had decided to write about my life's journey from Wiltshire, to Porto and on to the Holy Land; the awful battle and my imprisonment and eventual freedom. I left no part of my story out and as each new adventure began, I included that as well. On the right side of the page, I illustrated my story and adventures with vivid paintings.

I painted pictures of my mother, my school, and a full page showing the bullies, complete with their snarls, sneers and the curl of their lips. Fulke was portrayed as particularly ugly, as my hatred for him had barely cooled. I painted myself with my one good arm and a happy countenance. I wanted future generations of readers to see that despite my shortcomings, I was contented.

I drew the big, imposing castle in Wiltshire and my lord, dressed in his full armour, seated on his magnificent white stallion. I painted the seas and the ships, depicting the battle of Damascus from the description Hans had given me. A young Arab boy graced many of the paintings, growing larger as he gradually turned into a man. I even drew Era, or how I imagined him to be, writing his name without further explanation below his picture.

I grew passionate about colour, inspired by the fabulous paintings in the Umayyad Mosque. I could see all of the vibrant shades in my mind's eye and I reproduced them exactly as the originals. In fact, Yusuf took me back to the Mosque to confirm my accuracy. He was very excited about my creations. Every page brought to the fore the feelings and passions of the times I was describing, and my moods created their own colours on the corresponding illustration.

I worked on my book one day a week. I looked forward to my weekly visits to the bookshop, but that day disappeared in a whirlwind of deep emotions and sensual colours. I just couldn't believe how quickly the time passed and how much I became immersed in my work. This endeavour would take my entire lifetime, but I was determined to put my experiences and feelings into my huge book.

The moments when I translated my life into writing and vivid colours moved me into daydream mode. Shutting myself off from all sensations of the world, I wasn't aware of anything or anyone around me.

Until one momentous day. And then, my life was turned upon its head once again.

***

"The green is too light in those vines. It just doesn't look right."

I was startled into full consciousness. How could I not have been aware of this young woman standing next to me? How long had she been there? For a brief moment, I wondered if I had become subsumed into a trance state. Perhaps I should not leave the present by burying myself into my subconscious too deeply. Perhaps I would lose my mind in those depths and never get back into the moment.

My senses awakened and I inhaled the deep, warm perfume of lavender. Was I still in my trance? Was this my mother? No, the young woman beside me had brown skin, and her presence stirred in me feelings that were entirely new to me.

"This is how I saw the colours in the Mosque," I said, a little tersely. I didn't like this stranger criticising my work, but more so, I felt on the back foot thanks to the allure of her presence. "And I have put them into my book accordingly."

"Yes, I can see that, but the Islamic colours are not quite right. May I show you?"

"Hmm, all right, but please don't paint into my book in case I don't like your ideas. Use this scrap of paper." I tried to sound short and a little annoyed, but in truth, I was intrigued.

"Look, the colours need to be bolder and the patterns more intricate and detailed." She demonstrated her skills, and I was immediately fascinated by her work. All defensiveness flew away. She painted for more than an hour with fierce lines of concentration etched on to her lovely forehead. Her colours were not only stronger than mine, but blended much better, and I had to admit to myself that her detailed designs were far superior to my rather miserable offerings. Her art had an ethereal, almost spiritual quality that I was unable to produce. This was the effect I had been trying for weeks to create.

"I truly love your work," I said eventually, my voice now full of admiration. "Will you teach me your magic?"

"This is not magic. I attend the Islamic School of Art and I have been training to create these scenes for more than three years now. I am inspired by my religion. Yes, of course I will show you, but at the moment, we are strangers. What is your name?"

"I was given the name Crispin by my mother," I replied, stopping myself from referring to it as my Christian name. "But since I have come to live in Damascus, I have been known as Shiva."

She laughed, the sound as sweet as the most beautiful birdsong. "Shiva, of course," she said. "Yusuf's friend." It seemed my efforts to go unnoticed hadn't been as successful as I would have liked. "My name is Yasmine, which means fragrant flower."

Never had a woman been so aptly named. Her perfume was exquisite and intoxicating, and to me, she was as lovely as the most beautiful rose. Small in stature and rather demure, probably not yet out of her teens, she wore a light shawl, and when she turned towards me, I gasped with joy. Her face shone with an unusual brilliance and when she smiled, the sight was so sweet, I nearly melted.

When Yasmine and I started talking, I thought we would never stop. We wanted to learn everything about each other. Her family lived close by, she told me, and her father was a senior official in the local government. She was the eldest of six.

I showed her all the work I had produced so far in my book and my reasons for attempting the project. Fascinated by the account of my life, she asked if I would allow her to help me. Her beautiful artistry would only enhance what I had created, and I agreed.

Our partnership started that day. Working one day a week, we would continue with what had now become a joint book project.

***

When I told Yusuf about Yasmine, he became extremely excited.

"Shiva, I know her family. They are highly influential in the city. You must meet them as soon as possible. I will arrange it."

The days seemed to drag by between our meetings and I couldn't wait for the next time I would be in Yasmine's company. I asked her if she would take me to art galleries in the city so that I could learn more about the colours and cultural influences of her people, but in reality, I just wanted to be with her more often. In addition to the galleries, she took me back to the Umayyed Mosque and showed me colours and textures in the marble and stone I had not noticed before.

We grew closer and almost inevitably, we fell deeply in love. She was definitely the one for me. I had never known I could be so happy and content. Yasmine gave me a new confidence and direction in life, so much so I began to trust her judgement in all matters.

I grew to appreciate her many talents, but overall, her kindness. She could be tough and somewhat stubborn, but these were qualities we would need in the years to come. My life here would never be easy as I wouldn't be fully accepted by the people, and if I was to share that life, it had to be with a strong woman. Yasmine was ruthless with people who criticised me and was always supportive. I needed her by my side.

Yusuf was true to his word and accompanied me to meet with Yasmine's family. But it transpired that I didn't need the moral support that he offered, grateful though I was for it. Yasmine's family were as warm and accepting as she was, and they embraced me into their circle with love and enthusiasm.

Yasmine and I were married within a few months. Her parents provided a magnificent ceremony and a reception for over 100 people to celebrate the occasion. Yusuf made a huge fuss and seemed to be more excited than we were. But it was truly the happiest day of my life as I looked forward to many years with the woman I loved. Yasmine's parents had gifted us a house in the centre of the city and we would want for nothing.

My only regret was that my dear mother was not here to share my joy.

***

"Crispin," unlike Yusuf, Yasmine liked and used my given name, "have you noticed anything different about me in the past few weeks?"

"You always look lovely to me, Yasmine. What do you mean?"

"Our lives are about to change and will never be the same again."

A shiver of fear ran down my spine.

"What on earth do you mean? What's going to happen?"

Yasmine was a big fan of the dramatic pause. She stared steadily at me, her expression giving nothing away while my mind went through agonies of concern. Was she going to leave me? Had another man stolen her heart – a man with two good arms who shared her religion? Was she ill, dying?

Have faith, whispered Era in my mind. But patience had never been my strong point. Soon, I could stand the suspense no more.

"What, Yasmine?"

To my utter relief, her face broke into a huge smile. "You are going to become a father," she said simply, and my agony turned to ecstasy. I picked her up and swung her around with joy, and then set her gently back on her feet, concerned for her welfare. She laughed and assured me that she was fine, everything was wonderful.

Except, it wasn't. Yasmine went into hospital under the care of the same doctors who had looked after me. Within a short while, she began to deteriorate, and then became seriously ill.

I was asked to attend a meeting at the hospital. "We are very concerned about Yasmine," said a serious-faced doctor, "and we think we should abort the child. Her life is at serious risk. I need your agreement, Shiva."

I had no need to consult Yasmine. She loved this baby as much as if he or she was already in her arms, and nothing would convince her that terminating her pregnancy was the right thing to do. I told the doctor that under no circumstances was he to perform an abortion. To make my point absolutely clear, I told him that Yusuf would be coming to visit us at the hospital soon and was looking forward to the birth.

I had no doubt I was doing the right thing by my wife as well as our unborn child. Era was on my shoulder, whispering to me to have faith, and I had learned by now to trust him implicitly.

Nonetheless, the next few days were some of the worst of my life. Yasmine's condition deteriorated still further. I was at her bedside constantly and could only watch helplessly as she grew pale and her frame became painfully thin, although her stomach was still swollen. Her eyes developed dark shadows beneath them and her breathing grew shallow. She lapsed in and out of consciousness and I believed she was close to death. Sweat poured off her face. I could only pray to my God and hers for the safe deliverance of our child. And all the while, Era was giving me his usual positive encouragement.

The doctor came to me again and suggested he used a procedure that had apparently enabled the birth of the Roman emperor, Caesar, but I answered for both of us when I said that we would wait for a natural birth. It was common knowledge that such an operation caused the death of the mother. The answer was an emphatic no.

I sat by Yasmine's bedside for many days and nights. At last, an end came to her suffering, and as usual, Era had been right. It was positive.

Refusing to leave my wife for a second, I watched as her weakened body strained until, finally, a head appeared. In moments, the rest of a little boy slid out, screaming in outrage. The cord was cut, the baby washed and the doctors rested him next to his mother's cheek. Despite her weakened state, Yasmine cradled him in her arms and smiled contentedly.

Later, the leading doctor took me to one side. "You are married to a most remarkable woman, Shiva," he told me. "I have never seen such a determined fighter. She was going to bring her boy into the world and nothing and no one was going to stop her. I wouldn't want to be in your shoes if she ever falls out with you! What are you going to call him?"

I turned at a familiar footfall, seeing my dearest friend appear in the doorway. There had never been any doubt in my mind, or Yasmine's.

"Yusuf, of course," I replied, still looking at my friend. I had rarely seen such a big smile on his face.

Chapter 6

The Battle of al-Babein

Shouts ahead of me made me jump in shock. I was deep into my daydream and had lost concentration completely. Horsemen were riding towards me, waving their swords and screaming their war cries. To my surprise, they had already crossed the great river on a hastily made pontoon bridge and were making rapid progress.

I was furious with myself for drifting off. Now I might have wrecked Yusuf's plan for his first battle in charge and ruined our chances of success. I turned my horse around with great urgency and dug my heels into the poor beast's sides, racing off towards our army. I had a long way to go, but I didn't let up the pace, praying that my horse had the stamina to get back without collapsing.

After several hours, my horse was resisting and I knew he couldn't go on much longer, but I dared not delay. With Yusuf's words echoing in my ears, I didn't waste any more time looking back.

I asked my imaginary friend Era to support and help me. Once again, he didn't fail me. At last, our army came into sight and I saw the diminutive form of Yusuf in front of his forces. I raced up to him, waving and pointing to the approaching army behind me. At that moment, my horse collapsed beneath me and I jumped clear just in time. He had had enough and didn't move again.

Yusuf ran towards me and helped me to my feet, concern on his face. I was a bit shaken, but unharmed. Holding me up by my good arm, he looked at the huge dust cloud of the army approaching from the north. To my relief, I had been able to warn him and our army in time.

Vast hordes of enemy soldiers rode up towards us, now at a slower pace, their arrogant confidence in their superiority clear from their demeanour. Yusuf was in the middle of a valley with his army behind him. He seemed very exposed, but he calmly stood his ground and ordered his men to do likewise. I was terrified for him.

"Shiva, get yourself out of here. Climb up that hill and get away from danger. We will take over now. Thanks for the warning."

I felt guilty at his thanks. He would never know how close I had come to ruining his special day. I had to obey his command immediately and without question, so I raced up the side of the sandy slope and struggled to the top. Falling forward and looking up, I was horrified to see lines of our horsemen in front of me, waiting to spring Yusuf's plan to trap the Franj. I had to get myself behind them to safety or risk disobeying Yusuf.

As I moved up, a gap appeared in the line, and though I was somewhat embarrassed at my indignity, I managed to scramble through. A man walked up to me, led me into one of a dozen large tents, sat me down and gave me a large pitcher of water. I drank gratefully.

I looked towards the slowly approaching army, now around 300 paces away. The light white coats of the knights, some of them frayed and worn from years of use, swirled and billowed in the slight breeze, displaying large red crosses and covering their heavy metal armour. The effect was like a sea of foam and blood looming ever closer.

Hundreds of ugly square helmets, flat topped and barred to allow vision, moved forward, nodding in time with the solid tread of the knights' brutal beasts. Heavy metal shields hung from their necks, again with red crosses displayed. The men carried long steel-headed lances, steel axes, huge swords and vicious-looking black maces. The horses also had helmets with a grill and a sharp pike protruding from the front.

The men and horses looked massive and extraordinarily tough after decades of fighting and surviving in this harsh land and relentless heat. These were killing machines designed to crush any opposition in their path, their weapons the most terrifying and deadly the world had ever seen. The horses kicked up clouds of dust and sand, which billowed behind them for as far as I could see. The noise of hundreds of hooves tramping together made the ground reverberate in a terrible rhythm.

I was afraid that the mass of the approaching cavalry would obliterate our army and that Yusuf would be the first to be crushed. I shivered in dread for my friend and his loyal soldiers, but was impressed with Yusuf's coolness in this extremely dangerous situation. His men were clearly inspired by his courage.

Without warning, Yusuf shouted and turned the head of his horse around, ordering his men to do the same. I had a perfect view from my high position as they retreated from the enemy hordes. They rode away along the valley with the enemy in pursuit.

The ground gradually became steeper, but the Muslims on their light horses kept an even pace up the sandy slope. The heavily laden horses of the enemy started to slow and struggle at the incline. They were falling into Yusuf's trap.

Yusuf finally turned his horse around, facing the enemy, and raised his two arms into the air. This was the signal to his waiting cavalry on higher ground to his left and right to charge. I watched as hundreds, together with Bedouin on camels, raced down towards an inevitably terrible clash with the

Franj army. It struck me for a moment that they were charging against my people, those from all over Europe, including from my own country. I had to dismiss this thought and pray that Yusuf's soldiers would prevail.

His riders kicked up huge clouds of dust as they charged down the slopes from both sides. They crashed into the solid heavy mass of armoured men on their huge chargers. The knights were desperately trying to turn their horses to face their oncoming foes head on. The charging army hardly dented the near impenetrable legion of knights.

The noises of battle were horrifying: the shouts and piercing cries of the attackers, the roars and screams of terrified horses, and the clash of swords and spears against armour. The knights fought back, slashing and swinging their huge swords at the charging men and horses, causing terrible damage. Horses and camels fell, kicking and howling as they crashed to the ground with terrible lacerations and broken bones, taking their riders with them. Some of our men were able to jump clear and carry on the fight with their weapons. Others were chopped and hacked, losing limbs and heads, suffering appalling wounds and slaughter. I hated watching this savagery from my safe place on the hill, feeling guilty but thankful that I was not part of this brutality.

I heard a loud cry, which I rightly guessed had come from Yusuf. It was repeated down the line of the attacking men, and immediately his horsemen retreated on both sides. Mounted archers took their place and fired hundreds of arrows repeatedly into the mass of knights with deadly effect. This clever plan kept the archers well away from the enemy's huge swords.

Knights and horses fell, both screaming in terrible pain and panic. Another command and the archers withdrew, replaced by the riders who had had a short rest, refreshed by gallons of essential water. They charged with renewed vigour, this time running parallel to the lines of knights, slashing with their razor-sharp scimitars, then dancing out of range of the deadly broadswords. I was amazed at the discipline and precision of both sides of Yusuf's army working in tandem. I now had no doubt that Yusuf had the ability to become a great general and leader of his people.

At last, his army managed to break through the mass of knights and divide the enemy into two parts. His men surrounded the smaller front part and drove them towards Yusuf, who was easily able to overcome them. I guessed that he would now be able to capture some valuable prisoners, worth a high price in ransom, to pay for his cause. I was so impressed with his cleverness and abilities.

Fighting carried on for several hours. By the time the sun began to set, I could see there was likely to be no clear result to the bloody skirmish. The knights in the rear half of the enemy army gradually began to withdraw and turn their horses back towards Cairo. They increased their pace to a gallop and the attackers did not pursue them.

Even though there was no clear winner to the battle, Yusuf had gained the advantage. He had also shown great courage and leadership in facing and standing his ground against the massive army of knights. I was watching him from the top of the slope as he walked with his officers towards the battle area to view the mass of destruction. The numbers of fallen knights exceeded those of his army, but he cried tears of sadness when he saw his slaughtered men and horses. There were signs of life in some of his men. He made sure all his wounded were tended with great care.

One prone Syrian raised his right arm towards Yusuf, showing respect and devotion. Yusuf rushed towards him and held his hand, telling him that he and all the soldiers had been immensely courageous in the face of a fearsome enemy and had attacked with unrelenting heroism.

"You have served you country with fortitude today," he said. "Your children and grandchildren will tell stories of you, long after you have left this earth. They will tell of your extraordinary courage and resolve. You will become famous for evermore and in 100 years, people will talk about you in hushed tones. Your valour today will never be surpassed."

Yusuf was already an extraordinary leader. I shed tears of pride and admiration for my very good and loyal friend.

***

We stayed in that place for several weeks, burying the dead and caring for the wounded, many of whom returned to full health. Yusuf made sure that the captured knights were treated well and with respect, although stripped of their armour and weapons, they looked so helpless and harmless.

Yusuf had already sent out senior officers to negotiate substantial ransoms for the safe return of his captives and all had returned with promises of trunks of gold. He would now have the resources to further his ambitions. Eventually, we closed down the camp and travelled at a slow pace towards the wonders of Alexandria and its world-famous lighthouse.

Yusuf worked hard to eliminate his enemies and gradually took control of Egypt, the first stage in his domination and unification of the Arab peoples. He still had a huge amount of work to do to achieve his mission, but it was at this point that a highly significant change took place. From now on, he would be known by a name that meant righteousness of the faith, which indicated the great respect he had earned from all. It was a name that would echo down the ages, ensuring my friend a place in legend for the rest of time.

From this moment on, no one referred to our great leader as Yusuf. His name was Saladin.

Chapter 7

Home At Last

During the six years we were in Egypt, I acted as Saladin's assistant, armourer, groom, cook and advisor, among many other jobs. This was a great honour for me and showed that he trusted me implicitly. He had a huge family, with many brothers, cousins, uncles, and no doubt felt more secure with them close by, so he usually gave them key responsibilities. I was probably the only one in his inner circle who was not a relative.

But I badly needed a break, a long rest. Most of all, I was desperate to see Yasmine and our three children – since Yusuf's birth, she had blessed me with two beautiful daughters, both born with no complications at all. However, I wondered whether we would recognise each other after so many years. I certainly looked older with more lines on my face and I tired more easily. There was grey in my thinning hair, but I was fitter and stronger than I had ever been. The children probably wouldn't remember me at all, and that made me feel sad.

I was sickened by the horrible violence I had witnessed, perpetuated by both sides. Even though Yusuf – no, not Yusuf; I had to remember to call him Saladin now – was honourable and decent, if anyone crossed him, he would seek the most violent retribution. I had seen this many times and I respected him for it. At least his violence had some justification. He was also magnanimous in victory and incredibly generous to his enemies afterwards.

Nonetheless, I was ready to get away from his violent world for a well-earned reunion with my gentle wife. I sought an audience with him and made my case.

"Saladin, I desperately need to see my family in Damascus."

His reply was not what I wanted to hear. "I need you here, Shiva, to support me in many ways. I wouldn't know how to manage without you. You are hard-working and honest, and I need trustworthy people around me. Even some of my family members are not as honourable as you have been. We've been together for so many years and I wouldn't have achieved so much without you close by my side. There are still tall mountains to climb and wide rivers to cross."

Then he relented and his expression softened. "I know you hate the violence we encounter every day and would rather not be part of that. Shiva, you will return to your family next month and take a long rest. I will call for you when I need your services. You still have a great role to play in my life. I need your help to reach my destiny."

I couldn't wait to get back home to see Yasmine and our three children, but I was extremely apprehensive about the welcome I would receive. Would Yasmine be pleased to see me? Would she take me back into the family? Perhaps she had given up on me after so long. And would my children feel any love and affection for me? Would I for them? Perhaps they had found a new father figure. Would I settle back into the family home, or would I yearn for more adventure and travel?

I returned to Damascus together with a small group of soldiers Saladin had granted permission to visit their families. They had all given many years of service and I was grateful for their company and protection. As we drew closer, I became nervous and emotional about the reunion, and I started to dread the moment. Tears flowed down my face in anticipation.

Four figures were standing outside the house as I rode along the dusty street towards them. I almost fell off my horse in excitement and ran to them with my one arm open wide. We hugged each other with tears dripping down from five faces. We were all crying unashamedly, but with deep love and blessed relief.

My oldest child, Yusuf, named after my closest friend, was ten years old, only one year younger than my friend had been when he'd first come to visit me in prison. He was a beautiful boy with his mother's brown skin and my blue eyes. Our first daughter, Yasmine, was nine and had inherited her mother's beauty and long dark hair, as well as her name. Farah had been just a baby when I had left the family home. Now, at seven years old, she was sweet beyond compare with long flowing yellow hair, exactly the same colour as mine. I fell instantly in love.

Yasmine was as pretty as the day I had first met her in the bookshop all those years ago. She had put on weight, but this made her look even more beautiful. She was perfect to me in every way. I had wondered for so long what the four of them would make of me. I needn't have worried. Our family ties and the love we shared were enough to see us through the longest of absences and the toughest of times.

***

I settled back into family life over the next few weeks and loved being with my wife and children. But I didn't find it easy. I had long periods of misery, my dreadful experiences of war and violence having had a depressive effect on me, and showed moments of anger and stress to my family. I wanted to calm down over time and become a good father and husband, but my despondent mood never completely left me.

Although I spent as many hours as I could with the children and helped with their education and schooling, Yasmine and I found the time to resume work on our book. We recorded our children in pictures and words. I related my many experiences in Egypt while Yasmine painted the pictures of the dreadful scenes as I described them. And it was this work that finally helped me to come to terms with my demons.

The months drifted by. I was slowly settling into peaceful family life when Saladin called in unexpectedly.

"My great friend Shiva," he said as we hugged and laughed and cried. "How lovely to see you again. How are you?"

Saladin looked older and lines which had not been there before were forming in his handsome face. His head was covered as always, but his neat moustache and beard had streaks of grey, so I guessed his hair had gone the same way. His eyes were sunken and the huge responsibility he had taken on was clearly beginning to weigh heavily. I was worried that his health was suffering with all this work and worry.

However, nothing could take away from the pleasure of seeing my old friend again. We talked for hours and shared many memories.

"I haven't got long," said Saladin regretfully as the afternoon progressed. "I must leave before the sun goes down."

"But you have time to share my hospitality, I hope, Saladin." Without waiting for a reply, I called out to Yasmine to prepare a table fit for the ruler of the Arab world. I could see this pleased him. While Yasmine did as I had asked, Saladin made a huge fuss of our children, who squealed with excitement. Then he turned back to me, his face serious again.

"I have a new job for you, Shiva, a very important one. The Arab world relies on good communication and if this fails, my plans will collapse and fall. Communication must be accurate, fast and reliable. I have to know immediately when and where troubles arise. And I need to keep my people informed. We cannot wait for men on horses to deliver messages. Too much damage will have been caused by the time they arrive."

I was intrigued to know where he was heading with this conversation, feeling a buzz of excitement at the prospect of a new opportunity and purpose for me, but no more would Saladin say until he had eaten his fill of the magnificent spread Yasmine had prepared in a very short space of time. She left us alone, sitting on two cushions, giving the children strict instructions not to disturb us in any way so we could talk in private.

"As you know, we rely on pigeons for fast communication across our vast region, and have done so for 1,000 years or more," he continued once he was replete. "Unfortunately, this system has become seriously mismanaged and I suspect that there has been widespread corruption. This has resulted in messages being delayed or even lost, often with tragic consequences. I am not exaggerating by saying that my whole life's work, my holy mission to unite the Arab world, is at risk if this system fails. But if it is run properly, it will be the single most significant element in my success. I hope this gives you a clear idea of the importance I attach to good communications.

"I want you to take charge of the pigeon communication system and improve every part of it, so that every message is delivered quickly and replied to without delay. I want you to write the words to inspire every man, woman and child in the Arab world so that we can all rise up as one. You will travel across all our territories and do whatever is necessary to create a first-class service. You don't have long as nothing can delay my mission. Do you think you can do this?"

But Saladin didn't wait for me to answer. "I had to use the service recently and it failed to deliver my urgent messages on time. In some cases, they didn't arrive at all. We suffered a terrible defeat at the hands of hundreds of knights from Jerusalem and lost many good Muslims."

I was shocked at this news. "How many men did we lose?"

"At least 20,000 and maybe more, but we mustn't let this be known. We must play this down."

I had to think about all the implications in a few seconds. "Yes, of course, Saladin," I said. "I have no idea how to do this and what will be involved, but I will take on this task, starting today."

"Good. I want to meet with you before the winter so you can report back. If you need money, and you most certainly will, my brother Tanshah will sanction a loan. I know I can trust and rely on you. I have never had a moment's doubt."

I hid a gasp. This gave me only six months to complete the task, so I would need to work every waking moment of that time. I would have huge distances to cover and many new skills to learn. Could I do this to the standards Saladin required? I doubted it, but of course, I couldn't refuse.

Saladin needed to work hard and fast to re-establish his scattered forces and continue his seemingly never-ending mission. Before he went, he gifted Yasmine a beautiful golden necklace with fabulous jewels, the value of which would have been enough to support a large family for many years. Saladin was always extremely generous to friends. He was even know to be generous to his enemies.

***

I'd already known about the pigeon messaging service; everyone did and took it somewhat for granted, even though it was hugely important as it was the only way our people could communicate across the Arab world with speed. All the major cities were connected, and Saladin relied on the service while on the move so that he could report back developments or call for reinforcements. I made a mental note to visit my favourite bookshop to find out more information.

When Saladin left, I set to work immediately, starting by looking for the man responsible for pigeon communications in Damascus. His name was Omar and his business was very close to my home, but he was suspicious and deliberately unhelpful when I went to visit him. It was only when I said my orders had come directly from Saladin that he stood to attention.

I was amazed to see that he was running a large enterprise with hundreds of workers employed to look after, train, breed, transport and care for the pigeons. Dozens of cotes echoed with the soft cooing of the birds, but I wasn't impressed by the work Omar was doing. The smell from the area was appalling. Dirt and mess covered everything.

"Omar, how are the pigeons transported between the bases?" I asked him, wanting to find out more before taking any action. One thing I did know, though, was that pigeons could only fly one way: back to their home base.

"Those wagons over there are fitted with mobile cotes," he replied, pointing. "We employ a small army of drivers and riders to transport the pigeons, using horses and camels. These men are on the road the whole time and have only short breaks."

As we walked round the huge area, he explained all the different skills and people needed to make the service work.

"In addition to transporters, we also employ builders for the cotes, breeders, cleaners and supervisors. We had over 1,000 employees here last month, and the other twenty centres across the Arab world need the same."

I'd had no idea of the scale of the operation and felt rather daunted.

"How far can our pigeons fly?" I asked.

"Our longest journey is around 1,000 miles. We get quite a few dropouts on long journeys due to high winds, cold, tiredness, and we've had many shot down by our enemies. On one dreadful journey, we lost half the pigeons."

I watched as a fresh batch was released. Omar told me they were going to Tripoli, which he explained was quite a short distance of around 100 miles. I was fascinated with the details, but I hadn't appreciated the complicated logistics of running the service, and the huge number of people needed. Using the information he gave me, I estimated the workforce for the entire system would total over 20,000. Would I be able to cope with such a huge job? I was feeling overwhelmed, but I was desperate not to let Saladin down. Had he overestimated my limited abilities?

But I was sure that every aspect of the operation could be improved. I didn't like the state of the equipment or how the birds were kept. Were the men fully trained and motivated? I doubted so. I wondered if the other centres were like this one. How much money was being lost? Were the allegations of corruption true? I began to understand the issues Saladin had been talking about. I badly needed reliable expert help.

A man called Salman was the answer. On my request, Salman took a job at the centre, in disguise just in case he was recognised. When he reported back to me a week later, he was disgusted by what he had seen.

"The place is a disaster. I am surprised it can operate at all. Omar is ripping off the state and providing a very poor service. Everything is wrong. There is no scheduled cleaning programme and the animals are living in filth. They need much more space and are not being fed properly. They need good seeds, grain, fresh fruit and vegetables, but their food is inadequate and poor. I don't think the training programme is any good either. All these factors are very important for efficient and successful operations. I've never seen anything as bad as this before.

"These lovely animals need more love, care and nourishment. Also, the transport arrangements need total overhauling. It's going to be very expensive."

Expensive was not a word I had wanted to hear and my heart sank. However, Saladin's orders had been clear.

"Salman," I said, "I want you to take this place over, put in proper systems and employ people who will love these animals. I have the resources at my disposal."

Salman fired Omar and appointed a young man called Akeem. Within weeks, everything started improving, but I was warned that the operation at our site in Baalbek was in an even worse state. I travelled with Akeem and checked it out.

"Shiva, we will need money, urgently," Akeem told me, "a lot of it. How soon can you get it for me?"

I was dismayed, but not surprised to hear this.

"I need to return to Damascus to see my paymaster. Akeem, ensure that all expenditure is recorded accurately. I must be able to prove to Saladin and his team that we are good and efficient managers."

***

The moment I had been dreading was upon me. Tanshah, Saladin's brother, was extremely jealous of my influence and hated me. He had made my life difficult before and I generally managed to avoid him, but this time, I couldn't.

Saladin had put Tanshah in charge of Damascus, but the man obviously had no interest in his responsibilities. He was more concerned with enriching himself. He was a powerful man and I would have to be careful not to cross him. I dreaded having to deal with him.

As it turned out, I had every reason to worry.

I arrived at his palace, determined to strike up a friendly tone to ensure good relations. The size of it and the ostentatious prosperity amazed me. It was a huge marble building and I wondered how Tanshah was able to find the resources to build and maintain it.

In contrast, Saladin was extremely modest and frugal in his lifestyle, and gave away most of his possessions, which annoyed his wife who desperately wanted to live in splendour. He was happy to sleep in tents alongside his soldiers while on manoeuvres and expected no special treatment. And as far as I knew, none of the other members of his family lived in such style as Tanshah.

A well-armed guard took me inside, walking ahead of me. After a long period of time, we arrived in a vast room with perhaps a dozen men sitting on huge cushions, being served food and wine by scantily dressed girls. A loud growl greeted me as I walked in.

"Come over here, you, and state your business."

Tanshah, as fat as he was evil-looking, summoned me to stand in front of him. I introduced myself, even though he knew full well who I was.

"Saladin has commissioned me to look at the pigeon service in Damascus and elsewhere and improve operations..."

"It's not necessary," Tanshah snapped, interrupting me. "It's all working fine. I can't see why he needs you. Anyway, he hasn't told me about this."

As I had suspected, this wasn't going to be an easy or a pleasant task. I could hardly get a word in, but eventually managed to state my request. It was all in vain. With a contemptuous wave of his hand, Tanshah dismissed me.

I tried again a week later, asking him for money which I desperately needed for improvements to the messaging service so as not to let Saladin down. Receiving the same negative response from Tanshah, I returned home empty handed and shared my woes with my wife.

"Yasmine, I really don't know what to do. I suppose that I could contact Saladin, but I don't want to trouble him. Tanshah will not give me any money, though."

After considering the problem for a few moments, she said, "Well, we have the necklace Saladin gave me and we know it is worth a small fortune. Why don't we sell it and use the money for the pigeon service?"

It was a brilliant solution and I admired Yasmine for having suggested it. It must have pained her to part with such a lovely gift. She approached her family to determine the true value of the necklace and sell it, and a few days later, we had enough gold coins to run and improve the pigeon service for many months – at least until I had my next meeting with Saladin.

***

Over time, using the gold the necklace had fetched, I visited most of the twenty pigeon centres and made operational changes. Sacking many of the old team members, I set up a management team and we all worked hard to enhance efficiency. As we did so, we were able to improve economies and costs, and find better people to run the operations.

When I met with Akeem at the Damascus pigeon centre to review progress and check on operations, he had a surprise for me.

"Before we begin, Shiva, I want to show you something," he told me. He went inside the compound and came back holding a pigeon gently in his hands. "Take this beautiful creature, Shiva, and tell me what you feel."

Akeem passed the bird to me. I grasped him carefully in my hand and was immediately entranced. Even though I had been in the business for months now, I had never held a pigeon before and had taken no personal interest in these birds, only concerned about their usefulness to us. But Akeem was right, this was such a beautiful creature. I felt the softness and stillness of his body and was captivated by the intelligence of his bright eyes, communicating calmness and trust. I loved how his white feathers held a soft hue of blue. There was no fear in the bird at all; he conveyed nothing but a confidence in me.

"Akeem, I think I have made a new friend. He is so affectionate and assured in my embrace. We will be soulmates for ever. What is his name?"

Akeem laughed softly. "His name is Yusuf," he said, "so I knew you would take to each other immediately. I believe that now you are starting to develop a love for these birds who make the business work. From this love, we can continue to make improvements, which are desperately needed.

"I am sure you have noticed how plump and healthy he is. Smell him to check his cleanliness and notice how he treats you as an equal, unlike ordinary pigeons who flap away from you at every encounter. Put him down and let him follow you.

"Yusuf epitomises the distance we have travelled with our work. Can I suggest we rename our venture? How about *The Pigeon Post*?"

I liked the idea, which demonstrated that the system was now totally transformed from the shambles I had inherited. I asked Akeem to send out pigeons to all parts of Saladin's empire to launch the new name, statement of objectives, principles and targets for the business.

***

After six months, as expected, a message came from Saladin, requesting that I join him in a village nearby. What I was not expecting was to meet not with Saladin, but one of his aides. Unfortunately, my dear friend had been called away at the last moment. I didn't know the man who was waiting to greet me and disliked him instantly. One look at his cruel face told me there was nothing pleasant about him.

"Well, how is the pigeon service going?" he demanded aggressively, fixing me with an unblinking stare as he gestured to me to sit. He hadn't offered me refreshment, which was a telling omission. Nonetheless, I kept my tone even and polite as I replied.

"I have made radical changes here in Damascus, in Baalbek and in other centres, and I will visit more over the next few months."

"Do you have an account of the money you have spent?"

"Yes, I have it here." Taking a scroll of documents carefully from a goatskin hide, I opened it for him to check. He took it from me and spent some time scrutinising the entries, asking a few questions in a sharp tone until he understood the figures.

"Where does it show the money that Tanshah has given you?"

"He hasn't given me any money yet," I replied.

"That's not what he told us." This wasn't going well. "I think you have received the money and kept it for yourself."

"No, that is not the case at all. Saladin knows that I am scrupulously honest and always have been."

"Well, in that case, how have you funded the improvements?"

"I was forced to sell some jewellery," I said firmly, trying to hide my nervousness.

"And how did you get this jewellery in the first place?"

"Saladin gave me a necklace as a gift." I started to worry. This man clearly didn't believe me and perhaps now, Saladin wouldn't trust me either.

"Don't move." He stood up and gestured towards the entrance to the tent. Immediately, two heavily armed guards grabbed me roughly, forced me to my feet and marched me away. We entered an empty tent, where they threw me to the floor and left me alone.

Several hours later, my questioner returned and stood over me. "Have you changed your story?"

"No, no, I have told you the truth."

"You are just another lying Franj bastard. What are you doing in our country? And why have you changed sides? No, don't answer that. Just shut up."

The two burly men who had hauled me here earlier took me outside and threw me over a camel, tying my legs and arm together with a rope underneath the animal's body. A small escort rode alongside the camel, leading me away from the camp. I was extremely frightened, uncomfortable, thirsty and hungry, and I needed to relieve myself very badly.

Even in my confused state, I knew we were travelling into Damascus. Where would they take me? Surely not to Tanshah. I doubted I would survive if that were so. Thinking back to his opulent palace, I was certain he was embezzling the money he was supposed to have given me. I wouldn't be surprised if he was also stealing money from the city as well.

My worst fears were realised. I was taken to Tanshah's palace and thrown into a dungeon in the basement to lie on the floor in my own filth. Dangerously thirsty, I also ached all over; the guards had decided to throw in a few well-aimed kicks before they'd left me alone.

I was in a desperate situation. How could I get a message to Saladin? My own family was so close by, but I had no way of contacting them. They wouldn't know what had happened. I almost felt like crying in frustration and agony.

I heard a lock clank, then the door creaked open and someone walked into the cell. I peered into the dim light and saw the fat figure of Tanshah standing over me. He was smirking.

"I hear you have been telling lies about me," he sneered. "Well, we have a solution for those crimes. I will cut your tongue out, and then hang you. Maybe I will think of other ways to make you suffer as well."

With that, he turned on his heels and left the cell triumphantly.

I knew I was finished. Tanshah couldn't afford the risk of me getting to Saladin and telling him the truth. My friend would believe me, of that I was sure. I had to do something, but I was so thirsty, I couldn't think clearly.

Here I was in prison again. Thanks to Saladin's kindness, I had survived many adventures and close shaves since my last imprisonment, but even after decades of freedom, the horror and fear of my experience when I was fifteen had never left my mind. Surely, I wouldn't end my life here after surviving the last time. Would I? If it came to it, I decided I would face my demise with as much courage as I could muster, although I hoped I wouldn't suffer too much. I was not a brave warrior.

I didn't sleep that night. What would Yasmine and our children do? Would they be safe? I would give up my wretched life for them. In my deepest despair, I spoke to Era, my constant friend. Surely even he couldn't have any words of comfort for me this time.

But that's where I was wrong. Although I could see no way out of this horrific situation, he told me to keep calm and all would be well.

Chapter 8

The Assassins

The following day, three men came for me. They burst through the door and grabbed me roughly, hauling me to my feet, dragging out of my cell and down a stairway which seemed endless. Then long corridors and more stairs. I was already suffering after the roughness of my jailers, and this treatment added to my pains. My body stank, and I briefly wondered how these men could stand my lack of hygiene.

Were they going to execute me outside, because Tanshah didn't want any mess inside his palace? As long as they didn't do as Tanshah had threatened and cut my tongue out. I didn't think I could have stood that pain, I would rather be killed quickly.

Outside, rather than the hangman's noose, a group of four horsemen were waiting. Before one of them dismounted and covered my head with a kind of hood, I managed to have a quick look at their faces. To my surprise, they didn't seem hostile. Perhaps they didn't have intentions to take my life after all. Fortunately, there was no sign of either Tanshah or my cruel jailers.

I was hauled on to a spare horse, grateful that I was not tied over the saddle as I had been on the way here. We moved off at a steady pace with my horse being led by the men. I was still very smelly and desperately thirsty and hungry.

After a few hours, which seemed like days, we stopped and they helped me to dismount. They took my hood off and I was allowed to wash in a stream, then given fresh clothes. More importantly, I was given a leather water bottle, which I drained desperately and then topped up. What blessed relief!

I wanted to ask where we were going, but decided that it was better to keep quiet for the moment. I was so grateful that my life had been spared and that I was being treated better than I had been by Tanshah's men.

We camped overnight, moving on the following day. The men bought provisions in villages and towns we passed through, and they kindly shared these with me. Our journey lasted for so many days that I lost count. I had managed to start a dialogue with my companions, but they would only talk about our immediate needs and would not tell me where we were going and why.

We entered a huge city. Was it Baghdad? I asked, but the men wouldn't confirm this. I hadn't been there before and would have loved to explore the place. That would have to wait for another time, though. We travelled on, heading in a westerly direction. I was aware that every day I was moving further away from home, which made me sad.

"Tomorrow, we will be arriving at Alamut Castle," said one of the men eventually. "This is the headquarters of the Hashshashins. You will be their guest."

The Hashshashins – the Assassins. Everyone knew about these people and we were all very afraid of them. They hid in their tall castles, secure from the outside world, and carried out raids and killings against their enemies. Some of them disguised themselves as servants or advisors to enemy leaders and, often months or even years later, they would turn on their masters and kill them. Built on several craggy hills in Syria and Persia, the castles were impregnable. There seemed to be little anyone could do to fight back.

I wondered why I was being taken to Alamut Castle. Sure it wasn't for my health, I started to worry again.

***

By my reckoning, I had been here in Alamut Castle for over a month. I was well looked after, fed and watered, and had a room high up in the tower from where I could get a partial view across the huge valley. However, the slit window was designed so that men could fire arrows through it without receiving any in return, not for admiring the landscape. The room was well furnished and a good size; I even had a few books to read, but I was never allowed out.

An elderly man would unlock the door and let himself in at midday, bringing me food and water. He never spoke, although I tried to communicate with him on many occasions, asking him why I was locked up here and what was going to happen to me. I guessed that Tanshah was keeping me out of the way and denying that I had ever crossed his path.

Would I ever get out of here and see my family again? I began to despair and sank into a low state of depression, wondering what on earth I could do to improve my situation. After a while, I became numb to my fate and gave up any hope that I would be freed.

One morning, I sat in my chair, reading, as a thin ray of sun shone through my narrow window. I decided to contact my friend Era; I needed help desperately. He answered immediately and told me as always to keep calm and have faith, promising that all would work out well in the end. This time, I did not believe him.

A few moments later, I heard a noise that I couldn't identify immediately. I put my book down while looking around the room. The noise came a second time: the distinctive soft cooing of a pigeon. A beautiful bird was standing on the window shelf, looking at me. Could he possibly be from our centre at Damascus? Surely that would be too much of a coincidence.

He was a magnificent specimen. I spoke to him gently, and when I felt that he was ready, I walked towards him slowly and gathered him in my one good hand, checking the identification on his feet.

Yes, he belonged to us! He was part of our operation in Damascus. I was overjoyed. He was just as lovely and soft as the one I had held months ago, the one Akeem had named Yusuf. I looked into the trusting eyes of the pigeon and a spark of recognition passed between us. He *was* Yusuf, of that I had no doubt. I was extremely excited that he had found his way here to my room. How on earth had this happened?

Of course, I knew the answer and thanked Era. He had done his job well once again.

Yusuf's coat was as soft as silk as I stroked him gently. There were some crumbs left on my plate from my midday meal, which I offered him, and I poured some water into a shallow dish. He consumed both, and then cooed at me as if to say thank you. That was the closest thing I'd had to a conversation for weeks and I revelled in his presence.

But more than that, just as had happened many years ago when a small Arab boy had appeared at the window of my prison cell, with Yusuf came hope. I developed a plan to call for help. I would write a message to send to Akeen to pass on to Saladin, sure that Yusuf would fly directly to his home base. It was unlikely that he would go anywhere else.

Akeen would react swiftly as soon as he received my message. I had writing materials in my room and I composed a short message, tying it securely on to the leg of my new friend. But he would have the best chance of completing his journey if I let him rest tonight.

The next morning, I whispered to Yusuf gently, and then eased him through the narrow gap. I watched him fly in several circles around the castle. He came into view again, and then flew off to the west. I prayed hard to my God to grant him a safe passage and once again called on Era for support. If I was lucky enough to be successful in contacting Saladin, I knew rescue would come, but it would take a long time.

***

Yasmine became increasingly concerned when Crispin didn't come home. Two days had passed without a word from her husband, and she instinctively knew something was wrong. Badly wrong.

He had said he was going to meet Saladin and would be back that night or the following day. When he still hadn't returned a week later, she decided to take action. She walked to Saladin's house a few streets away, hoping to speak to Ismat, his wife. They had met before, but were not close. Yasmine found Ismat a little frivolous and superficial, obsessed with the luxuries of wealth. For her part, Ismat didn't understand Yasmine, not knowing why the woman was so interested in drawing and painting, and not interested at all in perfume and clothes.

Ismat was at heart a generous and hospitable woman, who welcomed Yasmine warmly. But when Yasmine told Ismat of her concerns for her husband, Ismat dismissed her worries. She didn't think that anything serious could have happened to Crispin.

"Saladin moves around the country constantly," she said soothingly. "Shiva... I mean, Crispin has probably had to spend time searching for him."

"Ismat, no," insisted Yasmine. "There is something wrong. I know Crispin and I am sure he would have sent me a message if that was the case. He'd realise I would be concerned. Please believe me, I would not have bothered you normally, but I just know something has happened to him."

Ismat nodded, recognising Yasmine's true concern. She'd had similar worries many times herself about her husband. She called a male servant and ordered him to take a horse and look for Saladin, starting at his local camp just outside the city. The servant was left in no doubt that if he delayed, he would be in serious trouble.

"Yasmine, I will write a note for Saladin and take it to Akeem at the pigeon centre. I will go now and make sure the same message is sent to every camp, anywhere Saladin might be staying. In the meantime, you must go home and look after your children. Please try not to worry too much. I will do everything I can without delay."

A week later, Saladin arrived home. He immediately sent dozens of horsemen across the land to look for Crispin, then visited Tanshah. After that, he called on Yasmine.

"I am truly sorry, Yasmine," he told her. "I will keep looking and I will never give up. Shiva is a good man and a great friend, I know he would do the same thing for me. You must keep calm and have faith," he added, unconsciously echoing Era's constant advice to Crispin. "I will send more men to the furthest parts of my kingdom. I will also send pigeons to every city and I will, of course, let you know the moment we have any news."

Yasmine asked about Saladin's visit to his brother.

"No news there, I'm afraid," replied Saladin. "Tanshah assured me that he has not seen Shiva since he first called on him and borrowed the money to finance the improvements to the pigeon system."

Yasmine raised her eyebrows. She now knew for sure that Tanshah was a liar; Crispin had never received one single coin from the man. Should she say anything? Yes, especially as she suspected Tanshah wasn't as ignorant of Crispin's fate as he claimed.

"Saladin," she began hesitantly, "I am reluctant to mention this, but I'm sure that Tanshah knows something about Crispin's disappearance." She then told him about Crispin's visit to Tanshah's palace. Furious, Saladin stormed from Yasmine's presence, leaving her wondering if she had overstepped the mark. However, she felt she'd had no choice. Crispin's safety, his very life could depend on her trusting Saladin now.

And the great man didn't let her down. Within two hours, he was back.

"You were right, Yasmine," he said. "I managed to force the truth out of Tanshah and I now know who is holding Shiva, but we don't know where. I also suspect, and have done for some time, that Tanshah has been embezzling funds from the city. How stupid does he think I am?" Saladin roared, startling Yasmine, although she now knew his anger was most definitely not aimed at her. "How else could he afford that massive palace and all that rich food that's making him into a fat lump? I will deal with my brother later."

The following weeks were a torture of uncertainty for Yasmine and her children, and for Saladin. His men rode throughout the Arab lands, asking for news, trying to find where the Hashshashins had taken Crispin, but no one knew. Or if they did know, they didn't want to say so. Every day, Yasmine's haunted eyes asked a question of Saladin. Every day, his equally sad eyes transmitted a silent reply.

No news.

It was the best part of two months before that changed. A lone pigeon flew in from the east, back to his home and his master Akeem. The man took the message from the pigeon's leg as the bird settled in for a good feed and a long rest, and read the words on the page, his expression going from confusion to understanding to elation.

When Yasmine heard that finally there was news from Crispin, that her husband was alive and well, she wept with relief.

***

I suffered terribly for many dreadful days, imagining a string of bad scenarios. What if my pigeon didn't make the journey? What if he was blown off course, or lost or dead? Had enemy soldiers shot him down to prevent messages getting through?

My mental state deteriorated further and I found it near impossible to think positive thoughts, spending hours writing down different ways I could kill myself. If the message got through to Saladin, would he have any influence on the leader of the Hashshashins? Would he have to pay a ransom? Would he bother to do so?

At that, Era intervened and told me not to be so stupid. I had to try to be positive.

Finally, my ordeal came to an end. I was taken from my room by two men and led through the castle, down the long path to the valley below. There, waiting for me, were dozens of riders, one leading a spare horse. The leader introduced himself and told me he had been sent by Saladin to bring me home. I fell to the floor and wept in blessed relief.

My homecoming was joyful. I was reunited with my beautiful family and we cried and expressed our deep love for each other. As I learned all that had happened back home since my disappearance, I realised that once again, Yasmine had proved herself to be a determined and highly intelligent woman. I did not have enough words to thank her. I was so fortunate to have her as my lovely, strong and faithful wife.

And I remembered to thank Era as well. If I hadn't, I'm sure he would have reminded me!

When I was fully recovered from my imprisonment, at least physically, I rode out to meet with Saladin at his camp near Acre. I still couldn't believe I had survived and my words of thanks could never be enough.

Saladin and I both cried tears of joy at being reunited. "Shiva, my good friend, welcome back," he whispered over and over again. It was only much later, as we sat in his tent and feasted together, that he explained what had happened.

"My brother Tanshah had paid the Hashshashins to keep you far from our lands, hoping we would give up on you," he said. "Which, of course, we never would! I have now banished him from my kingdom to a post in the troublesome country of Yemen and he will never return to these parts. You need fear no more."

One thing was puzzling me, and I gave voice to my thoughts. "Why go to all that trouble, though?" I asked. "He threatened to cut my tongue out and then have me hanged. Why didn't he do that?"

Saladin smiled grimly. "Because he's a coward, like all bullies," he replied. "He was terrified that I would find out if he'd had you murdered, and I would do the same to him."

"And would you?" I asked. "Even though he is your brother?"

"Oh yes," replied Saladin. "You, Shiva, are my brother. Tanshah is nothing to me now. But enough of him."

There was something else that was troubling me, though. "I am sorry," I confessed, "but when Tanshah refused to lend me the money for the pigeon centres, we had to sell the beautiful necklace which you gave Yasmine. We had no choice if I was to carry out your wishes."

"Don't worry, Shiva," said Saladin, smiling kindly. "We are already looking for the necklace and it will be returned to you."

I was sure that Saladin had had to pay a large ransom to get me released, but that was one thing he would never confirm to me.

***

It took much longer for me to recover mentally from my ordeal. When I became plagued by bouts of deep depression, despite being back with the people I loved, once again, Saladin arranged for me to see the same doctor as I had many years earlier.

He visited me at home. Yasmine met him at the door and led him to my bedside. He still had a rather morose appearance, but thanks to the years that had passed, he now had far more lines on his face too.

Yasmine left us together. The doctor conducted exactly the same thorough examination as before and took his samples, looking serious as he prodded, pushed, and massaged me. It tickled and I burst out laughing.

"This is no laughing matter, I can assure you," snapped the doctor. "I can make sure you're physically better, but it will take much longer to cure the damage you have suffered inside here," and he pointed to my head. Then he said I would have to visit a specialist doctor.

The next day, he introduced me to a man who didn't look old enough to be out of school. The young doctor explained that his treatment would involve hours of consultations with him asking many questions. He wanted to know everything about my life from my earliest memories.

The treatment started immediately. He showed me hundreds of pictures and objects and asked me what I thought they were and what they represented. Questions about my relationships and experiences went on for hours, until I developed a headache from the intensity. I felt confident enough to tell him so. He apologised, but didn't ease up.

There was no doubt that he knew his job well. When he had written down several pages of notes, including my answers and his thoughts, he told me that he could now decide on the treatments I needed. Some he could administer himself, but my best bet would be to seek help elsewhere.

I was very surprised to be told that he was going to send me many miles East, to a country I had never heard of. The journey would take months. He explained that Saladin had already offered to pay for everything, so his fees and the travelling expenses had been covered.

I was unsure whether I should go. I didn't want to miss another moment with my family, and I didn't want to take more time away from the important job I was doing for Saladin. Of course, I spoke to Yasmine to ask for her opinion before I made a decision.

"You should do what the doctor recommends, Crispin," she replied. "Saladin clearly agrees as he has arranged for an escort for the potentially dangerous journey. We will all miss you, but we want the best health for you. Go, but come back alive and well."

How could I ever live my life without her and her precious love and support?

* * *

We crossed seas and miles of tracks over steep mountains, experiencing many different types of weather: high winds, ice and snow, as well as fierce heat. After several weeks, we arrived safely at a very remote building. It looked like a monastery, perched high up on a cliff, and leant over a steep drop at least a mile above the valley floor. I couldn't even see where I would land if I fell, and so it took me many days to get used to the feeling of vertigo enough to feel secure.

My treatment began as soon as I had recovered from my journey. It involved hard days of learning. Brown skinned and with narrow eyes that to me looked like they were almost closed, my teachers were amazing men. They wore little clothing, despite the biting winds so high up in the mountains, and all had long hair and beards.

Having been suffering with bouts of intense anger since my return from the Hashshashins' cell, I was extremely impressed with my teachers' gentleness and kindness. Voices were never raised, and despite our precarious position, I felt extremely safe here. After all, who but the most dedicated soul was going to make the long, hard journey to this remote spot?

My teaching took place in a large room where musicians seated along the far wall played soothing music while I was instructed. I had no idea what the instruments were, but they filled the air with soft rhythms. It was very relaxing.

As the days passed, I was trained in various types of eastern discipline, including self-defence and mind control. Physical fitness was also part of the treatment, and sometimes the experience was extremely tough. As the only student there, I was aware that Saladin must have spent many gold coins to pay for this treatment for me, and once again I was in his debt.

The lesson I appreciated the most was called meditation. I had no doubt this would become a daily practice for me for the rest of my life. I was told it would give me a higher state of consciousness, whatever that was; what I did know was that I found it extremely beneficial for my state of mind.

It would be an exaggeration to say I enjoyed my time in the mountains. The food was nourishing, but not what I would call flavoursome; the accommodation was basic and comfort was rare. However, the time passed quickly and every day, I was aware that I had benefited from the teachings of the wise men who surrounded me. When the time approached to leave, I almost found myself saddened at the thought of saying goodbye to this hard but peaceful environment. The real world seemed a very long way away.

But the real world was where Yasmine was. It was where my children were, and my dear friend Saladin. Return I must, and I soon started to look forward to feeling the embrace of those I loved once more.

The most significant event of my whole stay happened on my last day. I was sitting opposite one of my teachers, a young man who was extremely inspirational and a great communicator, in the half lotus position. We had been silent for many minutes when his soft voice spoke words that shook me to the core.

"I see a young man sitting on your left shoulder," he told me. "He is your spirit guide and lifelong supporter. What is his name?"

"Era," I replied when I had recovered from the surprise. So, he was real after all. "He has been with me for as long as I can remember. I am sure he has saved my life many times over."

"Of that, I have no doubt. You are blessed and extremely fortunate. Very few souls have this privilege. You are the first I have ever met. Please listen to him and take his advice at all times."

"Yes, I do. I often wonder why I was chosen."

"That is for Era to know," said my teacher with a smile, his deep wisdom belying his youth.

That evening, the escort Saladin had arranged to ensure my safe passage arrived, and my teachers made the men welcome for the night, so at first light we could start the long journey back home. On the roads, I had time to reflect on my stay in the mountains. I felt refreshed and relaxed and so much better in my mind and body. The anger had gone and I'd learned skills I could use every day for the rest of my life. My view on the world and people had changed. All that really mattered, in this life and the next, was love. This would be my guiding light.

Love started with my family, my friends and my neighbours, and then extended to people from all countries. I couldn't wait to get back and hug my wife and children. And I wanted to put my new skills into practice.

Chapter 9

Cairo

Several months later, I received a message from Saladin, requesting I visit him in Cairo. He wanted a full update on the development of *The Pigeon Post*, including all the facts and figures, and gave me a few days to gather the information together. Then a dozen soldiers arrived to escort me – we had to pass through the Franj states, so we would be travelling with great caution.

After three weeks of hard riding, we arrived at Saladin's palace in Cairo. My friend welcomed me with his usual hugs and smiles, and invited me to a banquet, planned for the following day. The guest of honour would be the new Caliph, Al-Mustadi, who Saladin wanted to endorse. I accepted, of course. Saladin's banquet would be the most magnificent occasion in the Arab world, and I was honoured to be sitting on his right. The Caliph was on his left-hand side.

I knew that Saladin wanted me to talk to the eminent gathering at the end of the festivities about *The Pigeon Post* and its achievements. Fortunately, I had been forewarned and able to make plans. I, however, had a surprise for my great friend.

When the feast was almost over, hundreds of officials entered the vast room, each carrying a pigeon. One of the pigeons was presented to Saladin, who looked at me with some alarm.

"What is this, Shiva?"

I touched his arm to reassure him. "See what the pigeon is carrying," I whispered. "Look at his feet. Take the parcel."

Saladin reached out a hand and took the small cloth bag, opening it. Inside was a beautiful ripe red cherry from the high mountains of the Lebanon, almost frozen from its journey south. Saladin's eyes lit up with delight. These cherries were his favourite.

"How come, Shiva? I thought these birds just carried messages."

"This time, they are carrying a present for you."

His smile told me that he was hugely impressed and grateful, and I had no need to explain further. Tears of gratitude slid down his face. As the servants stoned the cherries and placed them into bowls, serving them to Saladin and the Caliph, and then the rest of the guests, everyone in the room stood and applauded.

The following day, Saladin asked to see me.

"Shiva, I am so pleased with the improvements to *The Pigeon Post*. I know you still have more work to carry out, but I have an additional responsibility for you."

I was intrigued to hear what his request would be, and if I'm honest, I was a little apprehensive too. When Saladin had an idea, it tended to be on a huge scale. And it was.

"I want you to use *The Pigeon Post* to spread news of my mission to unite the Arab world and rid our country of the Franj for ever. Could we meet up next month in Damascus to discuss how this should work?"

I knew what he really wanted. He planned to use *The Post* to his advantage, only conveying positivity even when the news was bad. As far as Saladin was concerned, there was no bad news in the Arab campaign, so my task was to use my pigeons to spread good news about him and bad news about his enemies. The messages had to be much longer than before and were to be sent out from conflict areas where he was leading his forces against the enemy.

I needed to work out the logistics of the project. Firstly, I had to source a paper which was as thin and light as possible, so that the pigeons could carry more sheets. I also had to find a way to impress the message upon several sheets of paper at once, so that we could write a number of news stories at a time. This would solve the huge logistical problem of transporting and accommodating numerous writers on our journeys. It was a monumental task, but Saladin had every confidence in me and I wasn't going to let him down.

"Shiva," he said, "I want you to work with one of my most able advisors. I think you already know him. I trust him totally and we are not even related!" Saladin grinned impishly. With my ordeal at Tanshah's hands behind me, we had taken to joking about it. I knew this was Saladin's way of dealing with his brother's betrayal. "I am talking about al-Qadi al-Fadil and he will advise you in your new position, spreading the good news about my mission. He is perhaps the most famous writer our nation has ever had. He is also an excellent and proven administrator and communicator, and fluent in financial matters."

I was pleased and surprised in equal measure. Of course, I had heard of al-Fadil and had met him on several occasions. He had been the Head Judge of Egypt and was well-known for his abilities and fairness in his rulings. Saladin was not exaggerating his skills. The elegance of his writing and poetry was world famous, so he was the obvious partner for me to carry out my new duties. He would know exactly how to craft positive news about Saladin and I would relay this to all of our people.

Once again, Saladin's judgement had been flawless, and I was amazed with his faith in me to deliver this project. My star was in its ascendance.

***

I travelled with al-Qadi al-Fadil to meet with Saladin, who was in the middle of a long campaign against Reynald de Châtillon, a Crusader knight. I had heard of him, but asked al-Fadil for more information.

"He is a cruel and bloodthirsty man and has been in many conflicts with Saladin," replied al-Fadil. "Reynald has attacked our peaceful caravans and has led his forces in daring raids against our holy places, Medina and Mecca. I would say he is our toughest adversary. We pray that Saladin eliminates this evil despot."

Saladin had spent weeks trying to capture Kerak Castle where Reynald was entrenched. Kerak was an almost impregnable fortress set on a huge hill, close to the Dead Sea and a short journey from Jerusalem. As we made our way to join our people, al-Fadil and I watched in fascination as a huge siege engine flung a massive rock high towards the castle wall. The air was sucked away from us, and the twang of the tense metal springs being released under extraordinary pressure was deafening and terrifying. It wasn't wise to be too close to this machine when it was firing. The pressures were so enormous that it could burst open, pulverising all within a close area.

Of course, it was even more deadly for those facing us high up on the looming rock of the castle. The projectile would smash open the walls as if they were made of paper, producing clouds of dust, annihilating scores of men and women hiding behind their stone defences. We could hear their cries and screams from where we were, around 1,000 feet away. The crumbling stones came crashing down on to the rocks and earth hundreds of feet below. I saw that even al-Fadil trembled at the power of these monstrous machines of war and the devastating effect they were having.

They were Saladin's mangonels, and he had seven of them. Mangonels had been used in sieges for centuries, although their design had changed over the years. These huge mangonels, the latest versions, were deadly. They had been made in our workshops in Egypt, and then dismantled into small parts so that camels could transport them to the siege. This operation needed almost 1,000 camels, an extraordinary logistical feat.

Their use did not guarantee the castle's surrender, but they would be a great contributor. The critical factor was to get engineers in to dig out the lower walls and foundations and place explosives, causing the walls to crumble. But this time, they could not get close enough to the castle.

"Surely the people in the castle will give up soon under this terrible bombardment," al-Fadil said to me, raising his voice over the relentless din. "I think you can safely write that in advance. Make sure you keep mentioning that Saladin is the rightful Sultan of our lands and that the Franj are the invaders. They have no right to be here."

Later, Saladin's brother al-Adil came to meet us, telling us that Saladin had been avoiding bombarding the highest tower.

"Reynald's wife Stephanie has sent boxes of food down to Saladin," he explained, "and by way of his appreciation, he wishes to spare her."

Already, I was amassing powerful stories to tell the Muslim world. Saladin was a decent man who displayed extraordinary chivalry, unlike the cowardly Franj and Christians who wouldn't even know how to spell the word. I would leave out the fact that Saladin had already started to retreat. An army of Franj was travelling from Jerusalem to defend the castle. It would make no sense to continue the siege at this time.

Al-Fadil advised me to write that Saladin had more important business to attend to in the north. He would take the castle when it suited him to do so.

"Never criticise our Sultan in print," he warned, as if I didn't already know. "Always find words to praise him and give reasons for his actions."

I nodded my head. I was getting used to my new role.

***

We didn't get back to Kerak until the following summer. This time, Saladin was even better prepared. Once again, I travelled with al-Fadil to witness the second storming of the castle.

"Look, this time there are nine of those huge machines," said al-Fadil, pointing. "And Saladin has built new siege towers and covered walkways to reach the walls. Now we can expect the engineers to load the base with explosives and force Reynald to capitulate." He looked at me, and I pre-empted what he was going to say.

"I will be sure to include all this in *The Pigeon News*." By this time, the name of our enterprise had changed, in line with its new role.

As expected, a terrible bombardment followed, but once again, Saladin was forced to withdraw. Yet another Franj relief force was on its way. With the help of al-Fadil's expertise with words, I managed to concoct a story that implied Saladin had won the day, that this second retreat was all part of his masterplan. I had several thousand pigeons ready to send my story to all parts of our lands and my scribes were kept busy for days.

We left and travelled with Saladin to the north to continue his mission. As we rode, I heard Saladin say that Reynald would never get away from him again. The Franj tyrant had carried out too many atrocities on innocent Muslims, and Saladin promised fierce revenge. I didn't have much hope for Reynald if my friend were ever to capture him – which, according to *The Pigeon News*, he most certainly would. It was only a matter of timing.

***

Saladin had been fighting for decades and the constant effort and endeavour were beginning to take their toll. When I received a message two years later from al-Adil that his brother was seriously ill and had asked me to visit him, I was dismayed, but not surprised. Saladin was only a day's ride from where I was at the time, near the Turkish border.

I was very worried about the state I would find him in and concerned that his life was at threat. As I walked into his vast tent, I saw him lying in a cot in the far corner, surrounded by around a dozen aides and members of his family. Al-Adil motioned me to one side.

"Before you go over, you should know that Ismat has just died. We haven't dared tell him as the shock may be too much. As you know, Saladin and his wife were very close."

Yes, I knew that. Saladin loved Ismat dearly and confided in her more than anyone else. He had many mistresses and a small army of children, although none by Ismat. I was saddened by the news. I had known Ismat well, of course, and Yasmine had told me how she had helped save my life years ago, when I had been abducted by Saladin's brother Tanshah.

I agreed that Saladin should not know about Ismat's demise until he had recovered. Al-Adil sent an aide to inform Saladin of my arrival, and then I was immediately taken to his cot.

I was shocked by his appearance. He was very pale with a strained look on his face. Dark shadows had formed under his eyes, and he seemed diminished somehow. He had never been a big man, but he was now so much smaller than he used to be and a rather sad figure. I was sorry to see my good friend in this state.

"Shiva!" he said in a thin, reedy voice. "How are you?"

"Saladin, your health is much more important than mine. How are *you* and are you feeling any better?"

"Shiva, I am very tired. How long have we been friends? I make it at least thirty-five years. In that time, you have taken a wife and now have three beautiful grown-up children and several grandchildren. I've lost count of the number of children I've got.

"I have always treasured our friendship and mutual trust. There are not too many I can say that to! I can still picture you through the prison bars, a hungry, sad and desolate boy. I was so pleased to be able to help you and you have repaid me 1,000 times over. I need to tell you how grateful I am. I fear that my days are coming to an end soon, but there is still so much to do. We haven't even taken control of Jerusalem yet and that is my dearest wish. I want to do so as soon as possible.

"I need to tell you that *The Pigeon News* has been an enormous success. Nothing has given as much advantage to our cause. Tens of thousands of Muslims who were against us are now supporting us. We have no need to go to war with any of them again. We can now bring all our people together to remove the Franj from our country. Thank you, Shiva, for all your great work."

With that, he closed his eyes and slept. His aide led me away to the entrance.

"It's not looking good for him, but we are working hard to aid his recovery," the man whispered when we were a respectful distance away. "It's better if you go now."

I left Saladin's tent with mixed emotions and walked to my horse. I was so sorry for my dear friend and fervently hoped he would recover. He had mentioned my family, whom I had not seen for several years. I had virtually abandoned Yasmine for the sake of Saladin and the work I had to undertake. But I had no choice.

Now, though, I needed to get back to her and beg forgiveness. I wondered how our children were doing. I was also thinking about our safety. If Saladin were to die, I would have no one to protect me and my family. I wasn't sure that any of his people would stand up for me. Even though I had given many years of good service to our country and people, I was still not one of them and never would be. I had adopted their customs, language and dress, and I was now indistinguishable from any of them, except for one thing. I had never changed religion and I didn't intend to.

I told my guards to take me to Damascus without delay.

Yasmine was kind, loving and forgiving once again, much to my relief. Our older children, Yusuf and Yasmine, had already left home and lived nearby in Damascus. Each had married and I couldn't wait to visit my two new grandchildren. Farah was still at home.

I couldn't stop crying when I was reunited with my family, partly from guilt at being absent from them for so long, but mostly due to a huge outpouring of love for all of them. They cried as well and declared their love for me.

My wife Yasmine was thriving, and was a very happy and proud grandparent. Most days, she told me, she travelled to the bookshop to add paintings and writings about our family and their lives to our joint creation. She couldn't wait to show me what she had done, encouraging me to update the words and pictures with stories from my travels and work. Of course, pigeons featured in most of the pages.

I asked her if we could bring our magnificent book home where I believed it belonged and she agreed immediately. She had arranged for one of the leading bookbinders of the city to encase the pages in soft light-brown calf leather. This was our most prized possession, so we displayed the work of art on a huge easel just inside the entrance to our house. We wanted our visitors and family members to see and admire its beauty.

Yasmine had painted many portraits of our children over the years, ever since they were small babies. I loved looking at their beautiful forms. She had captured their spirits and characters with great accuracy and skill, and I was reminded once again of her magnificent talents.

But my precious visit ended all too quickly when a message came through from Saladin. Before I left, I foolishly promised to spend more time at home in the future. Yasmine just smiled wryly as she kissed me goodbye. She knew full well that my word would be broken, yet again.

***

As I stood at Saladin's bedside, I was delighted to see and hear how much better he was. A little colour had come into his face and his breathing was steadier and clearer.

"Blessings on you, Shiva," he said, and I was pleased to hear that his voice had regained some of its former strength. "I hope you have enjoyed precious time with your family. You must tell me all about them later.

"Did you hear my Ismat has passed? I miss her dreadfully, but must get used to living without her. I valued her knowledge and wisdom immensely, and always took her advice before making any major decisions.

"Now, to business. That fiend Reynald has broken our truce with the Franj once again. He is the worst of our enemies and I have sworn to kill him with my own sword. He has been like a dagger in the side of our Muslim world, causing so much pain and sadness to our people."

"What has he done now?" I asked with some trepidation.

"He attacked a peaceful caravan of Muslim traders and killed their guards. He has taken many prisoners, locking them away in Kerak Castle, and he is treating them very badly."

I was extremely worried about the future after this dreadful news. It could mean all-out war.

Chapter 10

The Battle of the Horns of Hattin

I walked up the gentle slopes of Hattin with Saladin's eldest son al-Afdal, still only a youth of seventeen. He was so like his father in both personality and appearance, I briefly felt positive about the future. Al-Afdal had played an important part in this, his first battle, and Saladin had asked me to travel to the site so that his son could tell me about every stage of the fighting and the remarkable result.

I was finding the climb difficult and I was out of breath after the first few feet. I slowed the pace and al-Afdal had the kindness to fall in with my steps, just as his father would have done. Seeing the devastation on the hill around us, I was glad I hadn't been there to witness the horrible slaughter.

But I should have been at the battle with Saladin. I had been struck down with a horrible illness a few weeks before and had to be carried back home to Damascus and my worried wife. Yasmine had ordered my carriers to take me straight to my bed and sent for the doctor with instructions for him to come immediately.

He'd carried out his usual thorough examination without betraying his thoughts. Yes, he looked worried, but that was a normal expression for him. He told me I must stay in the same hospital as I had when I was young, so obviously, he thought my condition was serious.

Suffering terrible fatigue and fierce headaches, I was away from my duties for several weeks. When the doctor eventually released me, I had missed perhaps the most important battle of the past hundred years.

Now recovered, at least to a certain extent, I planned to write a detailed report of the battle for *The Pigeon News*. This story would be the biggest I had ever attempted. If I could get the tone right, it would have an enormous effect on morale in the Muslim world, and then we would have the support of even more men and money. Saladin had told me that his next ambition was to wipe out the Franj kingdoms and finally recapture Jerusalem after almost 100 years in Christian hands.

I needed to question Saladin's son carefully to get the full facts and portray the atmosphere of this crucial battle. The sun was burning hot as we climbed together. I looked up to see the twin hills on the summit; it was easy to understand how the place had earned its name. It resembled a massive bull's head.

Saladin's son pointed upwards to the unusual feature. "That is a long-extinct volcano, I'm told.

The larger horn has a broken rim and a huge crater, and this is where the Franj made their last stand."

The Battle of the Horns of Hattin had resulted in a massive victory for Saladin. I had already heard many of the details, but I wanted to hear them again from an eyewitness and visit the site to get the full atmosphere of this remarkable event. I asked al-Afdal what had been crucial to Saladin's huge success.

"Water," he replied. "We maintained possession and control of the water and made sure we kept the Franj well away from this vital resource. This was the single biggest factor in our great success."

"How did you do this?" I asked.

"We had a constant line of camels bringing skins full of water from Lake Tiberias. With this, we created small lakes up here and had all the water we required. The Franj needed vast quantities of water for their horses and themselves, and they couldn't possibly carry enough for their journey. They also had to keep their helmets and mail armour on for protection, increasing their thirst."

As we climbed higher, we had fabulous views of Lake Tiberias, although I knew it by a different name. This was the Sea of Galilee of the Bible, where my Saviour had performed miracles and preached to His followers. Of course, I did not mention this to my companion.

"And how did Saladin manage to tempt the enemy away from where they had been camped at Sepphoris? There, they would have had ample resources from springs."

"We besieged the castle at Tiberias where the wife of Raymond, one of the Franj leaders, was staying, to provoke them into travelling the twenty miles to rescue her. It was a tense time as they seemed to take ages to make their minds up."

I was having increasing difficulty talking as I puffed up the hill. "Why did they finally decide to go?" I asked him between breaths.

"I think there must have been disagreement amongst the leaders, but Raymond is a powerful man. When they set out on their fateful journey, Father was delighted that his tactic had worked."

"But why did they need so much water?"

"Don't forget this was July and the days were burning hot and humid, much more so than usual. Boiling in their armour, they were soon overwhelmed by severe thirst. To make things worse for them, we set fire to brushwood nearby, sending clouds of smoke in their direction. They were maddened by thirst, and to torment them, our men poured water into the ground in front of them!"

"It must have been terrible for them. I'm surprised they carried on." I was pleased to see that we had almost come to the top of the slope. My throat was dry, just imagining their suffering.

Al-Afdal carried on his commentary. "We made sure they couldn't sleep at night by playing loud music on drums and horns. This was another clever tactic." He explained how our men had the enemy hemmed in and bombarded them with constant arrow attacks. "We had brought in hundreds of thousands of arrows on teams of camels, with instruction to the archers to target the horses, as a knight without a horse is worse than useless. The men suffered terribly, the poor horses even more so."

"And did any get away?" I asked.

"Yes, Raymond. He took a big risk and led his cavalry towards our men. On Father's instruction, we stepped aside, letting him through, and then closed ranks again to stop more men escaping. Raymond and his men eventually got safely back to Tripoli."

"Why did Saladin allow this? It makes no sense to me."

"You know what my father is like. He believes that when he is chivalrous, his enemies will be kinder to him in return. Well, we all know he's a most unusual man. It's no secret."

Al-Afdal explained how the rest of the Franj cavalry and foot soldiers used their last reserves of strength to climb the hill, trying to reach the water, but when they arrived, there was none left. Our men attacked and many were killed.

"In one final effort, the Franj charged down the hill towards my father and me. At that point, it seemed as if they might win the day."

"You must have been terrified," I said, trying to imagine the dire situation.

"I have never experienced such fear. My father put his arm around my shoulders and told me to be brave. He is always so cool and calm under pressure, but this time, I saw him go very pale. However, we managed to stand our ground and push them back up the hill. They made their stand in the empty crater there."

He pointed upwards to the dome-shaped hill. I could feel the fear and desperation just from the tone of his voice. He was reliving the battle, blow by blow.

"At one point, I turned in great joy to my father, telling him we were about to win. He told me

189

angrily to keep quiet until the job was done. At that moment, that's exactly what happened."

I felt sick at the dreadful human destruction around me. Bodies were still lying on the ground in their thousands. Most of them were Franj, all their weapons and armour taken, but some were Muslims as well.

Al-Afdal told me that the few survivors of the enemy army had been executed, including the remaining knights. "These knights are the most dangerous in the world," he said, a little defensively. "We had to eliminate them so that they could never hurt us again."

Few bodies were intact. Limbs and heads had been hacked off. The stink from the mutilated corpses was appalling as their flesh was decaying, and I felt sick and dizzy having to breathe in the poisoned air. We stepped over these rotting human remains, trying to avoid the clouds of flies swarming the hill and the greater area around it, uselessly brushing off these filthy insects.

I didn't think that history had ever recorded such a terrible battle and hoped that I would never have to witness a similar scene ever again. I wanted to get as many miles away from here as I could. Al-Afdal told me that the estimates revealed that some 20,000 had been killed on that awful day. Many Franj had thrown their swords down, he said, and collapsed on the ground, burning with thirst and exhaustion. The fight had left them and they awaited their fate with resolution.

"Saladin must have been delighted and relieved with his victory," I said.

"Yes, my father knelt and prayed in thanks for his great day."

"And what happened to the Franj leaders?"

Al-Afdal explained that his men had captured them and taken them to Saladin's tent. Reynald de Châtillon had been among them.

"The man Saladin had sworn many times to kill for his treachery," I recalled.

"Yes, Father accused him of many crimes, including the breaking of peace treaties and the killing and terrible treatment of Muslims. I was sitting next to him. His anger was loud and fierce, and I was afraid. I had never seen him so inflamed before. He shouted at Reynald that he had attacked our Holy Cities of Medina and Mecca. Reynald didn't seem concerned and stated that this was the way wars were fought nowadays."

I was fascinated.

"'You have only one chance left,' Father told Reynald. 'You may convert to Islam or lose your life.' Reynald calmly refused and my father struck him on the shoulder, beheading him with one blow of his sword. Our bodyguards dragged his body away."

Despite the horrible violence, I was pleased to hear this. Reynald had been dishonourable, quite unlike any other knights I knew. He'd had it coming to him. I had already known that he had been killed; Reynald's head had been paraded through many cities since then, including Damascus. Huge crowds had gathered when it was brought there.

"We have also captured the most precious item of Christendom, the True Cross."

This would have been the worst blow for the Franj. It was the single most important symbol of their – my – religion. I had seen the cross hanging upside down, dangling from a spear while it was paraded through Damascus. Amid the frenzied cheers of victory from the inhabitants, I had felt a sense of terrible loss.

As we climbed higher, I saw several dozen men busy with a new construction site on top of the hill.

"What will this new building be?" I asked.

"My father has ordered a dome to be built here to celebrate. This will be called The Dome of Victory, and many will travel here and marvel at our great achievement. It will be a sign of our dominance over the land."

"What will Saladin do next? Will he subdue the ports and other parts of the Franj kingdom, or will he go straight for Jerusalem?"

Al-Afdal explained that this had been a difficult decision for Saladin and his advisors to make. He had dreamed of entering the gates of Jerusalem for many years and returning the city to its rightful place in the Muslim world, kicking out the Franj and Christians.

"It's been nearly 100 years since they took the city from us, spilling the blood of thousands of the faithful in the process. Now, Father would like nothing more than a peaceful surrender. But we must secure the ports first to restore our economy. Acre will be our first target and we are to meet him there in two days to help him. After that, there will be many more ports to take back into our ownership. Then the path will be clear to the greatest prize, Jerusalem."

We walked down the hill in silence and I contemplated the future. Surely the world must know that the balance of power had shifted in this country with the massive defeat of the Franj at Hattin. Many nations would be planning a return visit to attempt to restore our lands to Christendom and secure the Holy sites. We all knew that the second King Henry had sent vast sums to the Franj to support their cause. This was his penitence for the murder of Thomas Becket in Canterbury Cathedral several years ago.

Henry was now married to the lovely Eleanor, her marriage to her French husband having been annulled. I ached to see her again. Once more, I thought about my own safety and that of my family with the shifting sands of power. Would the Muslim world keep us here in safety or would these people destroy us? Would Saladin be alive to protect us or would he succumb to illness once again? If the Franj came here from Europe, would they consider me to be an enemy or one of them? I thought the former more likely. Would they execute my family and me as traitors or make us suffer a worse fate? I knew they were capable of terrible cruelty.

As I was considering my future options with uncertainty, I had a moment of clarity: I wanted to return to my own country and people. But would Yasmine share my vision of the future? I wasn't sure. Would my children and grandchildren come with us? Almost certainly not. They were from this country and culture. As Muslims, they would have trouble integrating into England's society. Anyway, why would they want to live in their father's home land and where would we all stay? Could I bear to leave them here forever and never see them again?

"What's the matter, Shiva?" al-Afdal's voice broke into my thoughts. "You look like you've seen a Jinn! We must hurry now as Father will be in Acre within days and he will expect us to be there."

I shook my head to clear my mind and walked briskly to the waiting horsemen. One of them helped me up into the saddle. As we rode fast along the dusty path, I considered my story for *The Pigeon News*, planning how to write the follow-up about our next military manoeuvres and successes.

***

We reached the magnificent port of Acre without incident, and I had time to reflect on the importance of this place. The port belonged to the Kingdom of Jerusalem and was the second largest city in our country. It was also the most prosperous port, trading with many countries around the world.

Al-Afdal and I rode towards Saladin, who was waiting to greet us with his men. I could see the tension in his face.

"Welcome to our latest conquest," he said. "This city has unexpectedly surrendered. The inhabitants had no means of protecting themselves, as we had killed thousands of their knights at Hattin. They begged me for mercy, which I have granted them.

"Al Afdal, this city will be yours. I urge you to treat the people with respect. No bloodshed. Free the Muslim prisoners and take the Franj wealth for our people. I will subdue the inland towns before taking the other ports."

Saladin asked me to travel with him as he and his army easily mopped up the nearby towns. These included Nazareth, home of the young Jesus. Once again, I felt a pang of longing to be back among my own people.

Saladin never stood still for long. He was already moving on, attacking more ports to control the economy of the country. Guy, the King of Jerusalem who had been captured at Hattin, was used to persuade the elders of the ports to give up without fighting. Some did, others did not, but Saladin soon wore down those who resisted. Together with his brother al-Adil, who had come up from Egypt to assist him, Saladin soon controlled all the territory outside Jerusalem.

While travelling with Saladin's army, I was trying to complete the articles for *The Pigeon News*. My first priority was to report on Hattin, but the news about the ports was urgent as well. I worked night and day to complete my essential task.

Tyre was the only port that had held out, which was awkward as it could enable entry for potential invaders from outside. Another European invasion could reverse all the gains we had made. Once again, we were in a dilemma. Should we move our army to secure Tyre, or should we go for Jerusalem? Tyre was well defended and would take weeks to secure, if we could achieve this at all. Saladin had told me privately that he was still concerned about his health and was desperate to secure Jerusalem before he died.

It was a decision we would all come to regret.

Chapter 11

Jerusalem At Last

I was present when a delegation arrived from Jerusalem to negotiate terms of surrender. We all gathered in Saladin's tent on the Mount of Olives.

"I want a peaceful surrender and all inhabitants can leave with their possessions," he told the delegation. "We will respect your holy places and your pilgrims will be welcomed."

There were nods of assent and the meeting broke up. But as we left, the most extraordinary phenomenon occurred. The sun dimmed, then disappeared. In the middle of the day, the land was plunged into darkness. None of us had seen anything like this before.

"Look, the Christians are all leaving as fast as they can travel," Saladin said when the light returned, pointing at the city below us. "But I predict that they will regard this event as an omen. They will renege on the deal to surrender the city."

This moment remains one of my most vivid memories of Jerusalem. Sitting high up on the Mount of Olives, we looked down on the magnificent spectacle of the greatest city on earth. In the centre was the huge, majestic Dome of the Rock, built over 150 years ago, a testament to the architects of Islamic beauty. This was where the

Angel Gabriel had taken the Prophet from the Sacred Mosque in Mecca to the furthest Mosque in Jerusalem. From there, he was taken to Heaven, and then transported back to Mecca. Saladin was physically shocked when he saw that the Christians had placed a huge golden cross on top of the Mosque.

Nearby was the domed roof of the Church of the Holy Sepulchre, one of the most precious and significant places of Christianity, where Jesus was crucified and buried. He was also an important figure in Islam, a prophet and a messenger of God. We saw the bell tower of the Hospital of St John and, almost out of our line of sight, the Tower of David.

My greatest memory of that moment was the richness of the gold. The bright sunlight shining on the golden stones confirmed to me that this was the most magnificent place I would ever visit. I was so privileged to be here and witness this.

As we sat in silence contemplating the importance of this moment in the history of Jerusalem, the sun was dying. Saladin was in the centre of our group with several of his relatives and generals around him. He gazed in reverence at this sacred city, as precious to Islam as it was to Christianity. Its return to the Muslim people had placed a huge responsibility on his shoulders.

However, as Saladin had so rightly predicted, the job was not done. Balian, a Franj knight who had miraculously managed to escape from Hattin unscathed, and was now the leader of the City of Jerusalem, had previously agreed to a peaceful surrender, but he and the people had changed their minds. They were determined to defend their city.

The Crusaders had attacked and taken the city almost 100 years ago and ruthlessly slaughtered its Muslim and other inhabitants. The story of this violence had been passed down from parents to children, and now their grandchildren had sworn vengeance.

"Balian has broken his sacred word," snarled Saladin. "This I can't forgive, and I am now forced to carry out the destruction of our city to force his surrender."

The following day, Saladin's men pounded the thick walls with forty mangonels. They continued this bombardment without success, while Saladin was considering his next move.

"I wanted to take this city peacefully and spare the inhabitants, but Balian has given me no choice," he told his generals. "We will move the assault to the north side. This was where the Franj attacked and broke through when they took the city all those years ago."

I could see the good sense in his plans, but dreaded the slaughter that would follow, together with the loss of the precious symbols of both religions.

With our mangonels bombarding the walls and our sappers working to place explosives in the foundations, we'd breached the city in three days. The current regime was doomed.

Saladin decided to take the city by storm. "They stole Jerusalem from the Muslims with bloodshed," he roared. "I will slaughter the men, and the women, I will make slaves."

After the breach, Balian came out of the city to speak to Saladin. He was taken to the Mount of Olives, where Saladin sat to hear his plea for the lives of his people. Balian was a tall, imposing figure of middle age, but he had been dishonest in his dealings.

"You have broken the promise you made to me," said Saladin, "and I can't forgive that."

But Balian had one more trick up his sleeve. "I have been released from my promise by the clerics," he said. "If you do not spare us, I will kill everyone in the city, men, women and children. I will also kill the many thousands of Muslim prisoners. The total number is 60,000 and I will slaughter them all. The religious symbols will be destroyed and the buildings knocked down."

This would be a shocking outcome, both for the people and the priceless artefacts and buildings. Saladin glared at the man before speaking in a surprisingly calm voice.

"Please withdraw while I consult my people."

The discussions went on for several hours. We could allow the people and the city to be lost to the world, but Saladin would get the blame for both crimes. We quickly devised a compromise whereby people would pay a ransom to be allowed to leave the city in safety.

Several days later, the process was complete. Saladin had secured the Holy City of Jerusalem for the Muslims once again. Another Franj kingdom had been erased from his country. In addition, he had spared thousands of Christian lives, in sharp contrast to the slaughter of almost 100 years ago, and released many Muslim prisoners. I saw the glow of satisfaction in his face. He had achieved his life's purpose.

As usual, I had a very tight timeline to write and distribute our momentous story amidst all the celebrations. But these were premature. A more terrible threat than we had faced before was approaching.

While the celebrations were continuing in Jerusalem and the work was going on to change the Christian places to represent Islam, I took the opportunity to escape for a few days to visit my family in Damascus. While there, I overheard several men in the market place discussing recent events, angry voices asking questions and spreading doubts.

"Why is Saladin sparing the lives of so many enemy soldiers?"

"He promised to carry out a slaughter of the Christians in Jerusalem as they did to us when they captured the city. Is he a weak leader?"

"Is he going soft? Their soldiers go free to attack us again. We are going to lose this war if he carries on like this."

Fortunately, I was not recognised. I certainly didn't want to be drawn into the discussions, but they revealed some truths. Saladin had a serious image problem which had to be resolved, so I decided to take it on myself to distribute positive stories to counter these rumours and opinions. I sent news articles to all corners of Saladin's kingdom to emphasise his belief in peaceful conquests, mercy, and a soft and charitable approach.

***

Just when we thought we had the country under our control, there were looming problems for Saladin to face in Tyre and Acre that were becoming more serious and urgent. Our forces were under attack from the Franj, and recent news reports indicated that a huge force from Europe was about to arrive to strengthen their armies. Perhaps we should have secured all the ports before overcoming Jerusalem after all.

Was Saladin losing his touch?

Tyre was still held by the Franj. Meeting Saladin's senior people outside the city on my return from Damascus, I joined in discussions with them.

"Of course, Tyre is under the control of Conrad of Montferrat," one of Saladin's advisors opened the proceedings. "It will be a hard job to oust him."

"Who is this fellow?" I asked.

"He is probably the toughest Franj we have come up against so far. A very well-connected nobleman, he is related to the Roman Emperor."

"They say he is handsome and courageous and fiercely ambitious," another advisor put in. "He came to Tyre and took command almost immediately. But I am sure he will be no match for Saladin."

"Have we launched an attack yet?" I asked.

"Yes, we have ten ships trying to blockade the port, but five have already been captured and the rest have fled. In addition, our land forces are being repelled constantly. We fear the arrival of massive numbers of Franj by sea, but our navy is neither skilled nor strong enough to block them."

The other advisors nodded. "We have bombarded them with siege engines without success," said one. "Saladin even used Conrad's father to negotiate a surrender – remember, we captured him at Hattin. Conrad said he would rather shoot his father with a crossbow!"

"We have tried to get the support of the Caliph in Baghdad, but to no avail."

This was a dire situation. After many months of fighting, Saladin was forced to withdraw. Tyre was now ready and able to receive the Franj ships. The consequences of this would be appalling.

I would have a difficult job to deliver good news this time. How was I going to put a positive slant on the situation? That is exactly what I did, but just like in Damascus, people everywhere were starting to doubt our great leader. I heard the whispers loud and clear.

"Saladin is to blame for this, you know. He let so many of their soldiers go after our campaigns in Jerusalem, Acre and elsewhere, and they are now free to come here and fight us again. His actions are crazy. He will be remembered for this failure."

Deep down, I could see that the whisperers were right, but I didn't make any comment, and this certainly would not be included in my news.

I travelled with Saladin while we took two Franj strongholds, Safed, and finally Kerak Castle at the third attempt. We also subdued the great stone city of Petra. These were extremely tough nuts to crack and took too much precious time. I could tell that the stress of the campaigns was once again taking a dreadful toll on Saladin's health. We were all immensely tired, but there was no time to pause.

We then travelled to the port of Acre, which we'd already occupied, but we urgently needed to repair and strengthen our defences there. We expected to complete the work in a few weeks, but no one anticipated we would still be there almost two years later.

This was a dreadful time for all of us. An army had arrived from Tyre, determined to capture the port. The Muslim population inside Acre was under siege from the Franj, who in turn were under siege from Saladin's army. The Franj were supplied by their fleet, while an occasional Muslim ship would break through to supply the city residents.

I urgently needed to communicate with our people trapped inside the walls, so used my precious pigeons to relay messages. The problem this time was that there was no way for my pigeons to return to us. They could only travel one way, and then they had to be carried back. So, I came up with a different plan to communicate with the city.

I sent for our strongest swimmers to report to me at my tent. Six huge men duly appeared. I gasped at the size and strength of the massive figures who stood to attention in front of me.

The leader spoke to me. "Master, we are the men you asked for. My name is Isa."

"And you are the best swimmers in the camp?" I asked.

"Yes, we have been navy divers for many years and carry out underwater repairs to our ships. And we often need to swim under the Franj ships to reach the shore. We can hold our breath for several minutes – much longer than the average man. Most days, we swim for many miles."

This was excellent news. "I need to send messages to our people trapped inside those walls. Could you do this?"

"Yes, sir," Isa replied. "We could also carry money and other valuables to our people. These items would be secured in our belts." He pointed to the thick leather band around his waist. "We would do anything for our beleaguered people."

And this was how we managed to exchange messages with our people trapped within the walls of Acre. It was a great success and I silently congratulated myself on my initiative. These brave swimmers were taking massive risks, but were achieving the tough tasks I had set them.

Each time the men returned, I asked them to report to me on their latest mission. I was amazed by their achievements, carried out in the most dangerous conditions.

"I can't thank you all enough for your great service to our Muslim people. I will ensure that Saladin gets to hear about your bravery, and I know that you will all be well rewarded."

But like all good things, this successful enterprise was doomed to come to an end.

***

One evening, Isa's men came to me as usual. But Isa was not with them.

"We have some bad news to report. Isa has been found dead on the shores of Acre, killed by the enemy. He was still carrying letters and some gold coins for our people."

"That's dreadful news," I replied. "I'm so sorry for you all. I have been very impressed with your work."

Feeling guilty about sending this good, brave man to his death, I wasn't so proud of my idea now. Should I abort the mission or risk losing more men? I decided a positive attitude was the right way.

"We must carry on," I told the swimmers. "This is essential for our trapped people. I can assure you that Saladin will look after Isa's family, and he sends his warmest praise and thanks to each and every one of you."

The siege of Acre was a two-year period I would much rather forget, but there are two episodes I can still recall many years later. In one of the clashes the two sides had, the Franj managed to break through our lines and reach Saladin's camp where I was preparing my latest story. The fierce fighting came right up to my tent, and I became involved in the struggle.

Two knights swung their blades towards a small group of our defenders who bravely resisted. I picked up a scimitar and swung it at the chest of an approaching knight, who skilfully pushed my weapon away with his shield. He then raised his massive sword and aimed for my skull, threatening to cleave me in two. Before he had time to start the swing, one of our men jabbed him in the back with his spear. He cried out, dropped his sword and collapsed on the ground, writhing in agony. He was dead in seconds.

Saladin had encouraged his army to fight back against the surge of men and we soon had the dangerous situation under control, much to my relief. As the enemy retreated, I helped our men to strip the dead Franj of their weapons and armour.

"Come and look at this, sir," called one of our men, the surprise evident in his voice. "This is the... um, man who almost killed you."

He took me to the body, which lay facing the sky. I looked down and shock overwhelmed me.

"But this isn't a man at all," I said once I had regained my composure enough to form the words. "It's a woman! I've never seen anything like it. What the hell are women doing out here? And why are they dressed as knights? Do you think they have been trained?"

"I don't know, sir, but I will find out. I think we should let Saladin know."

Over the next few days, we captured another woman dressed as a knight. On questioning her, we learned that dozens of women had been trained as knights and had travelled to swell the Crusader armies. Many were stronger and braver than the men! Not so noble was the fact the invaders had also brought 300 women with them to serve as prostitutes for their fighting force.

"What a great news story I can make of that," I told Saladin. "Who would have thought that Christians were capable of this?"

Saladin smiled with amusement.

The second episode concerned an alarming development: the Franj were constructing three huge siege towers. They were so big that we could see them from our position outside of the town. They must have been nearly 100 feet tall, much taller than the city walls. Using these, the invaders could easily beat back the Muslim defenders. The towers even had trebuchets. But we were blocked by walls and an army from getting to these monstrosities.

I spoke to Saladin in some concern. "I've never seen such huge towers. They are extraordinary. How many more will they be building and how long will our people be able to hold out?"

Saladin was in near despair. "If they capture Acre, the war is lost. Bring my engineers here and we will have urgent group discussions. We must destroy these towers."

The talks went on long into the night and throughout the next day. But the engineers couldn't agree a way forward. Saladin called for more experts to be brought from Damascus with great urgency. I sent pigeons to transfer these instructions.

Days later, a couple of dozen men arrived. Saladin explained the dilemma.

"I know you," he said all of a sudden, pointing to one of the newly arrived engineers. "Aren't you related to the master of the coppersmiths? I don't suppose you have any idea how to destroy the towers?"

"Oh yes, sir, I am Omar, his son. I have been experimenting with Greek fire, trying to increase its strength."

"Please explain," Saladin said. We all listened in eager anticipation.

"I will launch the Greek fire with trebuchets, aiming the steaming pots at the towers."

A small ripple of laughter came from our men, including Saladin's own engineers who had been unable to provide a solution. The noise grew to a crescendo, then one of the engineers spoke for all.

"This will never work. The towers won't burn, and we'll be a laughing stock amongst the Franj. And anyway, you will need to get into the city to access the trebuchets. How are you going to do that?"

But the man was adamant. He turned to Saladin.

"Sultan, can you get me and my equipment safely into the city? I can then prepare the Greek fire."

His engineers started to laugh and jeer again, but Saladin silenced them with a raised hand.

"Quiet!" he barked. "Not one among you has come up with a workable idea." He turned to look at Omar. "We have a way to get into the city, but it's very dangerous. If you are agreeable, my people will show you."

"I am agreeable," Omar confirmed.

Without delay, Omar was guided into the city through secret tunnels, the other men who had come from Damascus carrying his equipment. Saladin and I watched and waited with some trepidation, but for a long time, nothing happened. Then finally, flaming pots flew high into the air from inside the city walls, some hitting the towers. But they had no effect.

All went quiet for a while, apart from the odd jeer from Saladin's engineers, which he quelled with a glare. Then another stream of flaming missiles flew over the city walls. One hit the top of the first tower. The effect was instantaneous and violent. The tower burst into flames and exploded. The dozens of soldiers occupying it suffered terrible deaths. We saw their burning bodies falling to the ground. I will never forget their terrible screams.

Minutes later, the other towers were destroyed. Saladin was hugely impressed and requested that Omar be brought back through the tunnels to meet with him. He thanked Omar and offered rewards, but Omar refused.

"This is my contribution to God," he said simply.

I now had two fascinating news stories to relate to the Muslim world, which I wrote with great speed. My efforts helped us to gain even more soldiers from many parts, but we knew that massive reinforcements were coming across land and sea to supplement the enemy forces. And these would include one of the most terrifying, brutal, infamous and charismatic monsters the world had ever known.

Chapter 12

The King Arrives

King Richard, known as the Lionheart, had arrived at Acre. This man's reputation was already striking fear into the hearts of Christians and Muslims alike.

Richard the Lionheart was the son of Henry II and my beloved Eleanor of Aquitaine. As soon as her name was mentioned, a clear image formed in my mind of her beauty and magnificence. She was a widow after Henry's death two years earlier, although I had heard that they had been separated for years, and Henry had imprisoned her. She had given birth to many children, and several were leaders across the continent of Europe. And now, her sons had become Kings of England, and the second, Richard, had come here to torment us.

Our men could talk about little else. We became extremely worried about Richard's arrival and the rumours abounded.

"Have you seen him yet? They say he is red headed, very tall and immensely strong."

"He has been toughened by 1,000 battles and has never shown any fear."

"Richard has the spirit and heart of his mother and is a great leader of men. He is determined to seize Jerusalem back for the Franj."

"Did you know that he has already captured Cyprus? He has shown himself to be cruel and ruthless."

"I doubt he will be a match for Saladin, though. Saladin knows his country well and how to use it to his advantage. He also knows his people."

"Richard is a leader of a dozen armies from across Europe and many of his men are untried and untested."

"But he is storming the walls of Acre using his trebuchet machines with an incredible intensity. Surely they cannot hold out for much longer. He is certain to breach the city soon and imprison or kill all our people."

And so the gossip went back and forth. There was no doubt in my mind that everyone was unsettled and afraid of this man and the trouble he would bring. Saladin tried to calm the situation by talking to his people. I helped by playing down the story, sending positive messages across the Arab world.

Our situation outside the walls of Acre was becoming worse every day. Our greatest problem, which afflicted the enemy too, was disease. Illness was killing more men than the conflict. But those inside the walls were having a much worse time than we were, as supplies could rarely get through to them. Sometimes we were able to break the blockade of Franj ships, but mostly, the poor people starved.

There were some good moments, though, which helped me to keep morale high via *The Pigeon News*. We came up with a plan to disguise one of our ships as a Franj vessel, even dressing the men as Europeans and placing a few pigs on the deck to convince the Christians that we were part of their army. Surely, no Muslim would do this, even in these straitened times. I communicated our ideas to the Egyptian Navy leaders via the Pigeon Post.

They replied and said that it would never work. We would be found out and lose a valuable ship, many lives and tons of stores destined for our people imprisoned in Acre. Saladin told me to reply and insist that it would be attempted, putting his name on the message. This was now an order.

I was the first to hear the results of the exercise as a pigeon flew in with the news. I reported immediately to Saladin and his advisors.

"The plan worked even better than anyone could have imagined. The ship was halted by the enemy and the crew questioned, but they pulled off a remarkable deception. We managed to deliver a ship load of provisions to our starving people."

But, of course, the provisions ran out in weeks and the people became desperate once again. And then the inevitable happened. The constant battering and the fires under the walls eventually caused them to crumble. The Franj easily overran the city and all our people were imprisoned. We had failed in our attempts to protect and save them, despite two years of our best efforts.

***

I don't think many of our people realised it at this time, but Saladin was very ill once again. I was one of the few he trusted with the details.

"Shiva, I have campaigned and fought all my adult life and I have never stopped travelling. I am tired – no, I am truly exhausted. Acre has been a terrible disaster."

"But what are your symptoms?" I asked him. "There must be something the doctors can do. What treatment have they given you?"

"I have so many quacks fussing around me, but none seems able to find a cure for my stomach problems. They say I have colic, whatever that is, and that I should go away and rest. But how can I do that when we are under the gravest threat in our history? Now Acre has fallen, we can't stop these Franj hordes. Jerusalem is the least of our worries. Our Muslim peoples will be wiped from the face of the earth."

With my dear friend Saladin so very stressed about the worsening situation, I decided the most immediate support I could give him was to send for one of the doctors who had treated me in the Damascus hospital. He would be Saladin's best hope. I decided not to tell Saladin I was doing this, and of course, I put nothing about his worsening health in my regular news bulletins.

As I was leaving his tent, one of Saladin's advisors tapped me on the shoulder. I turned to face him.

"Have you heard about *his* health?" he asked.

"What do you mean? Whose health?'

"Richard's, of course."

I breathed a heavy sigh of relief. I was extremely worried that Saladin's woes had become common knowledge. But this was almost too good to be true.

"Well, what is wrong with him?" I asked.

"We are not sure because reports have varied. It seems that he has a severe fever, and some say his nails and hair have fallen out. No one seems able to put a name to his illness."

Thanking the man, I rushed back to Saladin's tent to bring him up to date. When I told him, far from being elated, he seemed very concerned.

"We must help Richard to recover," he said. "Please ask my brother al-Adil to send him a dozen bottles of our special snow water immediately. Make sure the water is as ice cold as the day it was brought down from the mountain. And get word to Damascus to send a doctor to Richard."

I was struck by the irony: the very plan I had made to help Saladin, he had put forward to bring relief to Richard. As always, I carried out his instructions immediately, once again amazed at his mercy and kindness. I had known for a long time that Saladin was the most extraordinary leader his country had ever known. His humanity always shone through, even in the direst situation. Who had ever heard of a leader sending his greatest enemy a doctor to cure him? It was unprecedented and once again marked him out as an exceptional and compassionate man. He would be idolised and worshipped for evermore.

I had been very fortunate to be able to call him my good friend for over forty years. My next news story would be one of my very best with a powerful message.

**

A few weeks later, Saladin summoned me once again.

"Shiva, I want you to visit Richard and lead our negotiating team. While you are there, try to find out all you can about his intentions and his health. I wonder how ill he really is. Can he survive this illness? Also, consult our doctor who treated him. I want you to describe to me exactly what you see and hear. This is essential information for me as I plan my next move."

I couldn't believe that Saladin was trusting me to carry out this very important mission. I had no experience of negotiation – but then, I supposed that my *Pigeon News* reporting involved some kind of negotiation and it had certainly honed my powers of persuasion.

I was full of trepidation as four of us – three negotiators and I – approached the Christian camp. I was leading the group as we were stopped at the entrance to Richard's tent by two of his knights and searched for weapons. Richard had already been told who we were.

Finding us unarmed, the knights went ahead into the tent to announce our arrival. The tent, or pavilion as the Franj called it, was enormous, and I was surprised how cool and airy the room was. I fleetingly wondered how they managed to provide this atmosphere, which was very beneficial for the sick, in such a hot country. Perhaps I could ask the question if the conversation went well, so I could then cool the air in Saladin's tent.

There was a smell of sweat and fever in the air, which was pungent with a miasma of spices and herbs. It was difficult to decide at first whether it was pleasant or not as I wondered if it would be beneficial to Saladin. Later, I would need to consult our own doctors about this. Incense lamps were hanging from the walls. The light was dim, and my companions and I blinked to adjust our vision.

The floor was covered in animal skins, stretched across the ground. Richard's shield bearing the three lions passant was propped up against a low cupboard. There were three magnificent greyhounds lying obediently at the foot of a bed. I had only ever seen creatures like these in my lord's castle.

The huge bed filled one end of the room and a massive figure lay right across the mattress. I looked again in surprise. He was truly enormous. For all the stories I had heard about Richard, none of them came near to describing his size. He must have been well over six feet, perhaps nearer to seven, but it was hard to tell. I guessed he had lost some weight due to the illness, but when fully fit, he would be a towering, frightening figure. His leadership skills were legendary, and I am sure he would have matched Saladin in many ways. But I was confident that Saladin could surpass him, especially in humanity and generosity.

I had heard that Richard's illness had caused hair loss, and this was apparent. A few remaining strands of his light red hair were brushed back and spread across the pillow. Beads of sweat ran down his pale face due to the fever that had taken hold. This was a sorry sight of a weakened giant, but the cruel face and ruthless lips remained.

This man was a monster, despite his condition, and I shuddered involuntarily at the danger my companions and I were exposed to. His reputation had determined that there were no limits to his depravity and ferociousness. If he wished, he could have us murdered in a moment.

I shuddered again at the huge responsibility Saladin had imposed on me. I briefly hoped that the next few minutes would race forward in one second, so I wouldn't have to suffer them. I was dreading the conversation.

I then had a vision of his mother, Eleanor, hovering just over his bed and I jumped in fright. The image was so real and lifelike, for a moment I was taken back to another pavilion many years ago, where I met and spoke with that magnificent lady. How could she have spawned this ogre?

"What's the matter, man? You look like you've seen a ghost."

I flinched as Richard's words brought me back to reality. I'd expected his voice to be loud, deep and booming, but instead it was thin and reedy.

"My apologies, sir, I was just adjusting to the light of the room after the brightness of the sun. My name is Crispin."

"I know who you are, but I was told you are called Shiva."

"Yes, sir, that is a nickname which has stuck with me for many years."

His next few words left me stunned. "My mother has told me all about you and how you saved her life many years past here in Palestine. She has asked me to give you a letter, but now is not the time. You will get it later. For now, we have more important matters to discuss."

Richard went quiet for a few minutes and seemed to have fallen asleep. The illness had obviously taken a terrible toll on his health and wellbeing. We waited in silence. His knights seemed to be used to his condition. They looked down on his body as he raised a drooping eyelid and spoke.

"Why hasn't Saladin himself come to negotiate with me? I am the leader of the Christians and should be speaking to the leader of the Muslims. Otherwise there will be no result and no point in talking."

"Saladin means no disrespect," I said quietly and clearly. "He wants to meet you and will do so when there is a conclusive agreement, not before."

"What we will agree today is a prisoner exchange," said Richard. "You have some 3,000 of our people captured from Acre and we have around half that number of your people in captivity. We need to agree the details and the date of the exchange. We also demand the return of the True Cross, which was stolen from us at Hattin."

"Yes sir, that has been agreed. We have shown your people that we have the Cross and we will hand it over as part of the settlement."

There had been a dramatic scene a few days ago when our army had shown the Cross to a gathering of Christian knights, many of whom had fainted at the sight of it. There was no doubt that this, the most influential Christian symbol in the world, was a powerful negotiating tool.

"We need to agree the timing of the handover of the Cross and the details of the prisoner exchange," I said. "We also need to agree which men will be exchanged. Of course, you will want your senior noblemen and we want ours."

"Don't bother me with the trivia! Detail is not the concern of a King. But I want ransom money from Saladin as well, every coin." After a pause, Richard went on. "Go and agree with my men which people will be exchanged. Write it down and make a copy for Saladin and for me to sign. I need to sleep now."

We were taken to another tent where we discussed all aspects of the exchange with Richard's negotiators. We spoke for twelve hours without a break. Eventually we had a draft agreement, which was signed by Richard. Then my companions and I were tasked with taking it back to Saladin.

After long deliberation, my friend also signed the paper. We had a deadline to achieve the exchange, which was only a few days away, so we had to start the process immediately in order to meet the agreed date.

However, we – Saladin's advisors – became more and more concerned. Saladin was delaying the exchange of prisoners with Richard, who was in turn becoming increasingly frustrated. We urged Saladin to action his part of the agreement, involving the release of Christian prisoners and payment of a high ransom, but he dug his heels in.

"Our senior people are not being exchanged and sent back to us, while Richard is insisting on having all of his," he complained.

I worked hard to resolve this issue, but both men were being somewhat obstinate. I begged Saladin to comply with the agreement, even though he did not have enough money to achieve the ransom terms. Instead, he offered Richard a small portion as a down payment. The negotiators and I went back to Richard, returned to Saladin, and then went back again, repeating the process dozens of times over the next few days. I was extremely concerned that the negotiations were going badly, mainly because of Saladin's intransigence and delaying tactics.

Richard finally ran out of patience. When the negotiators and I arrived in his tent, he told us to turn around and leave if we wanted to continue to enjoy the benefits of living without pain. But not using language I could repeat here. We shuddered at the power of his words.

The following day, we were forced to witness one of the most terrible events in the history of the world. More than 2,000 of our people were dragged out of the walled city by Richard's men and on to the field in front of our army, where the knights beheaded every one of them. It was horrific violence and I turned away in disgust.

Richard had demonstrated that he was capable of the most appalling brutality. But then, so was Saladin. He responded by killing hundreds of Christians he held in captivity.

This was the worst outcome after two dreadful years while we tried to save Acre from the Franj. I felt drained, empty of spirit and terribly tired. I went to my tent and lay on my mattress and hoped I could stay there forever; I had rarely felt so low. Even the meditation and other practices I had learned in the Far East failed to lift me.

But of course, I couldn't stay in my bed. After a few days, I received a message to visit Saladin.

"Shiva, the doctors have told me you are ill," he said. "It's time you went back to your family and had a good rest. You have done amazing work for our cause. Come back refreshed in a few weeks. I will arrange a team to take you to Damascus in comfort."

"But Saladin, it's you who should rest," I argued. "You have never stopped campaigning for years."

"I have a very real devil to deal with here," he replied. "I must erase Richard and his people from our country. I cannot rest until this is done."

Chapter 13

An Uncertain Future

And so, I travelled to Damascus. While I felt dreadful on the journey, I just couldn't contain my excitement. More than two years had passed since I had seen my family.

Yasmine welcomed me with open arms and quickly brought me up to date with the news of the family. There had been two more grandchildren arrive since I'd left, but her next words left me astounded.

"You also have a new son," she announced.

My mouth moved without any sound coming from it. I felt dizzy and had to sit down.

"It's all fine," she said calmly. "His name is Daniel. He is nearly two years old."

"Me Dan," a little voice called up to me. I looked down to see the most beautiful boy, still very small, with huge, intelligent blue eyes and a gorgeous smile. I wept as I knelt down to look at him, and then I picked him up, hugging him close to my chest. Tears flowed freely down my cheeks. Had I really been away that long?

Yasmine nodded in the affirmative. Once again, I had missed my own child's baby years.

"Yasmine, I promise I will never leave the family for so long again. I am so, so sorry."

"Crispin, you have no choice. Let's just make the most of this moment and do our best, spend time with our family. I have so much to show you in our book. Our children have been contributing too."

We spent the following days drawing and writing as Daniel played at our feet. As usual, I had many experiences of my own to express on to the pages, the worst, of course, being the appalling massacre. I painted the scene in graphic detail as my mind could never rid itself of the horrible images.

I had so much pain and anxiety to let go, but after many days of transferring my innermost tensions on to the paper, I felt a massive relief. Calm came over me in waves. Yasmine put her arms around me and hugged me. Then she led me to lie down on our bed and I slept more soundly than I had in many months.

Our home was the only place I felt at peace in the world. I wanted to hold on to these moments and live the rest of my life here with the family, but I knew this wouldn't happen.

"Saladin is sick," I told Yasmine in private, "and I don't think he will recover. He has endured more than anyone alive, has faced his adversaries with steadfastness and courage. It's hard to believe that he is only fifty-four years old. You would think he has lived 1,000 summers."

"Will he die soon?" she asked.

"Unfortunately, it's likely. And when that happens, I don't think it will be safe for you and me here in Damascus, or indeed anywhere in the Muslim world. Saladin has been a huge force for peace and unity and has protected us. But he has so many sons and brothers. There will be a huge scramble for power after his demise, causing much instability."

"So, what are our options? How do we protect ourselves?"

"There is less danger for you and our family. You are Muslims and belong to this country, but I do not, unfortunately. I may have no option but to leave."

"Well, that may be true, but if you leave this country, where will you go? Anyway, there is no chance you will be going on your own. I will never leave you."

"But what about our children? I doubt we can all leave together. Anyway, our older children have their lives here and their own children to consider. They will want to stay."

We spent many hours agonising about our future, but Yasmine never faltered in her devotion to me. Perhaps we should just stay here and take our chances. She was right: at the moment, we had no other options.

Despite the uncertainty, we didn't broach the subject again during my stay. I enjoyed some of the happiest weeks of my life at home, spending as much time as I could with my wife, children and grandchildren. But the time ran away far too quickly.

We weren't to know then that a huge opportunity and a solution to our problems would open up for us in just a few weeks.

***

Saladin sent soldiers to escort me to Jerusalem, where he was busy organising repairs to the massive city walls. I met him high up on the battlements on the south side of the city to discuss the Lionheart's likely next moves. Saladin still looked strained and tense, but to my relief, his health had recovered somewhat.

"You never know with Richard," Saladin said. "It wouldn't surprise me if he launched a full-scale attack, although I think he would be foolish to do so. It's very hard to guess his next move."

"Do you think he will venture south and attack Egypt? He would love to have the wealth of that country to boost his campaign."

"Yes, the thought has occurred to me. We just can't afford to lose Egypt. Remember the years we spent trying to subdue the country, fighting two enemies at the same time, the Franj and the Egyptians? Now I couldn't manage without its wealth to fund our campaigns against the Christians.

"But if we lose Jerusalem now, our allies will lose faith in us, so we must prepare for Richard's attack. The next stage in this game is negotiation, and while we are talking, we will wait for reinforcements. Richard is also waiting for help from his European allies.

"I want you to meet with my brother al-Adil. You heard about our battle with Richard at Arsuf?"

I had heard every detail, but I just nodded. I'd have to write another positive story, turning failure into success.

"It was one of the worst defeats we have suffered against the Christians. We followed them as they left Acre, going south along the coast. They made slow progress to conserve their energy in the very hot weather. Two of their ships followed them just

233

offshore, providing food and water and looking after their wounded.

"All along the way, we fired thousands of arrows at them and rode away before they could retaliate. We managed to kill or wound hundreds of their horses. I know we caused many casualties and much annoyance."

He went on to describe how Richard had halted his men at Arsuf, a wooded area near the coast. It was here that our army had attacked them.

"Their men held until we tempted them to break away. Then we attacked. Al-Adil told me this was the fiercest battle we have ever been involved in.

"My brother saw Richard in the midst of the fighting, an unmistakable figure. He has never seen such a brave and terrible fighter. Richard swung his longsword relentlessly for many hours, killing dozens of our precious people, maybe even hundreds, and he motivated his knights to fight even harder. Our men couldn't resist their ferocity and eventually, we were forced to retreat on our faster horses.

"Even though we lost, most of our men are still fit enough to continue our struggle. Shiva, I am sure you can call this a victory for the brave Muslim soldiers. We made a *tactical* retreat to enable us to fight another day."

But I knew the truth. This had been a humiliating defeat for Saladin.

"Now we desperately need arms, men and money from all parts of the Muslim world, not to mention the support of our Caliph in Baghdad. Positive news will be hugely beneficial for us."

The Caliph was the key to the success of our people, just as the kings and leaders of Europe needed the support of their Pope in Rome. I had witnessed the despair of Saladin when he was so often ignored by the Caliph. I wrote the most positive story with all the passion I could muster and sent it to all parts of the Muslim world, in the hope that this time, *The Pigeon News* would bring the Caliph on board.

***

After Arsuf, Richard sent his forces south along the coast. Saladin was worried that he might make a dash for Egypt, stealing our wealth from there. Others thought that he had different ideas.

A week later, I caught up with al-Adil in Egypt. "When he reaches Jaffa, which he will take easily, he will head inland towards Jerusalem," al-Adil warned. "If he takes our city, this will be a tragedy for us. First, we must get down to Ascalon to make sure he cannot move even further south. We have to take Ascalon apart stone by stone, so that

Richard cannot hold it. Then we have to double the strength of the walls of Jerusalem. We cannot let him take Jerusalem, or Egypt.

"This is a big game we are playing, and we must outsmart Richard. I have looked after this country for Saladin for many years and I don't intend to give it away now."

Then, he gave me my new orders. "Shiva, you must write more stories so that our people, especially the Caliph, understand how important it is to gain the support of our whole nation. We must put aside old enmities and unite with one accord. And Shiva – by the way, how did you get that silly name in the first place?"

"You must ask your brother sometime, when he is not distracted by war," I replied and he smiled. "It was his idea when we were very young and rather childish."

"I will be sure to ask him. More importantly, we are approaching a time of intense negotiations and I want you to work with me. We need to know when to speed up talks and when to go slow to allow more reinforcements to reach us. The winner will be the one who outsmarts the other."

We met with Richard many times over the next few months, usually in neutral land between Jaffa and Jerusalem. In the meantime, fighting continued with as much ferocity as before.

One of the later negotiating sessions stands out sharply in my memory. We arranged a large gathering with dozens of nobles from each side. Huge pavilions were built to accommodate the negotiators and the hot air of discussions went on for several days. During our breaks, lavish banquets were served by both sides, each trying to outdo the other. Afterwards, there were tournaments and tests of skills including horsemanship, polo and tent pegging, as well as displays of fighting skills. Both sides wanted to impress the other and no expense was spared. Even though neither could really afford the largesse, no one wanted to admit to a lack of resources.

It was a huge privilege to have been there at one of the most magnificent gatherings that had ever taken place. But the negotiations were exhausting. We got the impression that the Christians were keen to end hostilities.

Richard himself was once again suffering fevers and seizures, so he did not take part. As ever, there were serious disagreements among his people and European allies. They were all tiring from the relentless campaigning and perhaps even desired peace. We were also tired, but were very keen to hide this from our enemies, and yearned for peace as much as they did. At least, until our reinforcements arrived.

Richard wanted to hold Jerusalem, claiming that it was a Christian city, but history clearly showed that he was wrong. Jerusalem had always been a Muslim city and belonged to us. Richard also wanted to keep a huge area of the country, including the coastal strip, but once again we could not agree to this. Both sides were desperately looking for areas of compromise.

On the last day of this meeting, we had just broken off discussions and started the day's tournament when Richard arrived. He climbed down from his horse with some difficulty; we could see that he was still suffering. I was only a few paces away from him and noticed his face was now heavily lined and he seemed to be dreadfully tired.

His movements were slow and painful as he stepped forward to greet al-Adil. The two men had got to know each other well and had great respect for each other. Richard looked over at the tournament with some excitement, despite his weakened condition, and indicated that he wanted to become involved. The old warhorse could never resist a challenge.

"Adil," Richard boomed, "why do your people still use those piddling little swords? They are bloody useless, especially against a mighty English broadsword. I suppose none of you are strong or brave enough to swing a real sword. You little people would probably fall over."

He shook as he laughed at his own joke with a deep throaty roar. I thought that al-Adil would take offence and retaliate against these obvious insults, but he stood facing Richard with his arms folded and a big grin on his face.

"Here, try and hold my sword. Now take a swing," Richard challenged him.

Al-Adil took hold of the huge and heavy piece of metal and, with great difficulty, tried to wave it in a circular movement with his skinny arms – it nearly knocked him off his feet. Richard bellowed with laughter as he took it from the embarrassed man. I wondered how this was going to end.

Richard walked to a nearby table where one of our men had left his mace. He raised his sword above his head and swung it down with an almighty crash, breaking the metal club in two. The table suffered a similar fate. I was standing only a few feet away and almost jumped into the air with shock at the noise. Bright sparks shot in all directions.

"Now that is a real sword!" Richard said triumphantly and stood back for al-Adil and his men to admire his skill and achievement.

Al-Adil coolly instructed his aide to hold up a large piece of silk by the corners so that it hung down.

"King Richard, I challenge you to cut this flimsy piece of silk in two with your sword."

Richard laughed at the challenge, drew his massive sword back and swung it round in a strong sideways movement, aiming at the sheet. He succeeded only in pushing it to one side and it swung back intact. Richard howled in frustration. After two more unsuccessful attempts, he gave up. Al-Adil did not react.

Richard stepped aside and let al-Adil come forward with his scimitar. With one gentle swing, he cut the sheet neatly in half and the lower piece sashayed to the floor. He swung again and again until the sheet was in tiny shreds. I was worried about the poor aide having to hold the remaining piece of silk, but he didn't flinch, even when the blade came within a couple of inches of his hand. It was a very impressive display. Al-Adil had made his point well.

A broad smile spread across Richard's face, and he walked across to al-Adil and held out his hand. No more words were needed as the pair shook hands and embraced each other in mutual admiration.

***

Later that day, I was called to a meeting with Richard and al-Adil. I walked into the pavilion just as Richard was trying to persuade Saladin's brother to marry his sister, Joan.

"She is the Queen of Sicily, you know, a fine catch. And this marriage would make a brilliant alliance between our nations. You could become joint rulers of Jerusalem."

I knew that Joan had previously firmly rejected the idea of such an alliance and I was surprised that Richard was still pursuing it. In any case, al-Adil would never consider marrying a Christian woman.

"We have almost completed our negotiations," Richard announced in his usual thundering voice. Gone was the reedy whisper of our first meeting. "I plan to leave Palestine as soon as they are over. But first, Shiva – Crispin – whatever your name is, I want you to have the letter from my dear mother, Eleanor. She remembers well your selfless courage when you saved her life. I suppose that without you, I wouldn't be here – haha!" His laughter at his great wit boomed around the room.

"She told me to relay her grateful thanks to you, if we had the opportunity to meet. She wants to reward you for your actions and has ordered me to grant you safe passage back to England, should you wish to return. She also wants to make you Lord of Milton Castle."

I felt my legs go wobbly at his extraordinary statement. For a few moments, I was struck dumb.

"What has happened to my lord and his family?" I managed eventually.

"He has long passed and is without a legitimate heir. My mother has made enquiries and knows that you are his son."

"But I am not legitimate," I stammered. That my lord had been my father was a fact I had long known – how could I not have worked it out from the slurs aimed at my beloved mother by the loathsome bully Fulke? Or, for that matter, from the prominent nose that my former lord and I shared. But it wasn't something I had liked to dwell on.

"Indeed, but there have been no other claims, and she has decided that you will become the new lord. She will sort out the legalities – she explains everything in her letter. That is, if you want to take up this position – and it will be a huge responsibility. As owner of the castle, extensive buildings and land, you will be responsible for your staff and tenants, as well as your knights. I will be your King and your allegiance will be to me."

I listened carefully, making sure I took in every detail of this momentous news. I just could not believe what I was hearing. My mind was racing with the possibilities.

"Hubert Walter, the Bishop of Salisbury, will take you home," Richard went on. "He is here with me and is presently visiting Jerusalem. I suggest you go to see him to arrange passage. Saladin and al-Adil are both in agreement that you should be allowed to leave if you wish. I have ordered Hubert to take my army home.

"Now, I need to go and speak to my people and allies, if you can call them that. When I am fully recovered, I will go back home by land across Europe after a brief sailing. I couldn't bear to suffer another bout of that damned sea sickness."

My head was spinning. It was al-Adil who spoke next.

"You must travel to Jerusalem to meet the Bishop," he said softly. "And then go home to talk to Yasmine and your family to decide what you will do. Your work here is finished."

***

Days later, I told Yasmine all about my adventures and the extraordinary offer made by Eleanor.

"We have spoken of the fact we will not be safe here after Saladin has gone," she said. "There will be more wars and struggles for supremacy. You must leave these lands, but you will not go alone. I will go with you."

I knew how much it must have cost my wife to offer to leave her homeland for a strange and uncertain future. "Perhaps I *should* go on my own," I said, even though the thought of leaving Yasmine behind broke my heart. "I am sure you and the family will all be fine here without me. I could speak to Saladin, I'm sure he would move you to a safe place where you are not known."

I could not bear to think about leaving my children and grandchildren, but I knew my time in the hot Arab lands was coming to an end. The idea of taking Yasmine away from them as well was just too terrible to contemplate.

"Perhaps you were not listening to me, Crispin," she said, steel in her voice. "There is no way you are going on your own. We will miss our children and grandchildren dreadfully, but we need to start a new life together. They are settled here, they won't want to come. But little Daniel, we will still have him with us."

I had met the Bishop a few days ago as arranged. I was expecting some fat and crusty old man, but he was completely the opposite, many years younger than I was and very tall. He was kind and charming, and he told me that he had planned all the details of our return journey by sea. I was so pleased that he would be looking after us.

I needed to make some hard decisions, but I didn't think I had the courage to face this situation. Yasmine was so strong and determined, and I felt like a lump of jelly.

"I think it's best if I stay here and we all stick together," I blurted out. "I am sure we can find a way to survive and live well."

"Crispin, everyone will recognise you with your pale features and one arm. I doubt there is anyone else here who looks remotely like you. If you need convincing, go and visit Saladin. It's important that you see him anyway. You two have been the best of friends for over forty years. You have supported each other faithfully and have never wavered. I don't think anyone else has come close to this strength of friendship.

"Go soon, before it's too late. Most people now know that he is sick and weak after all those years of struggle. The country owes him an enormous debt, no one has ever done more for our religion.

But come back here as quickly as you can. We mustn't waste precious time."

As usual, Yasmine was right, and I had known this from the start of our conversation. She had always had the strength to support me and know best. I couldn't believe how unwavering her love was. Not many men experienced such powerful love. I knew, and was extremely happy to know, that she would never change.

We spent our remaining few days together updating our book. I wanted to add some drawings of the beautiful city of Jerusalem, recording the holy places of both religions. I also painted a picture of Richard, but it wasn't too flattering; I had exaggerated some of his features, making him look like a figure of fun rather than a mighty king. I was sorry Yasmine had not met him, as I am sure she would have made a truer to life portrait. She always had been a better painter than me.

Realising that Eleanor, or indeed the King himself, might see the book one day, I decided to amend my painting, making sure that Richard exuded strength and valour. I automatically touched my neck and hoped it would stay connected to my body!

***

Days later, Saladin and I met, and seated ourselves on large cushions in his tent. He had been fully briefed by al-Adil and his team, and had signed his name to the treaty agreed between his men and Richard's, but I was very concerned for my long-term friend. His frame was bent and shrunken. His scraggy beard and hair were now completely grey, and his eyes looked tired. I made a great effort to control my emotions, but one tear escaped from my eye.

Pretending he hadn't noticed my display of emotion, Saladin was all business. "It's not the best agreement we could have hoped for," he said, "but at least the invaders will leave us. The Christians have been given part of the coastal strip while we control the much larger part of the country and, importantly, Jerusalem. I think this compromise is a great achievement under the circumstances."

"The Christians will still be able to visit Jerusalem and their holy places," I replied. Bishop Hubert had told me that he had negotiated this concession from Saladin. "That is generous of you."

"Yes, it's a great compromise, but we are at peace, at least for the moment. It will be a huge relief when the Christians finally leave our country. We also retain Egypt. It was always my concern that Richard would rush down south and capture this jewel of our world. In that dreadful situation, he would have had the resources to attack and control our lands. That would have been the worst outcome."

He looked at me. "I am sure *The Pigeon News* has already relayed the good tidings of peace to all corners of our land."

I didn't need to reply. Of course, I had done my duty. I waited nervously for him to bring up the question of my future, but he wanted to reminisce some more.

"You and I have travelled many roads together and have had extraordinary adventures. We have always shared trust, honesty and respect. Do you remember the time…"

This was going to be a long meeting. But it was a privilege to spend such special time with this great man and good friend.

"There is so much to be done and so little time. We must remove all Christians still living in our country. We need to continue our work to unite our Arab and Muslim world. We are stronger together and weaker apart. Just imagine what we could achieve if we were all united. We could subdue the world and spread our religion to all countries.

"What a dream I have inside of me. Sadly, it will not be realised. I am not long for this world. The dream is almost over."

We were both silent for a few moments. Honesty had always been an essential part of our friendship. To disagree with Saladin's poignant words would have been a lie.

"Do you know how many brothers and sons I have?" Saladin asked eventually. "Many dozens. They will all fight against each other when I'm gone, instead of uniting and working together. Each of them wants power and will kill his brother to attain it, when they could so easily conquer the world by cooperating. And there is nothing I can do or say to persuade them on to another path. What a tragedy!"

Again, Saladin lapsed into thoughtful silence, his head lowered. When he lifted his eyes to my face, they burned with determination.

"In these circumstances, you and Yasmine are not safe here. You must take up Richard's offer. Go back to your homeland.

"Shiva, I want to die in peace. I want to know that you are safe. You have served me well, but above all, you have always been my trusted friend. No man has ever had a more faithful companion. I was fortunate to have found you in that dirty prison cell. I am also fortunate to have recognised your unique abilities and strengths, despite your disability. Shiva, you must go back to Yasmine and take her with you to safety."

I could see the tears welling in Saladin's eyes and felt my own tears also. We embraced for the last time, and then I turned and walked to my horse without looking back.

***

"Crispin, I have made a decision, and I don't want to hear any arguments from you."

I was back home with my wife, who was as determined as I had ever seen her. Yasmine had taken charge.

"We – you and I – are leaving together, and we are taking Daniel with us. Let the Bishop know so that we can travel with him, and we must hurry. We will see our family tonight."

That evening was the worst of our lives. Our entire family came together to the house to say goodbye, knowing we would never see each other again. We were fifteen in number, including our children and grandchildren. Yasmine had arrange a magnificent dinner, but the food stuck in my mouth and tasted like paper. I found it impossible to hold back my tears. I had to leave the room at one stage to wipe my face, but when I returned, we all cried together.

Only Yasmine remained resolute. She smiled and laughed and cheered all of us up. Once again, I was reminded of how strong she was and how lucky I was to have her in my life. She had brought up our wonderful, loving children almost single handed, ensuring they all became kind people who shared her brilliant soul. She'd always supported and loved me, despite my years of absence and my poor attempts at being a father. Did any man ever have a wife and family quite like mine? I doubted it.

Yasmine had persuaded me that our children and grandchildren would all be safe. None of them held a position in the ruling party and they were not known outside of their circle of close friends. They would have to move, of course, but they would be able to live anonymously.

I cannot even describe our parting that night. It's strange how people have the power to survive such mental torture. We block dreadful events from our minds. I wanted to remember sunny days, our family together in happiness.

"Crispin, we must take our Magnum Opus with us," Yasmine whispered to me as our family left us for the last time.

"What's that?" I asked stupidly. And then I realised. Of course, our beautiful book of colours, words and pictures containing the magnificent images of our children, forever captured on the pages. I wondered for a moment when she had named it and why those words.

Then I groaned at the inconvenience and effort this would take. It was difficult enough to ensure the safety of the three of us, let alone the transportation and protection of this precious family heirloom. But I didn't need Yasmine to remind me how essential it was to keep this in our possession, to remember our precious children and grandchildren and our love and experiences together. We would be empty and lost without this unique record of our family and history. This was our book, our heritage. We would guard it with our lives.

The following day, we set off with our few most treasured possessions, escorted by a group of Saladin's soldiers. I had sent pigeons to Acre to let the Bishop know we were on our way. There were already signs of trouble from Saladin's family, who could sense his end was near and that they now had opportunities for enrichment and power. The time had come for us to start another life, a new chance, even though I was now only days short of my sixtieth birthday – already an old man. We were looking forward to our future in a different world.

In the upheaval of departing from the place that had been my home for so long, it never crossed my mind to wonder at Era's absence. If he had given us so much as a hint of what the future had in store for us, we would never have left.

Part 2: Homecoming

Chapter 14

Back to Milton Castle

Eleanor was looking magnificent. Older, obviously, but she had kept her beauty, her immense charm and lovely presence. It was hard to believe that she was now over seventy. I loved her as much as I had at our first meeting.

I bowed deeply. She came towards me and, surprisingly, hugged me like a son and a long-lost friend. She kissed my cheek, which made me blush.

"Crispin, welcome back to England. We have been poorer without you. How are you and how was your journey?"

The journey had been truly awful, but I didn't want to bother her with the details. I was sure she had suffered many similar experiences during her long and adventurous life. For a brief moment, I was back in that boat and images of the terrors we'd faced flashed before me.

We had all suffered from seasickness, but as this was the first time Yasmine had sailed, or even seen the sea, she became so sick that I didn't think she would survive. She was unconscious for much of the time and had trouble holding down food or even water. Anything she consumed came straight back up. During the journey, she seemed to lose half her body weight.

For several days, we were chased by pirates and one of their ships got close enough to attach to ours. A handful of men boarded, brown skinned and armed with evil looking daggers. Hubert called all of us to arms. I was handed a small cutlass, which of course I knew how to use.

Hubert led the charge towards the enemy, shouting and screaming. Even God would have been afraid of him! We outnumbered them and they never stood a chance. The battle was over in minutes. Six pirates were killed or wounded; we threw them over the side and cut their boat loose. Three of our men suffered light wounds, but I was unscathed.

We reached Sicily without further trouble, greatly relieved to have a few days' break on land. Here, Hubert learned that Richard had been captured in Germany and set out to find him. We all missed his strong presence and leadership, and hoped he would get back to England safely. I in particular would need his support at home.

When we set sail once again, we hit terrible storms as we left the Mediterranean and entered the Atlantic. None of the sailors had ever seen such ferocious weather before. Fierce winds and relentless rain hit us with incredible force. The waves were massive, and each seemed to swell higher than the last. The skipper pointed our ship directly into the swell and none of us thought that we would survive the next mountainous wave. Our little ship managed to push its nose up, only to come crashing down.

I was extremely worried for Yasmine. Not for the first time, I regretted bringing her and Daniel on this long journey. I put my arm around them. They both looked so pale and exhausted, drained by the awful ordeal. I was terrified for us and our chances of survival.

I hadn't called on Era for some time, but now I did, begging him for his help. He didn't answer immediately and I began to despair. When he finally spoke to me, he told me not to worry, to have faith and all would be well. I tried to believe him.

Our skipper was brilliant and never wavered. This gave us all courage and confidence, even when the final big wave overwhelmed us and I thought we would sink. Tons of water crashed on to the ship, flooding the decks, living quarters and stores. We formed a line to scoop the water into buckets to tip over the side, but it was like emptying a pond with a small spoon.

But somehow, despite the terrible odds, we survived. I was hugely thankful when we reached

Portugal, where we had planned to stop, and I hoped we would have several weeks here for Yasmine to regain her health and strength. Unfortunately, we only had a few days. Hubert had left his assistant, Michael, in charge with orders to return home as soon as possible.

"I am sorry, Crispin, but we can't stay too long," Michael told me regretfully. "With Richard's long absence from England, there is much work to do. His brother John has been up to no good and is fomenting trouble, as usual. While the cat's away, the mice will play!"

I was so relieved when we finally reached Dartmouth without further incident, but Yasmine was still very poorly. I carried her to a small carriage where she lay for our journey to Hubert's church and residence in Sarum. In my relief that our horrendous journey had come to an end, I forgot to thank Era for our deliverance.

"We will spend a few days there," Michael told me. "Then we will visit Queen Eleanor in Winchester, for her to agree the legalities and process to take over your castle and estate."

* * *

Days later, I was standing alongside Michael in front of the great lady.

"The journey was as rough as we would have expected," I replied, jumping back to the present. "But it's a massive relief to be safely back in England, thank you."

"And how is your wife? This must be a very strange experience for her. I hear she is called Yasmine. What a beautiful name. Perhaps I should have called one of my daughters Yasmine."

"Unfortunately, she was very sick on the journey and has taken to her bed to recover. She apologises for her absence."

"No need, please send her our love and good wishes and tell her that we all are delighted to welcome her to our country." Eleanor turned to Michael. "Now, Michael, what news have you for me? Have you heard where my Richard is? I am desperate to know. Hubert's spies are looking for him all over Europe. We have heard rumours that he is in Austria."

"Sadly, Your Majesty," Michael replied, "King Richard has not been heard of since he left Acre. There's no good news to report yet, I'm afraid. As soon as I hear, I will inform you immediately."

"Yes, I know you will, and I thank you. When do you expect Hubert to return here?"

"Hubert has sent a messenger informing me that he hopes to be back in two weeks."

"Now, Crispin," Eleanor turned her beautiful eyes on to me, "Michael has all the papers and legalities prepared for you to take over your estate, and you are to do so immediately. In return, I demand your loyalty to Richard and me. I need your services to arrange my protection and I will call on you when I need your presence. Additionally, my son and I will need your support for our military operations."

Then her tone changed, becoming lighter and almost playful. "Now we have a very pleasant duty to perform."

Michael came to me and took my good arm, ordering me to kneel. He then handed a huge sword to Eleanor, which she raised to touch me gently on each shoulder.

"Arise, Sir Crispin, Lord of The Manor of Milton."

I rode back to Hubert's house in something of a daze. I knew I had been promised a castle, but I hadn't expected to be knighted, and by Eleanor as well! I would be fiercely loyal to her, and to King Richard.

I can't recall what words came out of my mouth, but I remember babbling away to Michael in my excitement.

"Yes, I am very pleased for you, Crispin," he replied when he could get a word in edgeways. "By the way, did you hear that Hubert will be made

Archbishop of Canterbury on his return? Now, let's get back to see how Yasmine is doing."

What a day of celebration. Hubert had become a good friend to me and I was delighted to hear this wonderful news from Michael.

***

Several weeks later, Hubert Walter and I were on our way to my castle. I can't describe the excitement I felt as we rode closer. I was returning home after more than forty years of adventures in foreign lands. I realised with a shock that it was more like forty-five!

I was so happy to be back in my home country, enjoying the cooler weather. It was such a relief after the intense heat I had suffered for so many years. Yasmine had hardly been outside since we arrived, and I knew she disliked the cold and wet of England. I desperately wanted her to share this moment with me, but sadly, she was still unwell, and Michael and I had grown more and more concerned about her condition. I felt guilty about bringing her back to my country, having had no idea that the journey would be so tough for her. If I had known, I would have insisted on us staying in Damascus and taking our chances. If anything happened to her, I would never forgive myself. Luckily, little Daniel was now well, despite suffering as much as the rest of us on the worst parts of our journey.

I was very reluctant to leave Yasmine again, but I knew she was in the good hands of Michael's doctors. Hubert and I were now concerned about what we would find when we reached Milton. He said that reports were not good, that a group of men had taken over the castle. No one seemed to know who they were or what their intentions were, but he was not surprised as the estate had been virtually abandoned over the past few years.

"We have been without a king for several years now and there is considerable unrest amongst the people," he told me. "Unfortunately, Richard's younger brother John is taking advantage of the situation and has made some unsavoury allies. Eleanor and her senior nobles are trying to stabilise the country, but law and order has broken down. I believe the current situation is as bad as it was during the civil war years back, when we had the terrible struggles between Stephen and Matilda.

"We need Richard back in charge to run this country with an iron fist and the rule of law, as his father did. Oh, how we miss him! I don't think John is worthy or capable enough even to touch his shadow.

"Richard appointed William Longchamp to be in charge of our country while he was away in Palestine, but the man has become greedy and hostile. There is now all-out war between him and John.

"However, we have more pressing matters. We are not far from Milton Castle, your home. I am concerned that your property may have been degraded and, more importantly, your people may have been attacked and harmed. There have been ugly rumours. But we must wait until we get there before making judgements."

Finally, we approached Milton, and the roads and landscape were immediately familiar. My heart beat faster with excitement and anticipation as we neared the castle. At first glance, the impression of the building was exactly the same as I recalled, but as we got closer, I could see evidence of decline and decay. Weeds and grass were growing out of control and trees had not been cared for. The land seemed to be impoverished, as were the people, who looked beaten and depressed. They did not even look up to acknowledge us as we passed.

"Hubert, I am extremely nervous about what we will find here. I'm even afraid we might be attacked."

"Don't worry, Shiva... sorry, Crispin, we are ready for anything!" Indeed we were. We had a small army with us.

As Hubert and I had got to know each other better, I had grown used to his jokes and knew he enjoyed teasing me. I smiled broadly. I liked and respected this good and clever man. However, anyone judging him by his language and actions would have considered him a most unusual man of God. To my mind, he was better suited as a military leader.

We were unopposed as we rode on to the drawbridge and straight into the castle. We entered the courtyard and saw no one. As we brought our horses to a stop with a clatter of hooves, a rather miserable group of men came out of the main building and stood in front of us. They looked tired and some were swaying. I realised that they were in an advanced state of drunkenness, which I deplored.

I recognised the leader immediately and looked at him with distaste and loathing. His bulging eyes and ugly hooked nose were unmistakeable, and I knew that this was my childhood tormentor, Fulke. He was much older, of course, and fatter, and had grown a number of ugly boils on his disgusting face.

I was interested to see how he was going to handle this situation. I was, after all, now his lord.

Hubert challenged him in a clear voice. "State your business, fellow. And who are these people with you? By whose authority are you here? Are you living in this place? Come on, speak!"

Fulke looked at him bashfully and for a moment seemed incapable of reply. Could he even put a sentence together? I wondered. Sweat broke out on his brow and his face reddened.

A huge man standing next to him fell unconscious to the ground, his trousers darkening with piss. I was disgusted, but perhaps not surprised. He did not move.

Eventually, Fulke spoke, or rather slurred. "This place belongs to us, and we have worked hard to care for the estate and the people. Who the devil are you?"

"It's none of your business, but I will tell you anyway. I am the Archbishop of Canterbury, and I order you and your disgusting drunken friends to leave this place immediately and never return here. If you disobey me, I will personally run you through with this sword and your wretched friends will hang. Now, get away from here before I finish you off now. Go on, clear off!"

The men looked downcast. As the brute Fulke led the way out across the drawbridge, they all shuffled behind him, two of them dragging their unconscious friend by his ankles. Fulke made some indistinct threats as a parting shot, but I was pleased that we had retaken the castle without any violence and so relieved they had gone.

After the men had left, Hubert and I dismounted and were greeted by a large group of people, mainly women, who I guessed worked in the castle. I recognised a few of the older women, who had been childhood friends. One in particular was familiar.

"Crispin, do you recognise me?" she asked, stepping forward. "I remember you and we have been expecting you. I am Mary."

Yes, of course I remembered Mary. She'd lived in the castle with her mother, the head cook. I recalled two children, running across the fields and fishing in the river. How long ago those days seemed.

"We are so excited to see you here," Mary said. "And now you are our lord! Did you recognise Fulke and his bullies? They took over the castle and treated us like slaves and animals. Anyway, less of that." Her eyes shone with excitement in her weathered face, which I remembered as being smooth and unlined. "I have something much more important to show you."

She took my hand and led me inside the castle. I couldn't imagine what was about to happen. We walked along familiar dark corridors and climbed the stairs. I remembered the way through my old home very well.

She led me up another flight of stairs, and I knew we were approaching the room my dear mother and I had shared throughout my early years. I was looking forward to seeing it again.

Mary knocked on the door. Pushing it open, she stood aside to allow me to go in first. There was an old woman lying on the bed, looking up at me and smiling. I had no doubt who she was.

I cried out in surprise and shock. My beloved mother held out her arms to me. I bent down, and we hugged each other as if we would hold on for ever. We couldn't help ourselves; we were both crying uncontrollably.

I just couldn't believe that she was still alive, and I thought of all those times when I was convinced she must have died. If only I had known the truth, I would have come home sooner. But then I remembered. I hadn't had that option.

***

Some days later, I was pleased to be back with Yasmine and Daniel. Bursting with excitement, I told them my amazing news. Yasmine cried with me. Daniel cried too, although we didn't think he fully understood the situation. I was desperate to introduce them to my mother, but Yasmine was not yet well enough to travel.

One of the proudest moments of my life came a few weeks later when Yasmine, Daniel and I, together with an armed escort, approached the gates of Milton Castle. The sun was high and fleeting through the clouds, and the air was pleasantly warm.

Mary and most of the people of Milton, it seemed, were waiting for us, and as we came nearer, they cheered and clapped and showered us with streams of coloured paper. This was the happiest day these people had enjoyed for many years, and they were determined to give us a rousing welcome. A huge boar was roasting on a spit and hungry children sat nearby, their mouths drooling in eager anticipation.

Small, colourful tents and stalls were arranged in a semi-circle to provide for the crowds. Some stallholders were selling all kinds of food, others offered games of chance and skill. A few were selling clothes and colourful materials. Flags and bunting added to the air of celebration, as did musicians playing fiddles, drums and flutes. A man was singing old songs of England's past.

Daniel squealed in delight as Yasmine carried him down from the carriage. He ran with great excitement to see the stalls and to play with the other children. She knew he would be safe here.

I dismounted from my horse and took her hand as we walked towards Mary and her friends, who were laughing and crying with delight at seeing us. They welcomed us with open arms. Mary took our hands and led us towards my lovely mother, who was seated on a chair by the castle wall. Yasmine and my mother hugged each other and their tears flowed freely, causing Mary and me to follow suit. We couldn't have had a warmer welcome back.

I hadn't been this happy for many years. Being reunited with my mother, being here with my beautiful wife and Daniel. I wanted this blissful state to last for ever.

Chapter 15

A King's Ransom

"Richard has been found. He is locked up in a castle in Germany, near Speyer, cruelly bound in heavy chains. He is the prisoner of the Holy Roman Emperor Henry who, along with other European leaders, is seeking revenge."

"Revenge what for?" I asked Michael.

"Well, Richard had fierce quarrels with the leaders in the Holy Land, particularly Leopold of Austria, who accused Richard of the murder of his cousin, Conrad of Montferrat."

I had heard the stories, of course. Conrad's murder had been a shocking affair, but none of us believed that Richard was responsible. Perhaps his captors wanted revenge for Richard's insult to Leopold at Acre, when he tore down his banner from the city walls.

"Can we rescue him from there?"

"I don't think there's a rat's chance in hell. All we can do is negotiate a ransom to get him back. We will be hearing about that possibility tomorrow."

We had both been summoned to a gathering at Winchester, ordered by Eleanor. I was looking forward to seeing her again, but due to the seriousness of the situation and her distress about Richard, I doubted there would be much opportunity to socialise. Michael had told me men and women from all over our part of the country would be there. I was riding alongside him, together with a dozen soldiers for protection. These were dangerous times. Nonetheless, I was pleased to be with Michael once again.

He asked me how I was progressing with the organisation of the estate.

"Well, it's a nearly impossible situation. I am trying to motivate my people to get back to normal. But we don't have enough resources to achieve much."

"What do you need?" he asked.

"I have too few horses, cattle and sheep, and hardly any chickens. And little food for the animals I do have. Grain seeds are very scarce and I have no money. All the dwellings need repair or rebuilding, and the castle is in a dreadful state.

"To make matters worse, my people have little hope and morale is low. I need money and resources, and more people. Truth is that I don't have any experience of running an estate or business."

"Nonsense, Crispin, that's not what I have heard at all. You ran a huge and complicated business in Outremer with little or no resources. Your enormous success has been spoken about with awe and great respect all over the world. You also played a vital role in creating a settlement and bringing about peace between our people and Saladin's."

"I didn't think all of that was common knowledge."

"We know more than you think. And the extraordinary thing is you were on the side of the enemy at the time! Unfortunately, there are a few who believe you still are, I am sorry to say, but only those with a particular axe to grind. Most people think positively about you and your achievements. They are pleased to have you back on our side! Sometime, I would very much like to hear more about your extraordinary life."

"Well, thank you for that, Michael. All I can really remember are my terrible struggles and constant fear. Apart from my lifelong friendship with Saladin and my relationship with my dear wife Yasmine, I didn't know who I could trust. But I never had cause to doubt them, not even for a moment. Without them, not only would I not be here, but I wouldn't have achieved anything."

We rode in silence for an hour or more. Over a refreshing ale and a nourishing dinner in a hostelry that evening, we spoke some more.

"Crispin, you should tell all the people about your life and achievements," said Michael. "Not only to inform them, but also to educate them about the world you have known. We have so many misconceptions about the Holy Land, the Muslim people and their religious beliefs."

I raised my eyebrows. "Michael, have I never told you about our Magnum Opus?"

"No, I don't think you have. What is it?"

I brought him up to date with the lifetime project I shared with Yasmine and the brilliant artwork she had contributed, how it was a full reflection of all parts of our lives and experiences in words and paintings. Michael became very excited by the news.

"I must see this as soon as possible," he said. "It could be an extremely valuable record of our recent history and a useful educational tool. Perhaps I could travel back with you to Milton after we have met with the Queen?"

"Of course," I replied. "However, I have to warn you that the work became badly damaged on the journey from the Holy Land after being soaked by the waves. We can show it to you now, but we will need months to restore it."

***

The vast hall was nearly full and the rumble of 100 conversations filled the space. At the far end was a raised dais with an empty throne, and behind this a closed door.

A chamberlain walked up the steps, faced the crowd and banged his staff on the floor, demanding silence. Moments later, he announced the presence of Queen Eleanor. He opened the door to let her in, guiding her towards her throne.

Eleanor looked magnificent: stately, imperious and magisterial. She was still very beautiful, despite her advanced years. I worshipped her and, within reason, would carry out any order she demanded of me. Her silk dress was the colour of ivory and if a working man toiled for forty years, he would not even be able to afford the sleeves! She was a woman of regal bearing and her dress flowed with her graceful movements.

She sat and waited in silence, so she could be absolutely sure that every one of her words would be heard by all.

"My lords, ladies and gentlemen, thank you for gracing me with your presence here today," she began. "Some of you may be aware that your great King Richard, my son and our dear brother, has been captured in Germany by that appalling and odious man Henry, whom I will not grace with the title of Holy Roman Emperor. He holds Richard in Trifels Castle near Speyer."

If someone had dropped a pin, you could have heard it.

"Henry is ungracious and extremely cruel. He has bound my son, your King, in heavy chains, so that he cannot make the smallest movement without extreme difficulty and pain. He has defiled him and therefore all of his subjects – all of you – in England and France. This is a man who has fought with you and for you in our countries and territories. A man who went on a dangerous pilgrimage to rescue our Holy Land from the heathen. A man who is good, honest, faithful and loyal to all of us."

A mutual voice of assent rose from 100 throats.

"This evil Henry will not release our King without a huge ransom, an amount we cannot pay."

"Let's get an army together and seize the castle and break down the walls," called a voice from the crowd. There was a mumble of agreement.

"We should tell the Pope to excommunicate the varlet!" shouted another voice. "He has imprisoned the defender of the True Cross."

"We must declare war on Henry…"

Eleanor raised her arms to call for quiet before any more voices could join in.

"Thank you all for your suggestions. We have, of course, considered all of these options and many others. Unfortunately, the only way to secure his release and safety is to pay the ransom."

Once again, there was silence while we all waited to hear how much Henry had demanded.

Eleanor paused. "The amount is 150,000 marks," she said finally.

A gasp ran around the room, soon turning into an angry roar. People starting asking questions they didn't expect to be answered, each one shouting louder than the last.

"Silence!" boomed Eleanor's chamberlain, banging his staff on the dais again. The room fell quiet once more.

"The amount of money required must be raised somehow," said Eleanor when she could be heard. "And I am asking – nay, imploring you all, as good and decent English men and women, to go out into the shires and tell everyone of this crisis. Beg them for gold, silver and jewels, or metals to raise this money. Tell them the future of England depends on them."

Raising her voice, she roared with all the passion she could muster, "We must get our King back home!"

With that, she stood and bowed to the company, signalling to her chamberlain to take her back the way she had entered the hall.

"That was a magnificent and impressive address, Michael," I said as the door closed behind Queen Eleanor. "What do you think?"

"Yes, it certainly was," he replied. "We must all get to work straight away. We have allocated you an area surrounding your castle. Would you visit your neighbours, churches, monasteries, houses – in fact, anyone able to donate? We need the funds urgently, within weeks rather than months."

"Yes, of course I will do what I can. Unfortunately, I am not in a position to contribute much myself at the moment."

"I understand that."

A tall man stepped forward and greeted Michael, shaking him by the hand and smiling.

"Crispin, please meet William the Marshal," said Michael as the newcomer turned to look at me. I was very pleasantly surprised. There were few men in the land better known than William, the most successful knight in Europe and a confidant of kings and queens. Eleanor trusted him above all others. William owned more land in England, Wales and Ireland than most, also being the Earl of Pembroke by his marriage to Isabel, daughter of Richard de Clare and Aoife Macmurrough of Ireland. His reputation was impressive.

"I am most pleased to meet you, sir," I said, holding out my one hand. "I am Lord of Milton Castle."

"Oh yes, I've been very much looking forward to meeting you. Perhaps I could call in to see you sometime?"

***

Michael and I had an uneventful journey back to Milton. I was pleased to be home once again and eager to see how Yasmine was.

I climbed the stairs to our room at the top of the castle, to find her asleep. Unfortunately, she was still unwell from the rigours of our journey and the shock of living in a new country. She was very pale and had frequent headaches, and I could see new lines forming around her eyes. We had been used to my sporadic health issues while in the hot lands, but Yasmine had rarely suffered. Now, she simply couldn't stand England's cold and wet weather.

Daniel was sleeping soundly in a cot next to the bed. My heart jumped when I saw him. He always looked so sweet and lovely, and had adjusted much better to the climate and country than his mother. He even enjoyed the food! Being so young, he had largely forgotten about his life before the journey.

I had left Michael downstairs to look through our Magnum Opus, after giving instructions to the cook to feed him well, and to open a good bottle of Bordeaux. Some time later, I joined him in the dining room.

"Crispin, this is the most wonderful book I have ever seen," he said enthusiastically. "It is more magnificent than I could have imagined, and the water damage is nowhere near as bad as you feared. We must show this to Hubert. I have so many questions to ask you."

We spent a couple of hours poring over the pages while I explained what had occurred in each place and how the paintings reflected our feelings.

"I had no idea you were such a talented artist," he said.

"No, no, I'm not. The best ones are Yasmine's work. We first met in a bookshop in Damascus when I started this project to reflect the stages of my life. Yasmine joined me and improved the work immensely with her paintings. We have been adding to our book for maybe thirty years, maybe more. Now we need to bring it up to date. I want to write about Richard and his imprisonment and the ransom. How on earth can we raise such a huge amount?"

"We still have the necklace Saladin gave me." A soft voice spoke behind us, making us both start with surprise. Unbeknown to us, Yasmine had come downstairs and was sitting at the table. I stared at her, uncomprehending for a few moments. She smiled back at me. "Remember how Saladin retrieved it for us after we'd had to sell it to raise funds for *The Pigeon News*? Now, I want to donate it towards Richard's release. Michael, you must have seen a painting of the jewel in the book."

Michael and I looked at each other in silence for a moment. Then elation filled me as I realised what a brilliant and appropriate solution this was.

"Yes, yes! Michael, take it for Richard. Show it to Michael, Yasmine."

Yasmine left the room, returning minutes later and presenting the jewel to Michael. He gasped and was silent for a few moments while he turned over the sparkling necklace in his hands.

"It is even more magnificent in reality than it was in your wonderful painting," he whispered, raising his eyes to Yasmine. "This is so beautiful and unique. It must be worth a king's ransom!"

We all laughed at his words. The irony was not lost on us.

"Crispin, we should travel together tomorrow, to show this to Eleanor," stated Michael. "She will be overwhelmed with gratitude for this gift."

***

"This is the most remarkable donation we have received to date." Queen Eleanor was gazing in awe at the jewel in her hands. "We are so much nearer our target now. I will have our jewellers value the necklace and let you know how much they estimate, but I am sure all of us will be amazed at its worth. Thank you, Yasmine, I hear that this is your generosity."

To my surprise, Yasmine had insisted on accompanying Michael and me to take the necklace to Eleanor. Her reply told me why: she wanted to make sure the true benefactor was acknowledged.

"No, Your Majesty," she replied. "This is a gift from our great friend Saladin. He would have been so happy to know that it is now helping to secure Richard's release. He admired Richard greatly and there was mutual respect between the two. They were both magnificent warriors and great leaders, but sadly, Saladin is no longer with us. Let us pray King Richard will be returned to us."

"Thank you, Yasmine." Eleanor was quiet for a moment. She reached for a handkerchief to dab away a tear. "I would like to have met Saladin. I hear he was gracious, generous and very humble, although ruthless to those who crossed him. I doubt if there will ever be such a leader in the East again. You are both fortunate to have known him."

Eleanor stood up to embrace Yasmine and then me as the three of us shed a couple of tears of emotion. This was a special moment. For a long while, we were lost in our own thoughts. Then Michael bowed to Eleanor and led us away.

***

Hubert called to see us at Milton a few weeks later. His first request was to view our Magnum Opus, which Yasmine and I had been working hard to restore after its difficult journey West. Of course, we were delighted to show him. We spent a few hours turning the pages as he gasped several times at the magnificence of Yasmine's paintings.

"Michael didn't exaggerate when he told me about your creation. Indeed, I don't think he came anywhere near to describing its importance to our nation and to the world. When you have finished the repairs, please let me know. With your permission, I would like to display this at Canterbury Cathedral."

"We never imagined that our work would be so interesting and valuable to others," Yasmine replied. "We should be able to complete the outstanding repairs in a few weeks, then we would be delighted to bring it to you in Canterbury. We would also like to create new pages, depicting our experiences here. There are so many pictures of Milton we have not completed yet. I am working on a painting of Queen Eleanor, but she is a difficult subject to do justice to. I also want to add a picture of you, Hubert."

"Well, you know how to flatter a man, Yasmine! But why?"

"History will record you as one of the most important people and influencers of this century, and the next one as well, I'm sure. Crispin will add the words to describe your life and deeds, and men and women in 1,000 years and more will admire your good works and your impact on our history."

"I am very moved by your words. I've never thought about my work in that way. I only consider the present day by day to the best of my ability. I still think you flatter me, but I thank you."

"Crispin has told me about William the Marshal. I would like to meet and paint him, too. From what Crispin says, he has also had an extraordinary life and I'm sure he will continue to add to our history." Yasmine then added, "If our work is to be displayed in Canterbury Cathedral, Crispin and I want it to be as comprehensive as possible."

Hubert nodded. "Quite right," he said. "Every year, many thousands of pilgrims arrive from all over the world to pay respects to Thomas Becket, murdered in this holy place by Henry's knights. I want these men and women to learn about our culture and history while they are there. This will be a tremendous way to pass on historical knowledge in words and beautiful pictures. I am looking for other educational tools as well, but none will be finer than your Magnum Opus."

"Crispin has told me about Thomas. He must have been a wonderful man of great faith."

"Yes, an extraordinary man. We will only see his like once. But this reminds me, there is a second message I have for you. William the Marshal will call on you in two weeks. He also wants to view your Magnum Opus. Later, he wants to introduce you to Prince John."

Dread manifested itself as an acute pain in my back and neck. It was a sensation I'd last experienced all those years ago in my appalling prison cell, when I learned from my German friend Hans that I might lose my only hand. I was hoping never to meet Prince John. I had heard that he was everything his brother Richard was not: dishonourable, cowardly and greedy. But I was also curious to discover for myself.

"There is a third matter," Hubert said. "Michael spoke to me about your estate and there is no doubt you desperately need funding. In fact, without capital, you could end up losing everything. And that would be tragic. I may have come up with a solution.

"I have spoken to a moneylender who could advance a considerable sum to you, enough to enable the estate to thrive and, in time, provide a return for you. Your people will earn good money for their hard work and will be able to pay rents to you for their lands. In turn, you will have money to repair and strengthen the castle and pay for knights to protect your estate. You will have to pay taxes, of course, and the King will require you to provide knights for his campaigns."

"Really?" I asked, surprised at this last point. "I have heard differently."

"If you elect not to provide knights, you will have to pay an extra tax called scutage. I would advise you to avoid this if you can. Also, you will need more knights to defend your castle in these dangerous times. And, of course, you will need to repay the loan, plus interest, over an agreed period. Gideon is a very fair man and I know you two can negotiate a good deal. I will act as guarantor for the loan, which will give him the security he needs. What do you think, Crispin?"

"I am very grateful to you, Hubert, this is most generous." Yasmine also thanked him and there were tears of gratitude in her eyes. She knew we could not carry on much longer.

I had heard about moneylending, of course. This was an occupation only the Jews in England were allowed to practise. It sounded like the solution to all our troubles.

"When can we meet Gideon?" I asked.

"I am sending you one of my best land agents to get the estate organised. He will bring Gideon with him."

***

Gideon was a small, wizened man with heavy lines on his face, which was partly covered by a huge dark beard, but he appeared to be much younger than these lines suggested. His back was bent, but not with age. Rather, I guessed, it was down to emotional strain. His eyes reflected a deep sadness, but there was a genuine warmth in his broad smile. Yasmine and I were most pleased to meet him and we welcomed him into our castle.

After two days of talking, Yasmine, Gideon and I concluded a very satisfactory deal. More importantly, we had become firm friends, and Yasmine and I were keen to learn more about him. The story he told us was heartbreaking.

A couple of years before Yasmine and I sailed for England, an angry mob had surrounded a tower in York where the Jews had gone for safety. The mob was determined to break in and slaughter each one of them.

"We knew that a terrible fate awaited our families and ourselves," said Gideon sadly. "We were left with no choice. The mob threatened to murder us or force us to be baptised. We decided to burn our possessions and papers so that they would not be stolen by these savages.

"We, the fathers, were forced into a position where we had to kill our wives and children before they were violated by the attackers. We then planned to kill ourselves. It was the most terrible day of my life. I have tried unsuccessfully to block the act and images out of my mind.

"I did my duty. But before I could kill myself, the fire got out of control. I was overcome by smoke and fell, banging my head on the stone floor. I was knocked out. When I woke, I wondered if I was dead. But I was the only survivor. Somehow, the flames had not reached me.

"The attackers came to where I lay, searching bodies for valuables, and I played dead. Eventually, they left, and I was able to crawl away. I had a dreadful few days trying to get away from the area and find another community of fellow Jews for safety. I don't know how I survived. I often wished I hadn't. I would rather have sacrificed myself to save my dear family. I recall my wife and children every waking moment in vivid detail, and my grief is endless."

For a moment, Yasmine and I were struck dumb by Gideon's awful story. We both had tears in our eyes. We were aware of the hatred and prejudice displayed by many people in this country towards Jews, but had never fully understood why. I wondered if it might have been because the Jews were often blamed for the death of Jesus Christ, but then Our Lord had himself been a practising Jew, so that made no sense. And He was crucified more than 1,000 years ago. As an outsider herself, Yasmine in particular felt empathy for the Jewish communities in our country.

Finally, she spoke kindly. "Tell me the names of your family," she said.

"Thank you, Yasmine. My dear wife was called Devorah. And our two lovely daughters, so sweet and innocent, were Miriam and the younger, Leah."

We waited in silence for Gideon to regain his composure. He closed his eyes in painful memory.

"Thank you both for your kindness and understanding," he whispered eventually. "Thank you for listening to me, allowing me to tell my story. It is a great relief to be able to express my grief to you."

I hoped this would help our new friend to recover, at least a bit.

***

After that day, Gideon visited us every few weeks to review our progress. We always paid him with the agreed rates on time, and over the months, our friendship flourished.

From the moment we first met Gideon, every aspect of our lives and livelihood improved. We were able to invest much needed funds into our estate and ourselves. Our people prospered as well, and our rental income increased many times over.

Hubert's land agent, Godwin, was a brilliant administrator and we were delighted to have him, but Hubert had made it clear that he was only on loan to us for a few months. Just before he left, I thanked Godwin for his excellent work.

"You have transformed our estate and we are so grateful to you," I said. "And to Hubert for offering your services."

"It's been a pleasure," Godwin replied. "Your people are now much happier. My only concern is that you haven't invested more into the security of the estate. You need guards and better defences. And, of course, you must have more of your own knights."

"Yes, you are right, Godwin. I do intend to invest in our security, but our funds won't allow us to do so at the moment."

"Well, don't leave it too long," were his parting words.

If only I had heeded his advice.

Chapter 16

William The Marshal

When William the Marshal came to Milton, he was leading a dozen knights, and I watched them coming from half a mile away. He was just as I had remembered him: tall and very muscular. There was no doubt about his Norman heritage!

I welcomed him warmly and was so pleased he had made the effort to visit us as he had promised.

"Hail, Sir Crispin. I am pleased to be here after so long. I have visited Milton Castle only once before, and it's very apparent that you have worked wonders. Or does the credit all go to your beautiful wife?"

William dismounted. I led him into my castle and Yasmine was there waiting for us.

"I am delighted to meet you, Yasmine," he said. "I hear you are the one who has restored this estate."

"No, no, it's down to Crispin and all the lovely people here. But we still have so much to do."

Yasmine handed William a large glass of Bordeaux wine to refresh him after his journey. She then led him to the table where our Magnum Opus was lying and left him to study the book while she took his men to the kitchen and made sure they received similar hospitality.

More than an hour had gone by before he spoke. "This is a remarkable work, Crispin," he said. "I commend you both. Now, Crispin, this is not the only reason for my visit. Prince John would like to see you within the next ten days. He is in Normandy now. I'm not sure what he wants to speak to you about, he probably needs to find out if you will be loyal to him. He doesn't want Richard to be released, and a rumour is doing the rounds that he and King Philip of France will offer the Holy Roman Emperor Henry a huge amount to keep him locked up."

I was horrified. "Surely he wouldn't do that to his own brother."

"Please believe me, he is capable of that." William watched my face as I digested that unpalatable detail about Prince John. Then he moved the conversation on to a new thread.

"Many people have told me about your adventures in Outremer in the Levant. You had the most extraordinary experiences. You must have known Saladin better than any man alive."

"Yes, they were amazing times, and I was extremely privileged to have known such a great man," I replied.

"Did you know that I was in the Holy Land as well a few years earlier? I fought for King Guy of Jerusalem with the Knights Templar. We were headquartered on the Temple Mount. Have you ever been there?"

I told him that I was in Jerusalem with Saladin when he won back the city for his people. William looked mortified and was silent for a few moments, no doubt reflecting on the terrible loss of the principal city in the world for Christians, the most important symbol of our religion.

"Were you at Hattin?" I asked him.

"No, I came back two years before that terrible battle. This was the worst time for our people in the Holy Land. But our defeat was down to poor leadership. I wish I had been there. Perhaps I could have persuaded the leaders to use better strategies. Even better if Richard had been there. I think the outcome would have been very different. Were you there?"

"Yes, but not until months after the event. I visited the site with al-Afdal, Saladin's son, who had been there with his father at the battle. He told me that the Muslim victory was simply down to water and how they used it for their maximum benefit. They kept the Christians away from water and all its sources. The Muslims burnt the brushwood on the slopes and the smoke blew towards the approaching army, driving them almost insane with thirst."

"I hadn't realised that this was such an important factor in our defeat. Why didn't we carry more water?"

"The amount needed would have been too much to carry, especially in the unusual heat that summer. The Christians shouldn't have left their water sources, but Saladin had lured them away."

William looked amazed. "Your knowledge of this, and hundreds of other events over those many years, would be incredibly useful to our people. Our scholars need to absorb this information and pass it on to younger people. It will teach us more about the past and might prevent future generations from making the same mistakes again. Have you portrayed Hattin in your Opus?"

"No, not yet, but I will speak to Yasmine. She can paint the pictures from my description while I write down the events."

***

The next day, William and I travelled to Southampton. We had so much to talk about, we seemed to arrive in minutes. This would be my first crossing to France and, unfortunately for my weak stomach, it was quite a rough day and the sea was choppy. I felt the sickness rising in my belly once more, but managed to keep my dignity. After all, this was nothing like as bad as the hellish journey from the Holy Land when I returned home with Yasmine and Daniel. Our sailors had completed this short journey hundreds, perhaps thousands of times, and their skills were legendary. I had no need to fear.

After docking at Le Havre, we spent a couple of days riding to Rouen with our company of knights. William and I continued our easy conversation and I was grateful for his company.

"Don't be afraid of John, Crispin. Yes, he can be prickly and abrasive. He is a well-practised bully, after all. He will try to intimidate and trap you, especially with your background and reputation. I will converse with him first. Then speak your truth without fear."

Of course, I had encountered bullies before. Nonetheless, I was grateful for his advice, which turned out to be good.

***

Two days later, we were seated opposite Prince John at a great table, and for the first time, I had an opportunity to observe him. There was no doubting that he was Richard's brother. In fact, he could have almost been his twin, although he was much shorter. But in John's case, his eyes gave him away. He certainly didn't have his brother's look of intelligence and self-confidence. Instead, there was a foxy, shifty look about him. His eyes flickered and blinked too quickly. I didn't feel I could trust him.

I had heard, from William the Marshal and from others, that John had a reputation for cruelty and instability. But he certainly had his talents as well. John was a capable and energetic administrator. I was intrigued to discover how this interview was going to play out.

As we'd hoped, John addressed William first. "Have you any news of Richard? Has my mother raised the ransom yet?"

"Not yet, but talks are ongoing. Richard will be freed soon."

"But how will that be possible, Marshal?"

"There is talk of using hostages to guarantee the final amounts. Have you been in communication with the Emperor Henry? And how are your talks going with King Philip?"

William had told me he knew very well that John was plotting with Philip to gain himself land in France. But before John could respond, a flagon of red wine arrived, which was very welcome. Slices of delicious beef followed, together with fresh trout, which I guessed was from the nearby river Seine.

"And where does your loyalty lie, Marshal?" asked John, speaking with his mouth full of food. "Who do you support? It seems you only support those likely to be the winners."

"Not at all, Prince John. I support the King and always have. I was loyal to Henry and his Queen, and to the young King Henry. Now that Richard is King, I am loyal to him, and will be to any future King or even Queen. Richard is alive and well and is likely to be freed soon, but if anything unfortunate ever happens to him, I will be loyal to you, if you are crowned King."

"So, even though I am looking after our lands while he is away, you are still not loyal to me?"

This wasn't going well. I could see that John was setting a trap for the Marshal.

"I repeat, I am loyal to the *King*, but in his absence, I am loyal to his regent. Need I remind you that Richard violently opposed your father, King Henry, and in a skirmish, I unseated him from his horse. I killed his horse, but I could easily have killed him. I believe that Richard then understood my loyalty."

This was a great answer and left John speechless for a time. The Marshal had shown that he was not afraid of John at all.

Prince John then turned his attention to me. "Sir Crispin, I am intrigued to know where your loyalties lie. Who are you loyal to? The King of England or the Leader of the Muslims?"

I did not hesitate with my reply. "I was fifteen years old, thousands of miles from home and badly wounded in a battle, thrown into prison, left to starve and rot and die, and a young boy set me free and saved my life, allowing me to have a future. Then, my loyalties lay with that boy."

"That's very clear, but who are you loyal to *now*?" he asked rather sarcastically.

"I cannot improve on the Marshal's answer, sir."

John then changed the subject. He asked me many questions about Saladin, Richard in Palestine and the other European leaders there. He was hungry for my knowledge and opinions. I answered as honestly as I could.

He then surprised me by asking, "Can you play chess, Crispin?"

The question threw me somewhat. I was aware that the sons of knights and military commanders were taught chess from a young age. The game helped them to learn how to develop tactics and strategies and, importantly, how to figure out the intentions of their opponents, so that they could overcome them in warfare and politics. However, I struggled to remember the procedures and rules. My friends and I had played sometimes in Milton before I left for the Holy Land, but I was nervous and unsure about John's challenge. On the other hand, I didn't want to disappoint him. I told him I could.

John and I played a game, which he won, but not before losing a few key pieces. It was a fair contest, but I could see he was a much better player than I was.

"Come on, Marshal, let's see if your game has improved."

The result was two to one to the Marshal. John thumped the table in frustration, but I could see that he had thoroughly enjoyed the evening and our company.

***

We left the next morning. I was very pleased to be going back home to Yasmine and my estate and, of course, to Daniel. There were so many problems and issues to overcome in order to run the business profitably, and pay the required taxes to the King, which seemed to increase all the time. And there were always petty squabbles and arguments to be resolved with the tenants. Prices of produce would fall just when we needed the income. The weather was a key factor, and it rained when we needed sunshine and was dry when we needed water.

I remembered from my youth that lords and barons were known for their constant complaining. They were never satisfied. Now I understood why. Nevertheless, I loved my people, the castle and estate, and was very happy with my good fortune at this stage of my life. Yasmine was beginning to settle into her new country and position, and I encouraged her to paint more pictures of her life here. These would later be added to our Magnum Opus, now on display at Canterbury Cathedral, along with a description and pictures of the Battle of Hattin.

Sadly, my dear mother had died recently, but we all celebrated her long and good life rather than going into mourning. I missed her dreadfully, but was so grateful to the Almighty that I'd had a chance to see her again after all those years, when I had given up hope. Yasmine had become very close to her and missed her almost as much as I did.

Daniel was growing up so fast and my greatest delight was to see his progress and happiness. He had little or no recollection of his homeland now, which Yasmine and I were relieved about. I made a mental note to ask the Marshal if he would take Daniel under his wing when he was old enough.

I wanted to spend as much time at home as I could, but the Royals were my masters and I had to provide men and money for their worldly ambitions. And I was required to lead those men.

I had only been back a few days when a rider raced up to the castle, informing me that I was required to travel with the Queen to Germany. She wanted me, and many other lords, to escort the ransom to free Richard from the Holy Roman Emperor. I cursed under my breath; I had so much to do at home in the coming days and months. But I had to do my duty.

After a brief goodbye to Yasmine and Daniel, I left with the rider and six of my knights. We were to meet Eleanor and the others in London, and leave almost immediately. I would, of course, be delighted to see Eleanor once again.

When we arrived in London, I revelled in her excitement at the prospect of seeing her son Richard again after so long. We carried the vast amount of money and valuables with us. We needed several carts to move these treasures.

"This is an extraordinary amount of money we are carrying," one knight commented to me. "It's the equivalent of 25 tons of silver! I've heard that while Richard's been away, the country has been doing very well, much better than most realised."

I gasped at this huge amount, amazed at how our lands could possibly contain so much wealth. Yet there was still more required.

"Have you heard?" the same knight said. "Philip of France and Prince John have told the Emperor that they will pay him 40,000 marks to keep Richard locked up, although they haven't raised the money yet. And he is seriously considering their offer!"

As it happened, when Emperor Henry realised that the huge amount we carried was available to him immediately, he dismissed Philip and John's offer and accepted ours. The cheers and noise and sheer happiness that heralded Richard as he was led towards us were indescribable, and I will always remember that special day in history. The highlight was when he rushed forward to hug Eleanor and they clung on to each other for many minutes, while the cheers from our throats reached a crescendo.

We were all now free to take Richard home.

After an uneventful sea crossing, the King was finally back in his own land. Leaving the celebrations to continue in London, I rode with my knights towards Milton, my excitement and anticipation rising.

But this day would become the worst of my life.

Chapter 17

A Terrible Event

My knights and I were only a mile or so from home when a small number of our people rode out to meet us. I felt a dreadful sense of foreboding, of doom, but it's hard now to explain why. Perhaps it was because they had no reason to come to us here. They could have given us the warmest of welcomes when we reached the castle courtyard. Perhaps it was their anxious and desolate expressions. Their heads were down and they were reluctant to meet my eyes.

What on earth was going on? Where was Era? If ever I needed him to tell me all would be well, it was at this terrible moment, but he remained absent.

The two groups moved towards each other in silence. It was as if no one had the courage to start talking. The familiar pain in my back flared up in response to my fear and dread. In a way, I didn't want them to speak. Whatever had happened, I just knew it was going to bring my world crashing down around me. I wanted to hang on to my last few seconds of normality.

But it was no good. I had to know.

"What on earth ails you? What has happened here? Speak, for God's sake."

Finally, one man had the courage to move his horse closer to us.

"Sire, we have suffered an attack on the castle. They have killed several of our people."

I fired so many questions at him that he went silent, looking as if he was about to flood with tears. Then in a stuttering voice, he spoke the words that broke my heart into a million pieces.

My lovely Yasmine had been killed, after being violated in the most brutal fashion by the leader of the attackers. His men had thrown her out of our bedroom window.

"What... what about Daniel?"

Through my fog of stunned shock, I was told that my childhood friend Mary and some of the other women of the castle had hidden him in the secret tunnel. Thankfully, he wasn't discovered. However, three of our men and women had been killed.

"They knew about him, though, and threatened us to tell them where he was," said the stammering man. "But none of us would."

"Who were they?"

"The same men you evicted from the castle. Fulke and his revolting henchmen."

I screamed out loud at this horrible news. Fulke! I should have killed the man when I had the chance.

"We have buried Yasmine's body in the churchyard."

I felt myself losing consciousness. The news was too much and overwhelmed me. Men rallied to my side to stop me falling off my horse, easing me to the ground.

I have no memory of being taken into the castle.

***

"We must track down these men and take them prisoner. They must be punished in the most severe way."

For a second when I regained consciousness, I had felt normal. Then the memories rushed back and the most intense anger I had ever experienced overwhelmed me. Not even my wise teachers on the Far Eastern mountainside would have been able to calm me.

With a series of barks, I ordered my knights to saddle up once again. We were going to find William the Marshal and ask for his help. One suggested we should leave it until the morning. I screamed in his face, insisting we went straight away without any delay.

We rode hard to Winchester, where we found the Marshal in his home. When I told him the dreadful story, he didn't hesitate.

"We will leave immediately. We cannot allow this lawlessness in England. Violent men like these must be punished. Don't worry, Crispin, we will find them. I will bring the full force of the law down on them. I wouldn't wager on their chances."

I will never forget the Marshal's unwavering support in my moment of greatest need. For a second, I saw a reflection of another dear friend in his face. The spirit of Saladin, I have no doubt, was riding alongside me as we set off to bring the vile Fulke to justice.

We started by visiting the local towns and calling in to taverns for information about the murderers. They had stolen some silver coins from my castle, enough to keep them in a drunken stupor for many days. We travelled to Salisbury, where we were directed to the local tanner with his own shop in the centre of the town. He had some information.

"I didn't like the cut of them at all," he told us. "They looked rough and evil, real scoundrels, although I know you shouldn't judge men by their looks. But I would have chanced a penny that they had been up to no good. They were flashing silver coins around and drinking from bottles. They were stewed drunk."

"When was this exactly and how many were there?" I asked.

"There were four of the varlets. They went to that tavern over there," he pointed, "let me think... must have been three days ago."

"Where did they go then?"

"They were seen heading west."

That was good news. Wilton was the next town and we could get there in less than an hour. We left immediately.

It didn't take us long to trace them to The Greyhound, a tavern in the marketplace. We were told they had been in there for many hours. And that much was obvious from the raucous singing coming from the establishment. My blood boiled. After the atrocity they had committed, I would see to it they would never sing again.

William told me to go in first. I recognised the evil Fulke and his three accomplices immediately, pointing them out to William as he came in behind me. His men strode over and grabbed every one of them and dragged them outside. Even in his advanced state of drunkenness, Fulke clearly realised it was futile to resist, and I had the satisfaction of seeing fear build into terror in his eyes.

"I would string them up now," snarled William, "but we must obey the law and give them a fair trial. We will lock them up in the local jail in the meantime. Fortunately, I know the sheriff."

Thanks to the power William wielded, the trial would take place without delay. I returned to Milton to encourage our people to testify, while the sheriff gathered together twelve good men and true to act as the jury, and a judge to preside over the proceedings. Mary didn't hesitate to come forward and others followed her lead. I brought four of the women to Wilton and they immediately identified the men to the jury.

They were found guilty and sentenced to be hanged the next day.

Hundreds of local residents came to witness the event. There was almost a festival atmosphere in the town, but I watched impassively as the men were dragged from the jail. My anger spent, I simply wanted to witness this foul scum eradicated from the world.

Fulke had sobered up overnight and he was being dragged along the ground, blubbering and begging for mercy, like the coward all bullies really are. The crowd jeered and booed and threw rotten vegetables at him. His boot had fallen off while he was struggling to get free and he cut a truly pathetic figure. For a second, our eyes met and I saw the silent plea in his. Remembering how much misery this fiend had caused, to me, to my darling Yasmine and to so many others, I made sure that one of the last things he ever saw would be my cold smile of satisfaction as I shook my head.

I watched him being hauled up to the scaffold. The jailers put the noose around his neck. In moments, he was swinging in the gentle breeze, alongside his three vile toads. I watched until his eyes bulged and his body slumped in death.

I thanked William and his men, and then left for home. My revenge was complete.

***

Daniel was the focus of my attention now. He was the only family I had left, so I was determined to protect and look after him. I wanted to ensure that he would have my support and guidance throughout his life, until he didn't need me any more.

Guilt was my constant companion. I had taken Yasmine away from her family to a strange country. She had never settled here properly or fully recovered from our most harrowing journey. She would never see her children again, or her grandchildren. And it was all my fault. I should have insisted that we all stay together in Damascus, but I was too weak. Perhaps I was scared for my own skin.

I hated myself. I had been a useless husband and father, hardly ever present during our long marriage. And now I had failed to protect her in our home in my own country. Godwin had clearly warned me to increase security of the castle and I had ignored his advice. Stupidly, I had decided that other matters were more important.

These thoughts were buzzing around my head like angry bees and I spent too much time on my own in my room. I became depressed and miserable and started to enjoy my wine too much as I sank into dark despair, seeing no way out of it. I had a dreadful time trying to sleep each night, and when I did, the nightmares were horrible. I could see that brute molesting my dear Yasmine, and then his henchmen throwing her out of the window, as if she were a piece of rubbish. She wasn't. She was the most lovely, kind, and honest person, and surely the best wife and mother anyone could wish for.

Days were little better. I clearly visualised a deep muddy pit in front of me. I was standing at the edge and I knew that if I fell into its depths, there was no coming back. That would be the end of me. And good riddance.

Eventually, it was my lifelong friend Mary who saved me, with the simplest of suggestions. She persuaded me to take long walks in our local countryside and forests.

"Go for several hours a day," she insisted. "I promise you will feel better."

At first, I was scathing, believing nothing would ever draw me from the dark place I had sunk into, but she was right. The fresh air was good for me, and the beautiful scenery and cheerful birdsong provided me with a distraction. Together with my many responsibilities on the estate and time spent every day with Daniel, my walks started to remind me that life does go on, no matter how bleak your circumstances. Gradually, I found some purpose in my miserable existence.

It was during that time that Eleanor sent me a beautiful picture of a woven coat of arms, which she had dedicated to me and my family. I was depicted riding a horse, my one arm holding the reins, and a flock of carrier pigeons were following me. I could now copy this on to a surcoat and make a banner which could be flown from my castle. This was a kind and magnificent gesture from her. I sent her a letter of thanks immediately.

I also had a letter from King Richard, expressing his sorrow for my loss and inviting me to his coronation. He had, of course, already been crowned, but he felt it was necessary, under the circumstances of having been away so long, to have a second coronation to assert his authority. Naturally, I pushed my depression to one side, at least temporarily, and sent him a letter of acceptance. The ceremony was to take place in Winchester. Together with hundreds of lords and barons from around the country, I would pay homage to King Richard.

I set aside funds for new fortifications for the castle and assisted with the heavy work myself. I hadn't realised how unfit I had become during the long weeks shut up in my room, and I benefited greatly from the exercise. The work took several months, but slowly, the repairs and additions strengthened the castle and secured the estate. Then I did what I should have done the moment Godwin made the recommendation: I hired extra men to guard the castle. Three sons of my tenants expressed a desire to become knights as part of our protection team, and I gladly accepted their requests.

Little by little, Milton Castle edged towards becoming an impregnable fortress.

***

Archbishop Hubert called in one day while I was working with my people on the fortifications. He was visiting nearby Salisbury and he knew my situation, of course. My bad news must have spread to half of the kingdom.

"I am so pleased to see that you have started to strengthen your castle and estate," he said, his face impassive. "This is a huge task, but in these days of unlawfulness, every lord should be doing the same. But I hope King Richard doesn't see this."

"Why ever not?" I asked in surprise.

"Well, he might think you are making too much money and withholding taxes due to him!"

I was horrified for a moment, and then smiled as I saw the gleam of amusement in his eyes. This was Hubert's idea of a joke.

"Have you heard that Richard has already left for Normandy?" he said. This time, his face remained impassive. These words were no joke.

"No, but I am surprised," I replied. "I thought he was going to spend more time here in England. Goodness knows, there is a huge amount of work to do here, firstly to restore law and order. He's been gone for more than four years."

"Yes, I understand that, and many agree with you. Unfortunately, he needs yet more money from his subjects to recover his lands in France. While he's been away, Philip and John have caused huge damage, and if he doesn't take action now, we will have no overseas territories at all."

"I wouldn't like to be in John's shoes with Richard coming for him. His disloyalty and aggression towards Richard have been appalling. What do you think will happen?"

Hubert paused for a moment. His next words took me by surprise.

"That's why Eleanor has gone with him. She will beg Richard to forgive John. My prediction is that she will bring about a reconciliation between the two. Yes, I know this seems extraordinary under the circumstances, but no one should ever underestimate Eleanor. After so many years of fighting within her own family, she is desperate for peace between them all. Has there ever been such a dysfunctional family?"

I was disappointed at first to hear this news. Eleanor had been Queen of England while Richard was away, performing her duties admirably, and I believed that we would need her here to keep the peace. But I could see that our immediate needs would be better served in Normandy.

"Well, if she can achieve peace between her sons, they will unite against Philip of France, and if this happens, I wouldn't give him a prayer," I said.

"Exactly! That's why, however unpopular Richard's absence may be amongst us, his move to Normandy is essential. He has a huge task ahead of him and John will be a great help. Also, don't forget that Eleanor has extensive lands and possessions there as well."

Then Hubert changed the subject. "What are your plans for the future, Crispin?"

"Well, I'm not too sure. At the moment, I have months, if not years of work to complete our fortifications. My doctor says that physically, there is nothing wrong with me, but the wounds in my mind will take time to heal. The scars, however, will never go away. When I feel ready, I will take part in life again, but I'm not sure which route I will travel."

"Don't forget that if you don't join Richard with your knights, you will have to pay scutage.'

"Yes, but at the moment, I would rather pay than leave Milton unattended again. I shudder to think what could happen. I will stay and complete my work here."

Hubert nodded. "When you feel you have recovered enough, we will speak again."

News came from France that Eleanor had achieved the near impossible. Richard had forgiven John, and both of them had fought their common enemies together with great results. They had regained towns and cities from Philip, who it appeared was now on the run. Richard was building a huge new castle above the Seine, which would protect Normandy for evermore.

I stayed at Milton, working hard on my estate, which was producing excellent results. The tenants seemed reasonably content, although they all moaned about the rents. I don't think there is a world where this is not the case! Yields improved many times over and we became well known for our wool. Overseas buyers would come by each year and for a long period, prices were rising.

Hubert visited us again on one of the rare occasions when he was in England. He had spent the past couple of years supporting Richard and John with their endeavours in France, which appeared to be gaining huge tracts of land and wealth from Philip.

"The Marshal has been in France for many months now, fighting for Richard," Hubert told me. "The King calls him the greatest knight ever, due to his many successes on the battlefield."

"Wasn't he a champion at the tournaments as well?" I asked.

"Yes, he was unbeaten on more than 100 occasions. An extraordinary feat." Then Hubert changed the subject. "Crispin, you have done great work at Milton since I was last here. The castle looks formidable. A modest army would have trouble breaking in. They would have to starve you out! I hear that you have done great work on the estate as well. Would you show me around?"

"Hubert, you must rest first, and then enjoy my hospitality. Then I want you to meet my successor, my younger son Daniel. I am keen for him to take over from me when he is fully trained, and I would very much like the Marshal to train him to be a knight. The problem is that he is still too young and I am too old, but I hope I live until he is ready. Then perhaps I will be blessed with a couple of years to enjoy retirement."

"I am sure you will live to witness many more sunsets. Perhaps in time, Daniel will take up the Cross and visit his homeland."

"That is my dearest wish. I will never see my children in Outremer again, but wouldn't it be wonderful if Daniel could? The trouble is that they would be on opposite sides!"

Hubert enjoyed a sumptuous meal that evening with Daniel and me. The following day, the three of us walked around my estate.

"I can't believe you have a market here already, Crispin," he said, impressed. "There can't be too many of this size in Wiltshire. My goodness, you are doing some trade here! I don't think I have ever seen so many multi-coloured stalls before. The effect is magnificent."

"Thank you. Yes, that was Yasmine's idea. She didn't like our rather drab surroundings and was always looking for opportunities to brighten up our estate. Hundreds of people come each week from all over the county to set up stalls and to buy and sell. I am so pleased with how well it has been going. It isn't easy to create a new market. I've had to hire a man just to run it and he is already begging me for a couple of assistants."

I showed him the fields and hills, which were almost white with thousands of sheep. In other fields, I showed him the cows that were brought in for milking twice a day, and a paddock full of chickens.

"You have created a paradise here." Hubert turned to my son. "Daniel, you will have a rich inheritance one day, but not too soon, I hope. Now I must return to my duties. No doubt Richard will be calling for me as soon as I get to Canterbury. No peace for the wicked."

"I didn't know an Archbishop could be wicked!" Daniel replied, rather cynically. "I thought you all spent your lives kneeling, praising God and giving sermons to the rest of us."

"Don't believe everything you hear, Daniel," Hubert replied with a smile and a wink. "Some of us are more holy than others. I doubt St Peter will be letting me in to heaven when my time is up. He will double lock the gates when he sees me coming."

We all laughed at his mischievous humour.

Hubert had always had a huge appetite, enjoying his food and drink enormously. We had cooked a whole pig on the kitchen spit in his honour. Over dinner, he asked me how my dealings with Gideon were going.

"Excellent, thank you, Hubert. We've had to recall him several times for more loans as we take on new projects. I have, of course, repaid him in full on each occasion, including his interest. His charges are very moderate and he is an honest man, and a great friend. He was most empathetic when Yasmine was m… died," I couldn't bring myself to articulate the word 'murdered' in front of my son. "The poor man understood my grief only too well."

"I knew he would look after you, and of course he would be able to relate to your dreadful loss," said Hubert kindly. "I don't know what England would do without the Jews and their moneylending. Our Kings certainly wouldn't be able to finance their ventures without them."

The following day, Hubert departed, waving to us until he was out of sight. Like Gideon, Hubert was a great friend and supporter, and I was so grateful to know him. In fact, without him, I don't think I would have succeeded or indeed survived back in my homeland. I hoped he would continue to be a mentor to Daniel for many years to come.

***

Over the next few months, I had time to reflect on my life. I still missed Yasmine dreadfully, but Daniel had given me renewed purpose. I wanted to leave him the richest inheritance I could.

Even more importantly, I was keen to give him the tools to survive without me. He would face many challenges, both in business and politics, and on the battlefield. He would undoubtedly be called upon to fight to protect his King and Country, but I also wanted him to be a decent man and a good

Christian. I therefore took a great interest in his schooling.

His teachers, the monks, said he was a good pupil, but could be lazy and disruptive at times. I told Daniel in no uncertain terms to buck his ideas up. I also wanted him to learn about the running of the estate and I made sure he spent time with some of the more successful tenants. I knew I was a worrier, I always had been, but he would need all the experience possible to prosper in the future.

My knights were delighted to have a new pupil and Daniel was at his happiest when he was in their company. Perhaps this was where his strengths were, rather than in the academic classroom. I reminded myself to speak to the Marshal when we next met. He would be an excellent role model for my son.

Yasmine had been a wonderful mother to Daniel and we both missed her influence on him, and indeed on all of us on the estate. Some of the women tried to mother him, but were no replacement for my dear wife.

With these thoughts filling my head, I hardly noticed a rider approaching me at great speed. When the thunder of hooves became too much to ignore any longer, I looked up in alarm. I had let my guard down, again. For a moment, I thought he was about to do me harm, then I recognised the insignia on his surcoat.

"Sire, I have been sent by Hubert to speak to you," he panted, drawing his horse to a halt. "There is dreadful news from France. Richard is dead!"

I waited while the man got his breath back. Dismounting, he gave me all the details as we led his horse to my stables.

"He was hit in the shoulder by a bolt from a crossbow. The wound festered, and within a few days, he was gone."

This was indeed terrible news. King Richard the Lionheart had only been forty-one years of age and had achieved a monumental amount in those years. He was the greatest leader our people had ever had, inspiring loyalty amongst all of us, and was at the forefront of every battle, fighting tirelessly against our enemies. Just as importantly, he had given stability to our country, and to the territories he controlled and owned. We were able to live our lives in peace and prosperity, safe in the knowledge that he would provide protection, a father to our nation and its peoples.

"Who was with him when he died?" I asked.

"His mother was able to reach him in time and he died in her arms."

I felt great sympathy for Eleanor. But the most important issue now was the succession.

"Who will become King in his place? Surely not John."

I had a nasty premonition that life would never be the same again for any of us.

Chapter 18

Travelling With Eleanor

The horsemen were heading towards us and their intentions did not appear to be peaceful. They greatly outnumbered our small band and I feared for my lady.

The sun was sinking down to the horizon and darkness would follow within the hour. I wondered who these riders were as I steered my horse in front of my lady to protect her, as I had done on many other occasions in recent months. Their lead rider spurred his horse ahead of the others, making his way towards me. He drew his sword and raised it high. His intentions were clear.

I tensed as he swung his sword at me, hitting my left side with huge force. The pain was intense. I was protected from serious harm by my heavy chain mail, but the blow was so strong, I was unable to keep my balance with my one good hand and I fell heavily and helplessly on to the road.

Eleanor rode forwards, holding her right hand up to prevent further aggression. A huge man riding just behind the swordsman also held his hand up.

Turning towards the other riders, he called out, "Stop, no fighting. They are too few to resist us."

I wondered what would happen next as the riders pulled up their horses. The only harm I'd suffered was to my pride. Pulling myself up into a sitting position, I managed to climb back on to my horse with some difficulty, and some embarrassment too. But I knew I was lucky to be alive.

We had just left Poitiers and entered the territory of the Lusignans. I guessed, correctly, that the big man was their leader, Hugh Le Brun. His forbears had tried to kidnap Eleanor some thirty years ago. William the Marshal had told me about how his Uncle Patrick, Earl of Salisbury, had been killed in the skirmish. He himself had been seriously wounded in the thigh and held in a nearby castle, but Eleanor escaped the ambush. She later ransomed him in thanks for his bravery.

Eleanor rode forward towards the vast figure.

"Eleanor, lovely to see you again," he said. "I wish to entertain you at a castle I own nearby. Please follow me."

I knew he was politely kidnapping her, but was helpless to stop it. As he led her towards his place, I followed at a distance with the rest of her entourage.

***

Eleanor asked me to be in attendance when she met with her captors in the dining room of Hugh's castle. I didn't like him at all. He was a revolting and despicable specimen, grossly overweight, and you wouldn't trust him with a market stall.

He demanded that Eleanor give him control of the vast and rich area of La Marche, which Henry had taken years before. Hugh made it clear that he would be holding her until she agreed to his request. Eleanor knew she had no other option. In hours, we were on our way again. I wasn't sorry to be leaving the place, but Eleanor had been humiliated by Hugh and I felt extremely sorry for her.

My visit to France had been planned several months earlier; a knight named Ralph de Marly, whom I had not heard of before, visited me at Milton to tell me that Eleanor had requested my attendance to protect her while she was there. After all these years, she had asked for me!

For a few moments, I had been speechless. My heart missed a beat. Surely this couldn't be true. She wanted a useless one-armed guard, and an old man to boot. If my calculations were correct, I couldn't be far short of seventy. There certainly weren't many people as active as I was at this age, but she had the pick of the bravest and strongest knights, and any and all of them would have come to her side with one click of her fingers.

"Sir Crispin, she insisted that she wanted you above all others. Will you come?"

"Yes, of course," I replied immediately, trying to recover my breath. "When do we leave?"

"Will you be ready tomorrow?"

I would leave now if she had asked me, I thought. I was entering into the winter of my life and the only ambition I had left was to serve my beautiful, wonderful lady. I had always worshipped and loved her; I would give up my life in her defence. Eleanor was my angel, my goddess, my Madonna, my Queen. I was her faithful servant and would always be so, until I breathed my last breath.

Of course, Yasmine had been my dear wife, honest, devoted and faithful, and a wonderful mother to our children until her horrible murder. I still missed her dreadfully and nobody would ever replace her. But my feelings for Eleanor were different, more complicated. At last, my life had a clear and desired purpose. I didn't expect anyone else to understand my passionate feelings, but I was eager to travel to my Queen.

That night, Ralph and I enjoyed a good dinner of spit-roasted duck with fresh bread and baked trout from my people's river, vegetables from our gardens. We washed down the delicious food with our local wine. I had recently started to grow grapes and was proud of the white we produced. Ralph was very complimentary about the fare, being the gentleman that he was. I was flattered to hear his praise.

My last task before we left was to ensure that Daniel would protected by his knights and well cared for by my people. He would be as safe as he could possibly be, but I still felt guilty about having to leave him.

***

After our unpleasant encounter with Le Brun, Eleanor was eager to continue our journey. She told me that her mission, if successful, would bring much needed unification to France and Europe. Her plan was to marry her granddaughter to the King of France's son, Louis Capet. I thought this was a highly ambitious but brilliant idea.

"John and Philip have already concluded the treaty and it's now my task to bring the girl to France for the wedding," she informed me.

"What is the name of your granddaughter?" I asked.

"Difficult to say. I haven't met my daughter's family yet. I last saw her when she was nine years old. Eleanor now has ten children and is married to the King of Castile. I will choose Louis's bride when we arrive at the Castilian court."

She was determined to secure her family's lands for generations to come. But I doubted whether her son John would keep the peace. He had a terrible reputation for causing trouble.

Hours later, we were travelling towards the Pyrenees, separating France from Spain. None of our party had been here before. I managed to secure guides in a local town to take us over the mountains. We would never have been able to find our way otherwise.

I couldn't have imagined that our journey would be so difficult, although it probably wasn't the best plan to tackle the mountain route in January. We had ice and snowdrifts to contend with and impossibly steep paths, and those coming down the mountains weren't any easier to navigate. Our poor horses slid and skidded, and some suffered broken legs. This was one of the toughest journeys I had ever undertaken and I hated the cold. At times, I wondered if I could carry on.

Eleanor was determined to get to Castile as quickly as possible and it seemed that nothing would stop her. She was extraordinary in her stamina and determination. We all made a superhuman effort to keep up with her, but many of us, especially me, had a terrible struggle.

Finally, we climbed down the last mountain, and laid out before us was a huge flat plain. Mercifully, the sun was shining. I find it hard to describe the blessed relief we all felt as we walked out into the unfamiliar warmth. But we still had several weeks of travel ahead of us to get to Castile.

***

The castle and court of Alfonso of Castile and his wife, also called Eleanor, were truly magnificent. The stonework was a light sandy colour and the architecture was impressive. I made a mental note to make some drawings so that we could copy the buildings at home.

We were all relieved to have arrived there safely as Eleanor led our party through the gates. Her grandchildren were lined up in the courtyard, waiting for her, her daughter Eleanor in front of them. Tears were in the eyes of both women as they greeted and hugged each other, holding on for several minutes, crying openly.

Eleanor, Queen of Castile, had lined her children up in order of seniority and was delighted to introduce each one to their grandmother for the first time. We were then all given comfortable quarters in the castle and were well fed and watered; the servants were very generous with the delicious local red wine. Our horses were also well looked after.

Our stay at this beautiful place was lovely and I was able to spend precious time relaxing and recuperating. Sitting in an archway in one of the courtyards of the palace, glorious sunshine warming me, I had a chance to reflect on my life and family.

Yasmine had been the best wife any man could have wished for, and I still felt the deepest guilt for taking her away from her family, her home, and her country. I had removed her from her blessed religion. Perhaps that had been a cruel thing to do.

We had left behind our beautiful children and grandchildren, taking only Daniel with us. Sweet Daniel. I hoped and prayed that my people would care for him and steer him on to the right path. He would have an excellent inheritance from us and I was keen that he should maintain and nurture our estate. William the Marshal had, as I'd hoped, promised to take Daniel under his wing. There was no better man in the kingdom to train the boy as a knight. Hubert had also kindly promised to guide Daniel whenever he had the opportunity, making sure he would grow up to be a good, honest and decent human.

I doubted whether I would see Daniel again. But as long as he listened to the advice from these fine men and acted accordingly, I was sure he would have a long, happy and successful life.

I thought about my good friend Saladin, how kind, considerate and loyal he had been to me. He'd always supported and protected me and was steadfast to the end. We had had a great life together and shared many extraordinary adventures, and I was sure that history would remember him with respect and admiration for his leadership and commitment to his people. His dedication to his nation was unparalleled. His achievements would be marvelled at until the end of time.

I missed my friend each and every day, just as I missed my children and grandchildren. I longed for them with a yearning and passion I hadn't thought I possessed. My feelings of sadness and regret at not having spent more time with them overwhelmed me, and tears flowed freely down my face.

A moment later, I felt a hand on my shoulder. I knew instinctively who it was; I didn't need to turn round. I could feel Eleanor's presence and I recognised the unique perfume she had specially made for her in Grasse. The heavenly scent filled the air around her with an essence of wild flowers.

We didn't need to speak. At her touch, I began to feel better and the tension in my body eased. My troubles melted like butter in a hot pan. A realisation came to me that worrying would achieve nothing. Everything in my life had happened for a good reason and nothing in the past could, would or should be changed. I had taken the right course. The only course available to me. That clarity of understanding made me feel a sense of contentment and acceptance. Era had been right all along. I should have faith and never give up hope.

Like Era, Eleanor had managed to calm me down and make me see the truth of my life and values. I was so grateful for her empathy and support. Moments later, she took her hand away and I was aware that she had gone back into the building. I was reminded once again of what a truly remarkable person she was, and I was so privileged to know her.

***

Days later, Eleanor took me into her confidence.

"Crispin, I have chosen the girl who will marry Louis. It will be Blanche. I am very impressed with her character and demeanour, and I believe she will be eminently suitable as Queen. She reminds me so much of me when I was her age. The other girl, Urraca, is in my opinion unsuitable. Our work here is done, but I am going to stay longer than I originally intended to."

Of course, Eleanor had no need to discuss this with me, a mere bodyguard, so I was extremely flattered to be party to her private thoughts and decision making.

"I love this place so much, it reminds me of my court at Poitiers during my youth. Watching the troubadours makes my heart leap and listening to the beautiful words of the poets stirs my imagination. This is a really splendid place, but unfortunately, we will need to get back to France soon to complete our mission."

After two comfortable and restful months, we finally left Castile for France, taking Blanche with us. I was dreading our return journey across the mountains, but at least the warmer weather had melted most of the snow on our path. Only the tops were white. Our main difficulty was that our way was regularly blocked by the pilgrims coming towards us, visiting Santiago de Compostela to worship at the shrine.

At last, we descended and arrived back in France, making our way to Eleanor's Palace, Ombrière, in Bordeaux. Again, we were comfortably housed, needing another good rest after our hard journey. Eleanor had plenty of time to coach and tutor Blanche so she would be ready for her difficult life to come. She had immensely valuable knowledge about the history of her family and her experiences as Queen to two Kings that she wanted to relay to the girl. It was essential she spend as much time as she could with Blanche to teach her diplomatic skills, so she would be able to steer her husband in the right direction: to benefit the Plantagenets as opposed to his people, the Capetians. And above all, to be subtle in all her dealings. Peace in her lands was Eleanor's top priority, along with the health and wellbeing of her family.

But it was Eleanor's own wellbeing that I was more concerned about. One hot afternoon, I saw her and Blanche sitting together on a bench in the gardens, in the shade of tall trees. They were talking as usual, and I hoped that Eleanor was making good progress with her granddaughter, but in mid speech, Eleanor slumped to one side and her head rested on Blanche's lap. I was momentarily frozen with shock. Had she had a seizure or passed out? Either way, I was desperately concerned, and I rushed over to help.

Blanche had her arm around her grandmother's shoulders and eased Eleanor back into a sitting position. Eleanor looked desperately unwell. I ordered some servants to help her to her room and ease her down on to her bed, making her as comfortable as possible.

After days of consultations, the best doctors in the land decided that my Queen had no known illness. They concluded that she must be extremely tired after many years of travelling and stress. She was ordered to rest for at least six months, but she replied, albeit in a weak voice, that she didn't take orders from anyone. That doctor was another one for the chopping block!

After several weeks' rest, she was well enough to travel to her beloved Fontevrault Abbey, stating that this was where she wanted to spend the rest of her days. We took Blanche with us. She stayed until the Archbishop of Bordeaux arrived to take her to Normandy for her marriage to the King of France's son, Louis.

I realised with great sadness that Eleanor's mighty powers were fading and the end might be coming soon. I was determined to look after her for the rest of her days.

Chapter 19

Final Days

Weeks went by in Fontevrault Abbey and Eleanor rarely left her bed. We tended to her as well as we could, and she was kept warm and well fed. The doctors still put her condition down to old age and exhaustion, but at least she was happy to be in her favourite place, which she had known since her childhood.

Eleanor's son, King John, visited us on two occasions and was delighted with the news about the royal marriage. He too was looking forward to peace in our lands, or so he claimed. He did not speak directly to me; in fact, he totally ignored my presence. This suited me well; he was a dangerous man to be around. I hoped he had forgotten ever having met me, but I was sure he had recognised me with my distinctive missing arm.

In contrast to King John, I was pleased to welcome William the Marshal at the gates. We had been in Fontevrault Abbey for a few weeks by then, and as I ushered him towards Eleanor's room, he told me briefly what was happening across France. Then I left William and Eleanor to talk together.

William and I met afterwards, and I was keen to find out more. We had heard so many rumours and I was sure the Marshal would know the true facts. I poured us both a large glass of the local wine, then settled back to listen to what he had to say.

"Well, King John seems to court trouble wherever he goes. He has decided to get married again. Yes, I know he's already married to Isabella of Gloucester, but the two of them despise each other and have produced no heirs. She wasn't even invited to his coronation."

"So, who is the lucky lady?" I asked.

"Well, he couldn't have made a sillier mistake. The poor girl – who is only twelve years old – is betrothed to Hugh Le Brun, the man who captured Eleanor. Hugh and his Lusignan barons are furious, and they are rising up against the King. In one move, John has wrecked the fragile peace which Eleanor has brought about. King Philip of France supports the barons, and so does John's nephew, Arthur."

Arthur was the son of John's late brother Geoffrey, and was therefore Eleanor's grandson. He had been furious not to be considered as Richard's successor, so I wasn't surprised he would take any opportunity to turn against King John.

"To make matters worse, John has decided to take his new wife to England to show her off to his people there. His enemies will relieve him of his lands while he is away. John has a dreadful habit of irritating people, turning them into enemies. I don't know why he does this – yes, I have told him this to his face. He does not have enough friends to achieve his goals. I fear he will lose everything this side of the narrow sea."

I couldn't help but agree with the Marshal's assessment, although my main concern was what would happen to Eleanor. I was extremely worried about her, especially as she was in no condition to fight back. William the Marshal would not be here to help protect her; he had to leave on urgent business. Nonetheless, I was grateful for his valuable time and information.

***

Many months later, Arthur, newly knighted by King Philip, was on the warpath. He was already attacking and taking towns and castles by force. I feared for Eleanor's safety, but I had learned never to underestimate her.

She called for me and I rushed to her room to find her sitting on her bed, fully clothed. She appeared to have miraculously thrown off the languor of the past couple of years. I was shocked, but pleased that she had made such a good recovery.

"My Queen, you should not be out of bed. The doctors were very clear about that."

"A pox on those quacks! I won't be told what to do, especially when there is a crisis and we might lose Aquitaine, and indeed all our lands here. If they give you any trouble, throw them out. The business of a Queen is far more urgent! That wretch Arthur is causing us so many problems and he needs to be stopped. Now, Crispin, summon the men and prepare the horses. We will be leaving today."

I knew better than to argue with her, but I felt a deep sense of foreboding and worry. My eighty-year-old Queen wanted to fight her grandson to stop him from capturing her precious homelands. What a terrible outcome for her family. I might not ever see my children and grandchildren again, but at least I knew they would not be fighting each other. As Hubert, Archbishop of Canterbury had observed, the Plantagents must have been the most dysfunctional family on earth. But this was not the fault of my dear Queen. I blamed the grasping, violent men in her family.

"We will be going to my castle at Mirebeau. There at least we will be safe."

I didn't think we would be, but again, I knew better than to say anything. The castle was not well defended and even a small force could break in easily. I was extremely concerned for Eleanor's safety, but we set out with our band of around twenty men. Eleanor insisted on riding in the centre of our group.

A rider had informed us that Arthur was leading a formidable force of knights and had joined up with the Lusignan barons. They knew where we were and where we were heading. Rumour had it that some Lusignans thought it would be a good idea to kidnap Eleanor for a third time. With her as hostage, they could get any terms they wished for, so their army was on its way to carry out these plans.

"Crispin, I want you to ride to John to warn him about the danger we are in," Eleanor ordered. We had heard that John was at Le Mans, leading a band of mercenaries, and was at last fighting back for his kingdom. His Norman army was far away, protecting his lands from attack by the King of France. "Go now with the greatest speed. We pray to God that you can reach John in time and he will rescue us."

I knew it was a hopeless mission, but nevertheless, I would carry out her orders to the best of my ability. No, I would do much better than that. I would have flown there if I had been given wings.

As I started out on my journey, dark clouds gathered and a gentle rain began falling. When you're riding, even a low drizzle is annoying. There is nowhere to shelter and you can't prevent your clothes and body getting wet. Usually, I had been lucky in life, but not this time. The rain was soon coming down with a vengeance, a force I had never experienced before. I was drenched and colder than I had ever been. I had no food, but at least I could open my mouth to gather more liquid refreshment than I could take.

I didn't think there was any chance of me getting to John in time, or of him coming to rescue his mother, but I had to try. I needed to race eighty miles to reach him and I was determined to do so as fast as possible.

I don't think I have ever moved so swiftly, even when I was racing back to warn Saladin of the enemy's approach in Egypt all those years ago. As usual, I started to worry. When I got to him, would John just ignore me? Or would he decide that the situation wasn't as urgent as I knew it to be? I was now so wet, I couldn't get any wetter, and beyond hungry.

I kept up my relentless pace and my poor horse started protesting. I urged him on. Several times, I called upon Era to help me. As always, he told me to have faith and keep going.

After a journey which felt like it had taken 100 years, I finally rode through the castle gates in Le Mans, demanding to speak to John immediately. But his knights didn't move until I had told them the full story. It was only when they had understood the urgency of the situation that they rushed back inside the castle.

Minutes later, John came out to see me. "What kind of trouble has my mother got into now?" he demanded. I updated him with the current situation, stressing the danger Eleanor was in.

"Your Majesty, she is about to be captured by Arthur and we cannot waste a minute."

John growled in fury and his voice became a throaty animal roar. He yelled for his commanders, who in turn mobilised a large army.

"We will leave for Mirebeau immediately," he ordered.

It was at that moment that exhaustion overwhelmed me and I fell unconscious from my horse.

***

I woke up two days later, just as dawn was breaking, feeling very hungry and thirsty. My body ached and was telling me that I had pushed myself too hard. It was surely time to start acting my age.

The wagon into which I had been placed had arrived at Mirabeau, but the soldiers had been well ahead of us. The battle was all over.

One of them related the story. "There was no sign of activity or sound as our men crept up to the one open gate of the town," he said as we shared a plate of bread and cheese, both of us eating hungrily. "At the last moment, we rushed forward, catching the enemy soldiers totally unawares. Many were still asleep in the courtyard, no doubt after celebrating their success too much the evening before. Our men captured their leaders and killed all of the soldiers."

John's men had done their work efficiently. I was so relieved to hear that Eleanor was now safe. She and her small group had withdrawn into the keep of the castle, expecting Arthur's men to break in and capture them. But Arthur had been so certain of the outcome, he had waited until morning, after resting and eating. He had not been expecting a rescue force.

I walked through the portcullis and was relieved to see that Eleanor was unharmed. She was amazed and delighted that John had come to her aid so quickly, and full of thanks and praise for my huge efforts.

"That horrible grandson of mine demanded my surrender and inheritance, but I managed to put him off while I considered the case and pretended to negotiate. I don't think we would have held out much longer, but," she turned and smiled at John, who was standing at her side, "you arrived just in time, as I knew you would."

John was seething with anger at the horrible distress caused to his mother. "I swear I will make that boy suffer so much that he will deeply regret ever threatening and insulting you like that. I will clap him and his Lusignan lords in irons. I will humiliate them. They will be carried by open wagon across my kingdom. Their countrymen will see them and will learn a terrible lesson. They will never challenge me again."

It was all too much for me. King John's words merged into a blur of sound and I collapsed again.

***

Eleanor was there when I woke several hours later.

"I am so proud of my brilliant son, John, and his achievement in our rescue," she said. "Another few hours and the soldiers would have awoken and attacked us. He made such a swift dash to protect his mother, he reminded me of his father. Henry moved around his lands with miraculous speed. Everyone was in awe of his extraordinary achievements, and only my Richard came close."

She paused for a moment in deep thought.

"John could be a great king, like his brother and father. He has displayed amazing qualities, which so far have lain hidden. I hope he puts his talents to good use to save our lands and defeat our enemies."

I wasn't as optimistic as Eleanor, but was prepared to give John the benefit of the doubt. Although the little he had done so far had not filled me with much confidence.

"Crispin, I want to go to Poitiers now, my home city. I want to hold court there and use all my influence to help my son and our Plantagenet rule. John has dealt with our enemies and they will not trouble us again."

She told me that she'd watched as Arthur and his conspirators had been carried past the castle in the wagon, bound in chains, as John had promised they would be. Arthur was sobbing quietly and she had felt sorry for him, as any grandmother would.

"He looked so young and vulnerable. But then I remembered his treachery and cruelty to me, and I can't forgive that. I don't feel any regret for his fate now. I just hope that John doesn't relent and let him or any of the barons go. They must never be free again to cause terror to our people and across our lands."

She'd had the particular satisfaction of watching Hugh Le Brun's face as his cart rolled past. He had tried to kidnap her twice, succeeding the second time. On this third attempt, he was thwarted by John.

"I have rarely felt such hatred for a man. He looked sour and beaten. I wonder if John should have humiliated them so much, though. He might lose support from their countrymen."

We rode in bright sunshine, happy to have been spared to enjoy more days alive in this beautiful, fertile country. Eleanor insisted I ride alongside her and we chatted happily, although it was quite apparent that our adventure had taken its toll on her, as it had on me. I felt so tired and I knew that further sleep, although very welcome, would not refresh me. Something had broken inside me and wouldn't be repaired.

***

We spent many months at Poitiers. Eleanor tried to garner support for John and assure her family's dominance in these lands, but as usual, her son had played his hand badly. He freed the Lusignan barons as they had promised to cause him no more problems. But they immediately reneged and joined their cousins in seizing John's castles and towns.

Then William the Marshal visited Eleanor, bringing more bad news. "It seems likely that John has killed Arthur, and some say he did the deed himself. Whether true or not, Arthur has disappeared and his supporters are furious, believing that John is the culprit. Philip is leading a group of rebels and has taken Castle Gaillard, which we all thought was invincible. John tried to take it back and failed, losing hundreds of his precious soldiers."

In some despair, Eleanor asked the Marshal what the likely outcome would be.

"I am sorry to say that it seems almost inevitable we will lose all our lands over here in France. I have strict orders to return to John in Normandy immediately. I believe our departure for England is imminent."

Eleanor replied with some passion, "But what about all our possessions, our castles, our towns and precious lands? Our family has fought tooth and claw to claim and maintain our inheritance. Henry and I devoted our lives to this cause, and my Richard also fought for his rightful lands. He risked his life in Outremer and later suffered so terribly in Germany."

William listened without commenting.

"John had our lands presented to him on a plate and what does he do? He tips the plate over and all our valuables fall into the dust. I can't believe how incompetent and careless he has been. And now he leaves his elderly mother to fend for herself, surrounded by evil rebels and enemies. Does he not care at all?"

William could only express his regrets. "My Queen, I am truly sorry for the way this has all turned out. You know I have fought for a different outcome, and when John has made mistakes, and there have been many, I have told him so. I have never held back!"

"I know, William, you have always been true and loyal, giving great service to me, my family and England. I sometimes wonder whether you should have been my son, instead of my feckless John. And now, William, you must do as he demands. I wish you safe journey back to England and good fortune. We will not meet again."

William departed, trying to hold back his tears. This was the end of an era and the world would never be the same again. I felt so sad for him, and for Eleanor.

***

Later, Eleanor called me in to her chamber.

"Crispin, we are finished here and there is no more for me to do. I want you to escort me back to Fontevrault immediately. I have done all I can to look after and promote my family. I have nothing else to give them. I will retire from all my duties.

"When we get back, I will give myself to God. I will take the veil, if I am allowed to do so. I have no energy left for this world, but hopefully I will be restored for the next one. Nothing will give me more pleasure than to serve God in my final days."

She turned to look directly at me. "Crispin, what will you do? Will you go back to England and your estate?"

"No, my Queen, I have sworn to serve you forever and will keep to my promise. I will stay with you."

After this exchange, we prepared to leave straight away. We rode side by side in silence, comfortable in each other's presence. I don't think I ever enjoyed a journey so much, filled with such peace and contentment.

By the time we arrived at Fontevrault, Eleanor was exhausted. She had no energy left and had to be helped down from her horse. Aides carried her to her room and laid her on to the bed. I asked the abbess to attend to her and to accede to her request to become a nun. She would have to get permission from the Bishop, but promised to seek this without delay.

I decided to stay with Eleanor and asked for a cot so that I could rest close to her. A team of nuns looked after her every need, while I fell into a sleep, not waking up until the next morning.

The sun shone through the Abbey windows, illuminating Eleanor's face. She looked so beautiful.

I would not last much longer in this world. Would I be remembered beyond the next generation or two? Saladin would be revered for evermore. Eleanor and her son Richard would be recalled with great respect by historians and troubadours many years from now. But what about Yasmine and me? Of course, we had left a piece of our own history which would tell our story. I wrote some notes into a book about the past months and years spent in France and Spain, in the hope that our Magnum Opus would be updated after I had gone.

In that moment, I prayed that our Magnum Opus would be preserved, so that generations to come would understand our lives and the extraordinary events of our time. Our pictures and words were evidence of a vital period of history. I wanted people down the ages to learn about the exceptional men and women, to know the truth about their actions and deeds. Their great achievements must never be distorted. Their lives had moved the mountains of history and our geography.

I silently thanked God that our Magnum Opus was safely held in Canterbury Cathedral. I prayed that it would remain there, honoured as a precious artefact, displayed to thousands of visitors until the end of time.

I was shaken out of my reverie as Eleanor woke.

"Crispin, please bring me some water."

I did as I was ordered. She drank half a flagon quickly, and I made a mental note to keep her regularly hydrated. I asked her if she wanted food, but she shook her head. She was asleep again in moments. I knew she was fading.

I felt so privileged to be with her in her last days. Determined to make her limited time as comfortable as possible, I did not allow any visitors to her bedside, apart from the nuns who were caring for her. She wouldn't have the strength to talk to anyone else. Of course, if John had come, this wouldn't have been my decision to make, but he had already departed for England. He had abandoned us and left his mother exposed to the thousands of rebels who were now raiding the countryside. There was no one to protect us. We could only hope that our enemies would respect our religious house.

In her more lucid moments, Eleanor would talk to me about her life and her family. Her recall of the smallest details of her past was extraordinary. She remembered her travels across Europe and the characters she had known. My life experiences paled into insignificance alongside hers.

She questioned me about her family. What did I think of Richard and John? Could she have done any more to make them better men? Had she been a good wife, queen, mother and grandmother? Did she lead her country with honour and dignity? How would she be remembered?

I was as honest in my replies as I could possibly be. When she suspected that I was trying to flatter her, she would immediately correct me. She wanted straightforward, truthful answers and was grateful when she received them. And she thanked me many times for my service and loyalty.

To share these precious moments and memories with this great lady was an enormous privilege. But gradually, she slept more frequently and for longer. Her end was approaching, and mine was too. We had both expressed our inner feelings and examined our lives together. We would leave this earth with love and hope in our hearts.

We drifted in and out of sleep – a happy and contented sleep, where we knew we had done our best and had served our fellow people as well as we could. I called on my spirit guide, Era, but he had left me. The time was now approaching for me to move towards my God. And I would be doing so with my Queen at my side.

The End

Bibliography

Church, Stephen, *King John, England, Magna Carta and the Making of a Tyrant,* Macmillan, 2015

Fripp, Robert, *Power Of A Woman, Memoirs of a Turbulent Life: Eleanor of Aquitaine*, BookLocker.com, 2010

Man, John, *Saladin, The Life, The Legend and The Islamic Empire*, Bantam Press, 2015

Meade, Marion, *Eleanor of Aquitaine, A Biography*, Frederick Muller Ltd, London, 1978

Penman, Sharon, *Lionheart, Passion, Intrigue, War and Deceit*, G P Putnam's Sons, a division of Penguin Group (USA) Inc, 2011

Penman, Sharon, *The Land Beyond the Sea*, G P Putnam's Sons, a division of Penguin Group (USA) Inc, 2020

Phillips, Jonathan, *The Life and Legend of the Sultan Saladin*, The Bodley Head, Penguin Random House, 2019

Scott, Sir Walter, *The Talisman*, Archibald Constable & Co (Edinburgh), Hurst, Robinson and Co (London), 1825

Spencer, Charles, *The White Ship, Conquest, Anarchy and the Wrecking of Henry I's Dream*, William Collins, Harper Collins Publishers, 2020

Other Books by Nigel Messenger

The Michmash Miracles

How Old Testament History Helped the British win a battle in World War 1

Two battles in Palestine 3000 years apart yet almost identical in every detail.

The first battle was recorded in the Book of Samuel in the Old Testament, where the Israelites were facing a huge Philistine Army, situated on a mountain near the village of Michmash. Jonathan, King Saul's son, finds a secret path to reach and outflank the enemy, and eventually wins an extraordinary victory.

The second battle takes place in 1918 when the British Army is facing the Ottomans in the same place and in similar circumstances. A British officer is reading the Bible the night before the battle and finds a reference to Michmash. He learns about the tactics Jonathan used 3000 years before and the secret path he found. Using similar tactics, he and his men try to achieve the same results as Jonathan did all those years ago.

Armageddon Revelations

Battles of Megiddo

Megiddo, the mystical Armageddon of the New Testament. Three momentous battles are described which took place near the ancient settlement in Palestine. Docker Nat Sullivan fights under Allenby during the campaign in World War 1. After falling seriously ill, he has vivid dreams fighting with Richard the Lionheart in the Third Crusade and with Deborah of the Old Testament, arguably one of the greatest generals of all time.

Nat returns to the London docks and rises through the Union ranks to become deputy to the political giant and statesman Ernest Bevan, General Secretary of the TUC. Nat, now a Labour MP, follows Ernest when he was appointed Minister of Labour during World War 2 and later his assistant when he was Foreign Secretary during the momentous post war years.

Three historic and portentous adventures helped shape the remarkable men of the twentieth century.

From Eden to Babylon

A filthy barge arrives in Basra full of near-dead British soldiers, wounded, starved and dehydrated without basic care and medicine, after the British surrender at the battle of Kut. A British Officer and his team take the desolate men off the barge and on to a steamer heading for Bombay and then by train to a hospital in cooler Northern India.

He recognises one gravely wounded man who had saved his life in the horrendous Boer War some years before. When this man's sister travels to India from England to nurse him back to health, she falls for his rescuer.

World War 1 action takes place in Mesopotamia, India, Arabia and South Africa and follows the adventures of a family who work and fight together and finally reunite at a family wedding in India.

Doctors at War

A family's struggles through two World Wars

The Great War in raging across the world and the British are fighting with their allies against the Macedonians.

In the hospitals of Malts and Salonika, two dedicated doctors are locked in an ongoing battle of their own. One, an active Suffragette trained in Edinburgh, faces a daily fight for status and respect, at a time when lady doctors were despised and distrusted. The other trained in The Royal College of Surgeons in Dublin and nearby hospitals. Both are strongly opiniated about their calling; a clash of personalities is inevitable. However, love flourishes in the most adverse of conditions – the two doctors go on to set up not one but two practises in London, as well as welcoming a daughter into the world.

As time goes by, war impacts on the lives of the doctors' descendants. Told from the point of views of various family members, the action leads the reader from the turbulent world of London during the Blitz to the code breaking genius of Bletchley Park, from the tense Battle of the Atlantic to the terrible Battle of Kohima.

Acknowledgements

"My very grateful thanks once again to my Editor Alison Jack for making my book so much better than it was. She has an extraordinary capacity for attention to detail, hard work and correcting my historical knowledge!

The cover design by Jason Conway of The Daydream Academy is a masterpiece once again and reflects the story in brilliant detail.

Thank you, Alison and Jason.

Thank you once again to my caring family and my very patient wife, Maura, who has an enormous capacity for supporting and encouraging me in my writing. She listens patiently as I read paragraphs to her. In minutes she is comfortably asleep on the sofa! She is my fiercest critic."

About the Author

Nigel Messenger has spent a lifetime working in the Hospitality Industry and now has his own consultancy company.

Apart from his family Nigel has two major passions – cricket and history.

"We often observe our leaders making dreadful mistakes, invariably due to their lack of knowledge of past events. We can all learn lessons from thousands of years of the past. History really does repeat itself.

I deplore the lack of history teaching in schools today. We should light the fires in the minds of young people, telling stories of the past to paint visual pictures. These stories show how the lives of their ancestors through the ages have been affected by extraordinary historical events."

Prior to Opus Magnum, Nigel has written four books about the World Wars. From Eden to Babylon, and Doctors at War, were inspired by the experiences of his family members in various parts of the world.

"They were not heroes, but ordinary people and families who carried out their duties, often under the most horrific conditions and deprivations."

Opus Magnum is the first book about historical fiction in the Middle Ages and will be the start of a new series from those times.

Nigel lives in Cheltenham with his family.

Nigelmessengerblog.com
Instagram: nigelmessenger2019

To join the mailing list please contact Nigel on:
nigelmessenger@me.com

Milton Keynes UK
Ingram Content Group UK Ltd.
UKHW041828081024
449420UK00004B/78